THE ART OF FALLING
FOR YOU

MAYA HUGHES

For Sarah for the countless hours spent walking and talking with me while I wrestled with Bay and Dare's story.

1

BAY

"If you deliver that baby in my room, I'll never forgive you." I brought in another box from the hallway. The new residence hall had been repainted white with a navy stripe running along the middle of the wall in preparation for the arrival of the Los Angeles Lions summer training camp.

Felicia cradled her rounded stomach, which seemed to have popped overnight, and opened a box with my name written on the side. The studio apartment for the Resident Director was mine now, since Felicia lived in the apartment she shared with her PhD-student husband.

"Every Franklin child going back three generations has arrived at least two weeks late; I think you're good."

I set the box down on my desk chair. "You're still thirty-five weeks pregnant. It could happen any minute."

"Then you get to take over as the residence hall director."

"Are you trying to get me to quit on day one?"

"You're my right-hand woman. You can't quit on me.

Can she, Becca?" She rubbed her stomach and looked at me with puppy dog eyes.

"Teaching her from the womb, huh?" I set down the boxes on the floor by my bed. "You'd think they'd at least give us real beds."

She laughed. "We're all in the skinny-ass bed together. Even the football players. You should be prepared to field a LOT of bitching about how they need the 'good' beds like we have California kings hidden somewhere."

"Why are they here anyway? I'd think pro athletes would be staying at five star hotels or something for training camp."

"Nope. The coaches like them here. Fewer distractions with campus mostly empty. It's easier to keep tabs on them, and there's no reason for them to leave. Gym, playing fields and food are all in one spot." She leaned in and stage whispered. "Plus, it's cheap." She shrugged. "Comparatively anyway."

"I have three more boxes."

"Get the cart. Why are you carrying them one at a time?" She unzipped my suitcase and lifted out a pair of my underwear. "I remember when I could fit into underwear like these."

I snatched them out of her hands and shoved them into the empty drawer. "Stay away from there and stick to the boxes if you insist on helping me unpack."

"Aren't I the boss?"

"The nosy boss."

I jogged down the stone stairs at the back of the building. At least I was on the ground floor and didn't have to trudge things multiple flights, but it had the downside of facing the quad where weekend revelers congregated. I'd have to rig up an elaborate pulley and bucket system to ward them off, although in the summer it would hopefully be better.

Being on campus was weird now. I wasn't a student anymore. I was an employee. Temporary employee. My final summer on campus. Graduation had been less than a week ago. I was a college graduate. I was a bona fide adult with no more excuses to avoid joining the real world. And I didn't feel any different. Well, except maybe the crushing dread of being an adult and not knowing what the hell to do with my life.

I grabbed the last box from my car and slammed the trunk closed. My temporary move-in tag hung from the rearview mirror. I'd have to go park it once I dropped off the box.

An older man in a wind breaker and khakis with a healthy glow that I didn't think came from tanning, but from a lot of time outside, stopped me on the steps up to the dorm.

"Excuse me, I'm from the LA Lions, they said I should look for someone in a lime shirt."

I looked down at my lime green Residence Hall Staff t-shirt. "That's me. What did you need help with?"

"Did you want me to get that for you?" He gestured to the box.

"It's not that heavy, and I'm only taking it over there." I nodded toward the propped open door.

"A few of our players are arriving early today and we only have the coaching staff keys. Could we get the keys to their rooms?

"Of course. The Resident Director and I can help you out with those. If you stop by Resident Director's Office right inside the main entrance with the room numbers, we can get you those keys. They finished setting up all the apartments and inspected them yesterday, so you're good to go."

He nodded and walked away.

I walked into my room.

"What's Dare?" She wiggled the notebook with brown curled pages in front of her face.

The box slipped from my hands, crashing to the ground. Text books and other random knickknacks toppled out.

"Did you chronicle games of Truth or Dare growing up? A bucket list?" She teased.

My ribs tightened as Felicia flipped through my worn green-and-white notebook. If only it were something so silly and embarrassing, something frivolous and forgotten. Instead, it was a cross section of my broken heart committed to the page. The edges of the paper curled and stained with tears I promised I'd never spill again.

I leapt over the box and spilled contents and ripped it out of her hand. "Don't look at that."

She jerked back.

My panicked heartbeat calmed now that I had the notebook safely in my hands. My breaths came out choppy. My fingers trembled around the tattered pages.

Concern radiated from her voice. "Bay, I'm sorry." She stared back at me, baffled, and I tried to calm down.

I set the notebook down, shoving it under a stack of text books. Sucking in a shaky breath, I turned and faced her with a smile plastered on my face. "No, I'm sorry. It's no big deal."

She clutched her stomach and I felt like an even bigger asshole.

A knock broke through the awkwardness in the room.

"Excuse me, Miss. I have the room numbers and one of our players has arrived already. He'll be right here." The older man with the grizzled face, but kind eyes stood in the doorway.

I dusted off my hands. "Yes, of course. This is Felicia, the Resident Director."

She smiled in her perfect professional way. "Nice to meet you." She shook his hand.

"I'm Hank. I'm the assistant tight ends' coach. And I didn't get your name."

"Bay." The deep, rumble of a voice shot through me like I'd been struck with an arrow.

In the doorway, a man stepped forward, looking both so different from the one I'd known my senior year of high school and so much the same that it hurt. A sharp stabbing pain in my chest.

"Dare."

2

DARE

She looked just like I'd remembered her. So much like the first time I saw her it almost brought tears to my eyes.

It had been too long. So long that, if it hadn't been for my sketchbooks I'd have sworn I'd made her up, that she was a figment of my imagination constructed to get me through the darkest days of my life.

But here she was, in the flesh. Breathing and staring at me with the same hatred and anger she'd shown the last time I'd laid eyes on her. But before that fateful day, when I'd splintered her heart and mine, she'd been the girl I couldn't tear my eyes away from.

~

Four Years Earlier.

My forearm ached. The reverberation of the blow I'd blocked had probably bruised the bone. He'd caught me off guard. I'd gotten sloppy, lazy. My own home wasn't a refuge, not when he was there.

Inside the garage, the swaying lightbulb overhead and choked panting were the only sounds.

The glossy shine of my football helmet reflected in my eyes, making the place flicker like a fucked-up night club. I bent, my fingers tightening around the bars of the face mask. I stared at my car with the engine still warm, panting, chest so tight I felt like I'd sprinted back to back a hundred-yard dashes.

The lock box I'd stashed my cash in sat on the grease-stained concrete floor busted open, the metal twisted and shattered. Instead of hiding it in my room like I always did, I'd gotten sloppy and left it out in the open. My vision blurred and got hazy. That fucking piece of shit.

Money I'd saved for the past six months to pay my way to the Titans Combine in Chicago in a month, which was conveniently when he'd be home next, was gone.

I'd scraped it together doing odd jobs, fixing people's cars and selling some of my old crap that I'd need to get rid of anyway when I left for college. If Aaron Smith hadn't fucked me over, so I'd needed to extract my fee through destruction, I'd have been home to hide this away before my dad had seen it.

As he took on longer routes driving his rig, our paths crossed less and less. Almost like every ten pounds of muscle I packed on in the weight room was another week he'd sign up for a longer trucking trip across country and stay out of the house. Good. I wanted him to finally be the scared one for once.

I picked up the box and turned it over. A quarter slid out into my open palm. Closing my fist around the metal, I launched the box through the air. The wall of tools on the other side shuddered and swayed. Both my hands clenched at my sides.

Air brakes from the trucker rig squealed outside the garage door. Tension gripped every part of me. Was he coming back?

The front door of the house banged open. My fingers tightened around the cold metal of the wrench beside me on the work bench. It was smaller than the one he'd used on me, but maybe this time I wouldn't freeze up, reverting to an eight-year-old kid when his boot steps hit the floor outside my door.

Stomping footsteps vibrated the wall behind me. My heart rate spiked, the throb traveling through my chest and threatening to choke me. Bile raged in my stomach, racing for my throat. Every cell in my body screamed for revenge, but I still sat there frozen, unable to move. The steps retreated again and the door slammed. Outside, tires ground the gravel in the dead-end street outside my house.

Shame washed over me. I should've run out there and taken his ass down. He'd always been bigger than me, but I was stronger. And quicker. And not drunk off my ass ninety percent of the time. I could knock him out and he'd never touch me again. Instead, I'd cowered in the garage, not even able to turn the door knob.

On the field, I never thought twice about knocking guys on their asses to get the opening that Bennet, our quarterback, needed, but my old man still paralyzed me.

Red rage clouded my vision and I let out a primal scream, wishing it could rip through the ceiling of the garage.

Crunching, smashing, pounding wrath unleashed on everything around me. A sound broke through the need to destroy. It continued, nudging at the edges of the blinding fog I'd slipped into, where instinct drove me.

The hammering of the blood in my ears slowed. I stepped forward, my shoes sliding on shards of glass. This snapped me from the haze and pulled me from the depths of my fury.

Staring up at me were a pair of eyes I hadn't seen in over ten years. My mom's sad gaze met mine through the shattered glass in the splintered picture frame.

I dropped the helmet and slid down the workbench to the floor. My sides were screaming, aching, burning.

I flipped the mangled frame over and rescued the picture. Shame ripped through my chest. The dull throb of the bruise on my ribs didn't compare to the lump in my throat.

Shaking off the haze and standing, like I'd broken through roots that had sprouted from my feet, I surveyed the rest of the damage. The glass glittered in the swinging overhead garage light and *tink*ed to the concrete floor.

Even in a blind rage, my car had been spared the brunt of my anger. A couple scratches, but no real damage I couldn't fix on my own. I grabbed the broom and cleaned up the glass, pieces of splintered wood, and bent and twisted metal. Unlike my old man, I cleaned up my own messes. The scrape and shower of glass into the trash can were the only sounds in the garage. What had I heard before?

No one was hurt. I repeated the mantra in my head. My dad didn't care about the outlet for his frustrations for his fucked-up life—namely me. It's what happens when you're the reason someone's wife was taken from them.

At least I only took my shit out on inanimate objects. They didn't bruise or bleed, not that he cared.

I could make it out now. Music.

The sound started over, louder this time. It wasn't someone's radio. The melody started and stopped like a car that hadn't had a key in the ignition in a long time. Drawn by a tug in the center of my chest, pulling me with a string I didn't know I had, I walked to the back of the garage.

I opened the door leading to the back yard. Shielding my eyes from the last gasps of the setting sun, I searched for the source. It was coming from my back yard. Correction —her back yard.

Bay Bishop sat on her back steps with her eyes closed swaying as her fingers plucked and strummed the strings like nothing could rush her through the melody. But it wasn't her guitar playing that drew me out of the fog of rage.

With her chin tilted toward the sky, her voice carried across our two back yards. Her hair was down, not like the ponytail she always wore. Inky waves of hair spilled down her back. A massive sweatshirt swallowed up half her body. The guitar was in her denim-covered lap.

Her left foot tapped to the beat and she rocked along to the melody.

The lyrics were lost in the wind, but the power of her voice, sweet and strong, powerful and vulnerable, hit me hard. Although she'd come to town a few years ago, her move into the vacant house behind mine was new, right before the beginning of our senior year.

I hadn't said more than a few words to her since she moved to town, even though we'd shared two classes every year since our sophomore year. We'd had a couple group projects, but as those always went, someone barged in to take control, hoarded all the information and then complained that no one else contributed. Not that anyone ever expected me to, so I'd sit back and let them freak the hell out and run through the playbook for my next game in my head.

Bay never treated me like a brainless moron. She never treated me like anything. She'd never even spoken directly to me.

What the hell was up with that? Six classes over three years and not a sentence? Most people vied for my attention.

She'd nod or shake her head, but I didn't even know if she'd ever said a word to me.

I leaned the broom against the doorway and wiped my bloody knuckles on my jeans. The throbbing increased with each heartbeat. I needed to ice them, but I couldn't move from my spot.

The slope and dip between our back yards meant the fence was more of a dividing line than a privacy barrier. Her back steps were clearly visible, almost raised up higher, like Mother Nature was giving her a platform to perform.

She hadn't been out here before. I couldn't have missed her voice. It was warm and full, and it wrapped itself around me and hit me in the center of my chest. An after-the-flag tackle.

Standing in the doorway, I needed to close the door. My fingers gripped the edge of the splintered, weather-beaten wood, but I couldn't take my eyes off her. The song was filled with hope and longing for a better time. A happier time. Although it felt like I'd never had those sunshine-filled careless days, her song made me believe I had. It created memories to a past I'd never lived, and left me hopeful that maybe there was a place where I'd find peace.

She smiled, almost laughing as the lyrics poured out of her. She repeated the chorus again, cycling back to it, trying to find the next verse. I could listen to the words on repeat for the next hundred years. She stopped, looked down at the notebook beside her, and then up.

Closing her eyes, she restarted at the chorus. Her fingers plucked the strings starting and restarting.

The break in the music sent a ripple of longing through me. My knuckles throbbed along with my arms and my side.

I craved the next note. Needed it like I needed my next breath.

Her eyes snapped open and she froze, staring back at me.

I'd been caught. Somehow this was worse than if I'd accidentally caught her changing in her bedroom.

A sharp honk broke through the hypnotic call of the melody curling deep in my chest. It severed the connection like someone clipping through a power line with a set of bolt cutters.

I peeled my fingers from the door frame and backed away from the sounds stirring something I couldn't name.

Slamming the door, I shook off the feelings coursing through me. I grabbed my jacket off the floor and rushed outside.

"What the hell took you so long?" Knox banged on the hood of his car.

"You honked less than twenty seconds ago."

"That's twenty seconds of prime drinking time." He slipped back into his car through the driver's side window and revved the engine. Knox 'always ready for a fucking party' Kane wasn't known for his subtlety.

"I'm sure you'll make up for it." I climbed into the passenger seat.

The car peeled away from the curb a fraction of a second after my foot left the asphalt.

"I sure as shit will." He thumped his fist against the ceiling and screamed out the window, shaking his head.

I grabbed the steering wheel, straightening us out on the road. "Asshat, can you not kill us before we get there?"

He dropped back into his seat. "An undefeated season. 4-time state champions. We're gods!" He screamed out the open window.

"Gods who can bruise and bleed." I slammed my fist into his shoulder. The bruise on my left side would bloom overnight, and the color would darken under my shirt minute by minute like all the others. The adrenaline was still coursing through my body, slowing the pain edging closer to the surface, but in an hour, standing would suck. And practice tomorrow would be brutal.

"Jesus." He glared and rubbed his shoulder. "We're not on the field anymore. The season's over."

My stomach knotted, twisting into an angry knot. It was over. My chances of getting drafted were getting slimmer and slimmer with each day. What better way to prep for my destitute fade into oblivion than with a blowout party where everyone woke up the next morning praying for death?

At least with the season over, the team didn't have to drag ourselves to the field for practice and puke twice during the warm ups where coach made us run backward while we chugged pickle juice. No, it would only be me.

Spring football was for the rising seniors, but I'd be right alongside them, grasping for the last of the light at the end of the slowly-darkening tunnel.

He tilted his head and grinned at me.

"You're fucking insane. Just get us to the party in one piece."

∾

Some girl danced in front of me, trying to tempt me off the couch. Her face was vaguely familiar, but it was hard to tell when most of the girls here had gone to the school of duck lips and highlights.

The second she found out I wasn't playing it cool with my draft prospects and instead had none, she'd find a new guy for private dances. Good thing I wasn't interested. Blocking her out wasn't hard. She was mainly a vague shape with flailing limbs, but she was getting a bit too close. I drained the last of my beer, shaking the bottle in front of me.

"Get me another beer." No please. The usual hints —avoiding eye contact and holding a conversation with everyone but her—hadn't worked.

She smiled wide, grabbed the bottle and rushed to the kiddie pool filled with ice to retrieve another one. The heat in the room had crept up over the past hour. Sweat rolled down the back of my neck. Why the hell was I even here? Everyone knowing I'd be stuck here while they all locked down college spots would be the final nail in the humiliation coffin. I'd rather puke after every scrimmage play than let anyone see me sweat.

"She's ten seconds from whipping out your dick and blowing you in front of everyone."

"My dick and I are in total agreement. That's not happening."

"This is Bethany we're talking about. She's hot as fuck."

She bent at the waist, running her hands through the ice bath looking for a bottle opener even though there was one on the wall in front of her. Her skirt rode up showing off the curves of her ass cheeks.

Knox's jaw was nearly on his lap and he and his dick

seemed in total agreement about what to do with the Bethany situation.

"Then you sleep with her."

"If that were an option, I would, but she's dead set on you."

"She's going to have a shit night, then."

"You're not the least bit interested in getting one of the hottest pieces of ass in school?"

I got up from the couch, wincing and biting the inside of my cheek. Fuck that hurt. "Not even a little bit."

Bethany bounded up to me with the open bottle of beer in front of her like an offering. "If it isn't my favorite tight end with the tightest end." She bit her lip and flashed do-me eyes.

"I need to take a piss. Can you give that to Knox? The whole college scout situation has him on edge. He's got so many teams after him, even after signing his recruiting letter, he doesn't know what to do."

Her eyes lit up. "Sure."

I glanced back on my way to the kitchen. Knox did have his pick of schools. He'd had a banner season and colleges were always looking for a stellar wide receiver to up their throwing game. He'd signed the letters, but the deals from other schools kept getting sweeter.

Knox mouthed a thank you with Bethany perched on his lap. He'd better never say I didn't do anything for him.

As a tight end, protecting my quarterback and punching a hole through the defensive line for the tailback to do their thing made most people think colleges were beating down the door to get me. They weren't—anymore. The fire in my stomach flared. My bones throbbed. In my entire football career, I'd missed one game. One game a year ago. The only game that seemed to matter and I'd spent it spitting up blood on the bathroom floor.

I'd be stuck in this shit town forever. All my talk of leaving in a few months sent the anxiety skyrocketing. I couldn't be in my house much longer. The urge to leave rode me hard. Who cared about a high school diploma? But these were my last couple months to get in front of any recruiter. Being a walk-on wouldn't work, since I'd been rejected from most schools I'd applied for as a regular student. This was my only out. My only chance to not end up as a guy who used to be someone back in high school.

Proof I wouldn't just become some has been who'd wind up drinking himself into an early grave, if the people around him were lucky, taking out his anger at a failed life on anyone within striking distance. I wouldn't be that bitter POS no one gives a shit about. I was going to find a way to get out and prove I'm nothing like him and never will be.

Snagging a six pack from the fridge, I headed out into the back yard.

The cold snap was back. Spring had tried to make a breakthrough, but winter wasn't having any of that. My breath hung in front of my face, slicing through my thermal shirt.

"The party's inside, Dare." Bennet came around the side of the house with his arm around a staple of the football fan club. Her hair was plastered to the side of her head and his fly was down. So much for some quiet time.

"I know, just getting some air." I slammed the edge of the bottle down on the stair behind me. The bottle cap flew off and disappeared between the gap in the wooden deck.

"When are we partying at your house? You've been holding out on us this season. It's your turn soon."

"Been busy." I'd also needed to repair the holes in the

living room, hallway, and bathroom walls before I'd let anyone over.

But my participation in the underage drinkfest wasn't a request. I'd be expected to play party coordinator before our June 3rd graduation. The date had been seared into my mind. The date I lost everything.

When the quarterback was also the coach's son, the coach who was my only shot at escape, he got away with way more trash talking than anyone else. His arm was a cannon, but so was his mouth. He'd been snapped up sophomore year just like I had been. Only his escape route hadn't been blocked by an alcoholic trucker with a wicked right hook.

The party rotation had made its way through everyone whose parents were never home or didn't give a fuck, which meant I'd already hosted my fair share this year.

I headed back inside. A clear head was a dangerous thing. I ran plays in my head, drilling them until the moves were ingrained in my muscles and I could run them in my sleep. In a few weeks, I wouldn't have football. I'd be done. Washed up at eighteen.

Four hours, three beers, and two dance partners later, after the prescribed attendance time, I searched for Knox. And I found him, crashed in one of the bedrooms with Bethany. At least one of us was having a good night.

In front of the house, I zipped up my jacket and stared down the street. The walk wouldn't be too bad. The soreness in my side and arm would be killer at practice tomorrow.

"Dare, you need a ride?" One of the guys from the team called out.

The three miles seemed a lot longer when there was a warm, fast ride at my fingertips. "Yeah, thanks."

Ten minutes later, we climbed the hill to my house.

"Is that The New Girl?" The defensive lineman stared out his window.

Bay? I shot to the window.

She rode down the street headed away from her house.

I checked the time. Where the hell was she going on her bike at one am? Not to the party I'd just left.

She'd never even driven by a party I'd been to since she moved to Greenwood.

Her coat flapped behind her. The pink gloves stood out against the pitch-black night.

The question swirled even after I got home. The stillness of the house comforted me. No Sports Central blaring from the TV. No rattling liquor bottles or house-rumbling snores. Even the smell of grain alcohol was dissipating from the broken-down recliner. I threw open the windows to air the place out. Only blissful silence.

The melody from earlier came back to me. The one that had been easy to drown out with thumping bass and drunk seniors doing their best to recreate every teen movie they'd ever seen in one night.

I stared out my window at the dark house behind mine. Had she snuck out her window?

A girl like Bay should've closed her school books and turned in without giving a thought to the alcohol-induced havoc happening across town.

A girl like Bay had a voice that could tap into emotions I didn't even know I was capable of feeling and make me crave them like an addict looking for his next fix.

A girl like Bay would want nothing to do with someone like me. And I needed to keep my distance from a girl like that.

So, what the hell was a girl like her doing riding her bike

away from home this late at night? I lay in my bed, staring up at my ceiling.

She faded into the background, never wanting anyone to pay attention, but there was a voice inside of her. Not only the one she sang with, but the melody that thudded in my chest like the perfect 50-yard pass. She might try to blend in, but if anyone else heard her sing a single note they'd never forget her. In less than three minutes she'd made me feel scary things I should run from.

Why did the need to know what other secrets she was hiding have me twisted up in knots after a single song?

3

BAY

Closing the backdoor behind me, leaving the warmth of our overtaxed heater behind, I sat and rested my dad's Martin guitar on my lap. Wasn't it supposed to be April?

The first hint of not-absolute-crap weather and I needed to get outside. Freak snow storms, icy rain, hail, blistering winds and pelting rain had stretched deep winter far beyond when I'd have hoped for a ray of warm sunlight.

Beggars couldn't be choosers. At least the ground wasn't sopping wet.

I jumped at Mamma Mia blaring from my phone.

"Hey, Mom."

"Hey, sweetheart. My shift's about to start, but I wanted you to know there's a plate—"

"For me in the fridge. I know, Mom. We've been doing this for months now. Even if you didn't have dinner for me, I can make it myself. College is less than six months away." Six long months.

"Why are you reminding me? Are you trying to kill me?"

"Think of the freedom when I'm not around to keep you tied to this place."

"It'll just make the house emptier. What are your plans for tonight?"

"Homework. Maybe watch some TV." Guilt banged in my chest, but I kept my voice steady.

"It sounds like you're outside."

Dammit, caught. "I had to take out the trash."

"Okay." She drew out the word like I'd crack if she made it three syllables long. "Be safe and make sure you—"

"Lock up before I go to bed. Yes, mom. I know. I'll be on my own next year. You don't have to worry. Have a good shift and I'll see you in the morning. Love you."

"Love you."

There was an edge of suspicion in her voice. Getting caught coming home at 3am six months ago might've had something to do with it. It was my fault; I never left before eleven pm anymore. If there was an issue with her shift, it always happened before then. So waiting meant less chance of getting caught. It also meant sometimes I turned up to school looking baked and barely coherent. I'd been lucky none of my teachers had sent me to the counselor's office for a talk.

We'd both had to adapt to the new life we found ourselves living in a new state without my dad. And we were still adapting. The never-ending challenge of figuring out what the hell this life was hadn't slowed down one bit. Four moves in four years. At least I'd stayed in the same school for the last three moves crisscrossing town. I still wasn't sure if it was a blessing or a curse. At least the new house cut the trip down to forty minutes when I snuck out. I'd been grounded twice, but it wouldn't stop me. Especially since I felt on the edge of a breakthrough. I was so close to finally overcoming the stalled sounds that caught in my throat before I swallowed them back down again.

"Love you too, sweetheart."

Guilt gnawed at my chest like a feral badger. My fingers slid across the strings, bringing out that squeaking twang.

I tugged my sleeves further down, covering most of my hands. With the sun disappeared behind my house, the evening chill seeped in even colder.

The picture frames hung on the wall by the door. In this house there was enough room to display them all and the landlord had been cool with nail holes.

In the first cherry wood frame were me and my parents. They'd made me wear a pink cone party hat, even though I'd been turning thirteen. We'd recreated the picture every year since. The one below it is just me and Mom with two giant cakes in the shape of a one and an eight. Our theater director had poked fun at me for showing up with a giant eight cake. But everyone in the stage crew and drama club had devoured it in minutes.

I stared at the last picture in the bottom row. It was one of the last pictures of all three of us together. He'd have been forty-one today. Usually on his birthday, Mom and I would pick out a cake together and find the worst present, usually personalized with "World's Best Dad." He'd open and fawn over it like it was the best gift he'd ever received.

Leading up to today, Mom had worked back-to-back twelve-hour shifts. Even more than usual. She always got this way when winter weather got stuck in the seasonal change limbo and the day crept closer like the thawing frost.

She'd slip into an immediate sleep after her shower. If only we could all be so lucky. It was harder to sleep now. There was a constant buzz in the back of my head, like I'd left the oven on or the garage door open. Opening my closet,

I'd fished out the only thing to calm the static in my brain. The familiar grooved feel of the worn handle of the case quieted the ringing, but didn't end it completely.

Unable to second guess myself, I'd grabbed the guitar and brought it out here. The dark grain of the wood contrasted with the light smooth body. The mahogany sides had a few nicks and bumps from my dad's time lugging this thing from gig to gig and studio to studio. Sometimes I'd gotten to tag along, always running my hands over the strings and smiling at the tiny twang before he'd sat me on his lap and taught me how to play.

I rested my forehead against the smooth side of the body. My fingers instinctively went to their positions on the strings. The metal bit into my flesh. Calluses hard-won over years of practice had softened in the almost thirty-six months since I'd picked up his guitar—my guitar now.

Filling my lungs with air, I let go of everything. My heartbeat, the crickets chirping and the slow strum of the strings my only focus. I fell into the rhythm of the music, letting the notes bring me back to a time before, when I'd never known what it was like to lose someone. After three years, I could finally bring myself to hold the guitar. Now I needed to play it.

Singing into the darkness, my voice carried on the gentle breeze. I was rusty, but the lyrics poured out of me like an unstoppable waterfall. Tag in the backyard. Sunday breakfasts with Marky Mouse—Mickey's slightly disfigured cousin—pancakes. The Mickeys always came out a bit wonky, and you couldn't tell if you were looking at a two-headed mouse sharing one ear or two incredibly disproportionate ears on a poor lopsided mouse head. The hours he sat with me, never getting angry or giving up, teaching me to play.

I love you, dad.

The words flowed through me. Through my slitted gaze, a figure moved. I could feel the heat of the gaze on me. Normally, this was when my vocal chords would clamp down, but I kept going, focusing on those words and the shadowy figure watching me. The last note rang out and I opened my eyes fully to see who had intruded on a moment no one else had seen in years.

I blinked back the tears pooling on the edges of my eyelids. The dam hadn't burst, but a release valve had been turned, letting the churning storm of emotions in my head settle down so I could breathe and think.

Over the fence, his movement broke up the shadow cast around him like he'd become a piece of the garage, still and focused.

My back jerked straight and I stared at the figure watching me in the dark.

Dare.

His form enhanced by his short-sleeved shirt was lit up in the darkened doorway backlit by a single hanging bulb in the garage. Smooth tanned biceps strained against the door jamb. He'd fit right in on whatever college team recruited him. Put him next to a college senior and not many people could tell the difference. From the five o'clock shadow to the piercing glare, Dare had never met an opponent he couldn't face down.

He was chiseled, in an 'I'll sweet talk you with bloody knuckles' kind of way. He was the epitome of the boy from the other side of the tracks, only instead of a motorcycle, he drove a muscle car.

We'd lived behind one another for more than six months and this was the first time he'd ever looked at me. Well, not the first time. The very first time it had been with a different level of intensity, biting and harsh. This time it was something else...

My stomach flipped. The wings flapping inside weren't butterflies. Maybe hummingbirds or sparrows—way bigger than the gentle flutter of delicate butterfly wings.

His gaze seared into mine across both back yards, and then he was gone. The slam of the garage door echoed in our nearly silent neighborhood.

Hello to you too, neighbor. Nothing had changed since I had first laid eyes on him.

Grabbing my guitar, I stared up at the night sky. The inky, cloudy mix threatened rain at any second. A fitting end to an already emotional day.

Back inside, I grabbed my dinner and headed to my bedroom.

I scribbled down a few more lines in my notebook. Running over the lines again, I waited for those feelings to come to me.

I'd sung for Dare. Well, not technically for him, but I'd sung while he was there. I'd known deep down it was him, even before I took in his entire form. Why had I been able to sing in front of him?

I dreamed of music, but dreams were all I could have when I couldn't even sing in front of anyone else. Every time I'd tried I kept coming up empty, until tonight. I'd hoped to make my dad proud by living his dream; instead, I'd been relegated to living his safe path.

I stared at the pictures on my desk. Our happy little family limped along now. And in a few months, I'd be gone too.

∾

The shrill screech of my alarm burst through my sleep. I shot up from my bed, fumbling for my phone. Fast or efficient wasn't how I'd describe my method for shutting it off.

I pitched forward too quickly and hit the floor with a thud. My phone shot under my bed like someone had attached it to a cord for comedy's sake. I snagged it and shut it off. Silence reverberated in my room without the nails-on-chalkboard squawk erupting from my phone. Rubbing the sleep out of my eyes, I yawned and went through my routine.

Got dressed. Left a note saying I was sleeping over at Piper's in case Mom came home early. Bundled up.

Every click and clank of my bike sounded like a thunderclap. I wasn't even sneaking out. It wasn't like my mom was upstairs.

I clipped my helmet and hopped on my bike. My bag tucked against my back, I set off down my street. A car met me at the top of the hill and my heart skipped a beat. But it wasn't my mom's gray sedan; it took the corners efficiently and sailed through intersections.

In the eighteen months or so I'd been sneaking out, I'd only been caught twice. The wind blasted my face, numbing my cheeks, but excitement drummed in my chest.

With one earbud in, I rode the nearly-silent street. The blocks got more compact and less sprawling. Winding roads shifted to straight ones that had been snapped down by a city planner. I flew past darkened store fronts. Liquor stores and pharmacies were the only things lit up.

I reached my destination: a nondescript stairwell with a green door at the bottom.

I hopped off my bike and grabbed the frame and handlebars, carrying it down the steps.

The door opened when I hit the last stair. A shadow fell over me.

"I was wondering if you were going to show tonight." Freddy crossed his arms. His salt-and-pepper beard fell almost to his upper chest.

"Like you could get rid of me so easily."

"If only I were so lucky." He held the door for me, grabbing my bike with one hand and hanging it up on the wall rack he'd mounted for me like I'd handed over a pamphlet.

"You singing tonight or working?"

A lump lodged in my chest like a hot burning coal. He'd heard me sing before, back when my dad was alive. Every time he asked the question, and every time I wanted the answer to be singing, singing my fucking heart out like I used to, but I couldn't. The notes lodged in my throat unless I was singing alone, and what good did that do for me when all I wanted to do was get up on stage and sing? I hadn't sung in front of anyone since my dad died. Except for Dare. I hadn't choked up like invisible fingers wrapped around my throat squeezing the air from my lungs when he watched me. I'd kept going, almost like I was unable to stop. But that was there, and this was here.

"Working." That pit in my stomach came roaring back at the thought of playing in front of someone else. Well, another someone else. I'd already played in front of Dare and didn't want to repeat that sensation. I swallowed down the lump in my throat.

He shook his head, walking off. I followed behind him, waving to the other techs and producers as we passed.

Gold and platinum albums dating back decades hung on the walls.

"Shouldn't you be happy?"

He scoffed. "No, cause then I have to pay you."

I patted his shoulder. "It also means less work for you."

"More. I've got to go behind you and check all your work." He pushed open the door to the smallest booth in the studio.

Now it was my turn to scoff. "And how many times have I made a mistake?"

His grumble was my only reply.

On the other side of the double-paned glass, a guy sat behind the piano crammed into the space, scribbling on the sheet music in front of him. "It's his first time. Be gentle with him."

"I always am."

He folded his arms across his chest and held open the door. "Does your mom know you're here tonight?"

I kept my eyes on the sliders and knobs in front of me. "Of course."

"Jesus, you're the world's worst liar. If she calls the cops, I'll tell them you broke in here."

"Broke in and started sound mixing demos for artists who've paid for booth time?"

He shrugged. "Kids these days are crazy." The door closed silently.

I shrugged off my coat and set it on the couch wedged in behind me. Ashtrays filled with abandoned joints and beer bottles covered every flat surface that wasn't the mixing boards. Home, sweet home.

I flicked on the intercom into the soundproof room. "You ready?"

The guy in the beanie and jean jacket jumped. He shielded his eyes trying to peer into the darkness on my side of the glass.

I flicked on the light and waved.

His head jerked back. "Are you twelve?"

"Eighteen, I assure you. You paid for two hours and the clock's ticking. Should we start?"

His gaze narrowed and he nodded skeptically.

I flipped the lights off on my side of the glass, checked my levels on the soundboard and pressed record. "Ready when you are."

4

BAY

The weekend was over too quickly—not because I hated school, although it wasn't my favorite, but because avoiding Dare would be impossible, since we shared three classes. I was also sleep deprived from my late-night trips to the studio, and there'd been a close call when my mom called the house phone just as I was closing the front door. She almost never called that late, and hadn't in the nearly eighteen months I'd been sneaking out. But every so often she would, always saying the call hadn't gone through to my cell. For twenty heart-pounding minutes after I hung up, I waited beside the phone to see if she'd call back.

As tired as I was, my thoughts kept drifting back to Dare.

Had he heard me play? Was he laughing his ass off at how terrible I'd been? My stomach clenched, knotting and churning.

Strapping my helmet on, I shoved the last of my pop tart into my mouth. Brown sugar, cinnamon, and I had a daily breakfast date.

Food was fuel, right?

The move had at least made it easier for me to bike to school. At our old house, I'd been stuck riding the bus, which none of the other seniors seemed to do. Piper, my best friend—pretty much my only friend—and I sometimes seemed like the only ones who hadn't gotten a cool new car the second we got our licenses and had to find alternate means to get to school. She and I had bonded over our shared distrust of the high school hierarchy. It probably had something to do with us not registering on it at all.

Wind blasted my glasses against my face during my final downhill stretch. Greenwood Senior High waited at the bottom, a not-so-glowing beacon with a line of cars cruising into the entrance.

I weaved my way through the cars lined up to enter the school parking lot. Off my bike, I entered the crosswalk and a car honked, revving their engine.

"Hurry up, TNG." A guy called out of his driver's side window before laughing with his friends in the car. "Or are you going to choke again right here in the parking lot?" He wrapped his hands around his throat making choking sounds.

I clenched my hands around my handlebars. Three more months. I only had to put up with this shit for three more. For some stupid reason, I'd thought I could try to take part in the talent show my first year here. Sing a song for my dad. To show him he wasn't wrong about me and I could do it.

The plan was to fling myself up on stage and force the music out of me. That had crashed and burned and the heat of the flames of embarrassment continued to lick at the back of my neck three years later.

I'd run off stage. And they'd never let me forget it,

cementing my new non-name when someone scribbled down TNG on my intro card. And it had stuck.

Cliques would posture and preen beside their cars until the late bell rang. I'd overslept in hopes of catching a stomach bug, or possibly Ebola, and not needing to go into school today.

I'd have to stop at my locker before class, which meant I'd be stuck in the hallway crush as everyone remembered why we were actually here in this 1970s-cinderblock building with barely-functioning heating on a Monday morning.

Brand new cars and clunkers filed into the lot. It looked like I wasn't the only one late today. The back row was reserved for the football team. The furthest from the building and the closest to the football field.

They laughed, high fived and threw around footballs like they didn't get enough pigskin time during practices and games. My gaze skittered over them, fear racing down my spine that I'd lock eyes with Dare. But why would he ever want to be caught looking at TNG?

I parked, locked up my bike, and headed into school, leaving the Greenwood Grizzlies crew behind. The hallway was decorated with banners and flyers for all the end-of-school activities. The senior trip, spring musical, prom, end of the year talent show. But the biggest banners were for the post-season Bedlam Bowl football game of juniors vs. seniors that took up more space than any other school activities even though they were scrimmages between our own team. That's how much they ruled this school. Their practices got top billing over everyone else.

I spun the combo lock on my locker. Suddenly, someone slammed into my back, knocking my forehead against the painted metal.

I shoved my body back, rubbing my forehead. I turned around, but whoever it was mixed in with the rest of the school pouring into the hallways. I don't know which was worse, that someone had done it on purpose or that I hadn't even mattered enough to register on their radar of objects to avoid.

I jerked my locker open. Down the hall people parted. No bowing or fanning with palm leaves? What a surprise. Small towns loved their sports, and a winning sports team? It was shocking that there wasn't a rose petal and glitter requirement. Even after three years in this town, the hero worship never stopped confusing the hell out of me.

At the front of the pack, Dare walked with a confidence some of the teachers didn't even have. He wasn't the quarterback—Bennet never let anyone forget his position on the team—but that didn't stop people from fawning all over Dare.

I turned, rummaging through my locker. Today's math homework that I'd finished last week and stashed here wasn't in my math folder. A corner of the paper stuck out from the barely-there gap along the side of my locker. Using pincer fingers, I bit my tongue, focused on extricating the paper without ripping it. Re-doing it before class wasn't an option. There was no time. Why were we being assigned actual work at this point in the year? Hadn't everyone submitted their applications already?

"Letterman jackets for today's parade, huh?" The lockers rattled as Piper slid into her spot beside me. The football player hallway parade was an unofficial Greenwood Senior High tradition. Every football player received a navy and yellow letterman jacket at the start of the season. One of those bumped anyone up the social stratosphere of the school by at least ten rungs. The players didn't even let their girlfriends wear them.

I'd made the mistake of walking through the social hierarchy peacock show on my first day here and was nearly tackled by the head cheerleaders. It hadn't been the worst moment of my first day, when I'd showed up still puffy-eyed, three days after the funeral, and determined to distract myself from the new reality that felt too foreign to even absorb.

The Greenwood cheerleaders took their points of pride, taking up the flank positions a little behind the guys, striking poses while they cat-walked down the hall. Just like they did at pep rallies, with the plastic smiles that hid their more sinister lizard-people strength.

"Brand new ones." She nudged her glasses higher, squinting through the lenses that magnified her eyes to look anime-huge. She joked that standing beside me, hers made mine look chic.

"How can you tell?" I slipped my homework safely in my class folder.

"They're the championship jackets bought in time for the trophy ceremony in a few weeks. They got a second batch of new ones after the championship last year, too. Where have you been?"

"Sorry, I'm not up-to-date on all my Greenwood Athletics gossip." I grabbed the rest of my books from my locker and slammed it shut, spinning the combination lock. "You leave stage crew with thirty splinters a day from reusing plywood from the '80s for set pieces and I'm running the risk of mild electrocution every time I run the sound board for the plays, but the thirty guys on the football team deserve new letterman jackets twice a year."

Her fingers bit into my arm. "Dare is looking this way."

"No, he's not." Please don't let him be looking my way. I sent up my silent prayer to the god of high school survival.

"Holy shit, yes he is." Her grip tightened.

Was she trying to pinch my bones?

"Piper, holy crap." I yelped and yanked my arm from her grasp.

"He was definitely looking this way." Her gaze was trained at the mob of people over my shoulder.

'This way' as in at me? Why would he look at me? Because of my music? That had to be long-forgotten locker room fodder already. The New Girl that lives behind me plays music. It sucked and it was hilarious watching her nearly cry on her back porch. It was so terrible, I slammed the door closed trying to block it out. Which was worse? Laughing at my expense or not knowing I was alive at all?

I turned slowly, like a serial killer was standing beside me with the knife raised over my head. The low thud of shoes against the slick linoleum floor signaled their arrival to my row of lockers.

His neck and shoulder breezed past me without a glance or nod of acknowledgement.

Piper adjusted the straps to her backpack. "I swear, he looked at you."

"Probably trying to figure out where he'd seen me before."

"You never talk to him ever?"

After my first day in the hallway? I'd been happy to avoid him at all costs. "Why would I? I'm surprised you do. People still call me The New Girl."

Her forehead crinkled. "You are, though."

"I've been here for over three years! How does that make me new?"

"You're one of the new*est*." She shrugged. "Small towns are weird like that."

"No shit. Plus, my actual name is a whole syllable less than calling me The New Girl. You'd think people would want to put less effort, not more, into mocking someone."

She looked back at me over her shoulder, waving her unicorn-topped pencil at me. "Weird or not, Dare was totally looking at you."

"So what? Maybe he liked my shirt." I tugged out the bottom hem of the Hamilton t-shirt Piper had bought me for my birthday and did a twirl.

"You're right. I'm sure he's looking for fashion advice."

I laughed at her deadpanned reply.

"He did beat the shit out of Aaron Smith's car over the weekend."

A hazy image of a nondescript guy with hair and eyes flittered through my brain. "He did?"

"Yeah, the guy owed him money or something and wouldn't pay up." She closed her locker.

"What an asshole."

I laughed at her incredulous look as she zipped her bag.

"Right? Who doesn't pay someone money they owed?"

"I was talking about Dare."

"I can't say he doesn't give people a heads-up about his terms."

"Terms for what?"

"I think he fixes cars sometimes."

All his time in his garage made more sense. "The guy didn't pay, so Dare wrecked his car." She shrugged like it made all the sense in the world to destroy someone's stuff because they couldn't pay. Talking and working out a deal seemed like a better plan.

"Removed the rearview mirrors, added a few more dents and maybe flattened a tire. I didn't get the full details."

"That was the Cliffs Notes version?"

"I only gathered bits and pieces of the info. I'm sure we'll hear more by lunch."

My stomach began the telltale destructo war path, but I had my supplies locked and loaded to keep me from an emergency wardrobe change.

The rest of the day went by like every other day. Classes. Class bells. Lunch. PE conveniently right after the twenty minutes when we all shoved food into our faces before we were booted out of the cafeteria. And more classes.

I shared three of those classes with Dare, including P.E. I'd never been someone who swooned over the hot guys. Generally, they were all Grade-A assholes and I didn't think he'd be any different. But this time I couldn't stop myself from looking at him. He was the only person who'd ever heard me sing other than my parents and Freddy. What did he think? Did he hate it? Run screaming into his house because his ears bled from the sound of my voice?

Did I even want to know what he thought? Why did it matter to me at all?

5

DARE

"Travis Maze 81!" Bennet shouted over the rumble of the band and muted clack of shoulder pads hitting each other. We were packed in at the line of scrimmage. Thirty-seven seconds left in the final half and down by one. The rising seniors and juniors and I were the only ones playing for glory, rather than just playing to keep from getting hurt and maintaining reflexes.

It was a post-season game. An exhibition match of sorts, but I wasn't going to stop and let up. Most of these guys already had their ticket written, but mine was still flapping in the wind.

My fingertips dug into the wet and freezing grass. Clouds from the inky black horizon blew against my face. I ducked my head, preparing for the collision.

Funneling my rage and fury, I had one objective. Lay out every person in my path who wasn't wearing a red jersey. I inched my cleats deeper into the ground, preparing to leverage my weight and protect my asshole QB from decimation.

We put our bodies on the line for the small-town glory

and college dreams. Some did it for money and fame. I mean, I wouldn't turn them down, especially not the money, but I'd sure as hell like to know everything in my life wasn't a mistake. That I had one thing I could do well enough to make it big.

Adrenaline raced through my veins. I bared my teeth at my opponents. Demolish. Dismantle. Destroy. The blood pounded in my ears like a metal concert.

A deep breath and I snapped, rushing forward and colliding with the bodies in front of me. I'd destroy anything in my way to gain as many yards as it took to complete our play and clear the path for Bennet's throw.

The ball landed in the hands of Knox, already in the end zone. Overhead, the scoreboard clock ticked down. The final seconds disappeared from the game clock. We'd done it.

I stared down at the prone bodies of the assholes who'd thought for a second they could make it past me. For that reason alone, I wanted to rip their damn heads off. I loomed over them, chest heaving.

Trumpets blared. A body knocked into mine. I flung my elbow cracking it into the thick pad.

"Fuck, Dare. It's me. Your teammate." Bennet shoved my shoulder.

Standing in the center of the field, I closed my eyes and steadied my breath, letting the hammering rush bring me back to my own head where I wasn't all instincts teetering on the brutal edge of control.

"What did I tell you about tackling me after a play?"

"So fucking moody." Bennet glared, walking to the sidelines.

I braced my hands on my hips, letting everyone else pile on one another at the sidelines. The crush of bodies and hits outside of the called plays sent a skitter of unease up my spine. I needed space, especially after a game like today's, brutal and hard-won. It took me time to come down from the impulse to destroy.

Knox jogged up to me. There was an uneasiness in his stance, poised and ready to get out of the way.

I sucked in a breath. That he even thought I'd go after him—it curdled my stomach. "Good catch, man."

His shoulders relaxed and he yanked off his helmet. "You think anyone's scouting this late in the season?" He stared up into the stands.

"At this point, does it matter?" If they were, I hadn't heard a word from them. The sniffs had gone stale long ago for me. It was stupid to even get my hopes up.

"There can always be a better offer." He grinned and dropped his gloves into his helmet.

We left the field and headed into the locker room. It wasn't so much a locker room as a holding pen for our gear and duffels. No place to shower and barely enough room to change. The locker rooms at the college I'd visited were palatial compared to this. Their own gyms, saunas, support teams, cafeterias.

Freedom.

Too bad I wouldn't get to experience it.

We boarded the bus to head back to Greenwood, still sweaty and drained.

A hand landed on my shoulder. "You going out after this?" Knox leaned over the back of my seat.

"You seriously have energy after the game we played?"

He bounced up and down like an overactive puppy. "Bethany's going to the after party with the other cheerleaders. Since when are you not up for a bit of oral gratitude?"

"I'm tired. I'm going home. Don't do anything stupid."
My stomach growled.

"You know me." He plopped down in his seat.

"Exactly." I shoved my headphones back in my ears and
rested my head against the freezing window, letting the
rhythmic cadence of the street lights and rocking of the bus
chassis drag me under into a dead sleep. More like letting
myself pass out after the exhaustion. Keeping myself in
check on the field was as punishing as throwing myself at
the bodies of my opponents, but I wasn't doing anything to
jeopardize my last shot at signing the recruitment letter for
a college scholarship.

After getting off the bus, I headed to my car. I flipped on
the overhead light and checked my wallet. Moths might as
well have flown out. I flicked open my glove compartment
and center console. Nothing.

My stomach made angry rumblings, pissed off at my
body being pushed so hard with no fuel injection. Maybe
there was some food at home.

But my stomach faded to the background as I got to the
intersection ahead of my house. Instead of turning down my
street, I went around the long way. I rolled past Bay's street.
All the lights were off in her house and the car wasn't in the
driveway. Was her mom not home? Or was Bay out partying? Maybe The New Girl had a wild side no one had seen
in the past three years. Maybe she biked three towns over to
let her freak flag fly.

I shook my head. What the hell had her song done to
me? And why was I driving past Bay's house after midnight
in the first place?

When I got home, the house was quiet. Opening the
fridge, I stared at the vast emptiness. Shit. I should've taken
Knox up on his offer. The cabinets were also almost bare. A

lone box of Cap'n Crunch that might as well have had cobwebs on it stared back at me. Handfuls of stale cereal it was.

A knock jerked me out of my liter water chug to quiet my stomach.

I opened the door.

A kid who didn't look familiar stood back a step and stared up at me with fear in his eyes.

"What?" I said through the last handful of crunch berries.

He glanced down my street.

"Someone said you could help me out."

"I don't have any drugs." I moved to close the door. Of course the poor kid eating fucking cereal at midnight was a dealer.

"No, it's about my car. My mom's car, actually, and she'll murder me if she sees the dent." He glanced over his shoulder to the car in the driveway with a girl in the passenger seat.

I dusted off my hands and narrowed my gaze. "Let me see it."

Staring at the side of his car, I let out a low whistle and squeezed the back of my neck. I crouched down and shook my head. "Wow, you really did a number on this."

"Fuck, I'm dead. She's going to kill me." He scrubbed his hands over his face and the girl hugged him.

"I can fix it for you. But it'll cost you."

"How much? Anything."

"Five extra-large Gitano's pizzas."

"Five!" His voice echoed down the quiet street.

"That's my price if you want this taken care of before your mom wakes up."

"Fine, I'll get them after you fix it."

"Payment up front. Then I'll fix it." I crossed my arms over my chest and glared.

"Okay," he sputtered before getting back in his car.

And that's how I wrangled myself a week of meals through a three-minute suction cup job on the side of a tan sedan.

I climbed the steps and got out the key to my bedroom. Mine was the first door at the top of the steps, facing the back of the house. I unlocked the padlock and flicked open the hinged metal strip before turning the knob. I'd installed this the first time I came home to find my room ransacked. Even when I was sure he was on the road, the peace of mind to calm my worries that he might be destroying my shit whenever I left the house.

In the shower, I rested my forehead against the tile, letting the water flow over my sore muscles. The grime and sweat from the game washed down the drain. At least these aches and pains washed away so much easier than the other bruises I'd earned at home—the ones that didn't come with padding and ref whistles blaring when things were out of control. I'd been prepared for these. They didn't come in the dead of night or when I wasn't braced for my dad's ire.

With a towel wrapped around my waist, I opened my bedroom window. Frigid air rushed in and I bit out a curse. Why the hell had I done that? The answer tucked itself in the back of my head, trying to hide even from me.

I dropped onto my bed, flexing my hand. Water dripped from my hair to my bedspread. Every few seconds my gaze drifted to the house across the way. A light was on now.

I shot up from the bed, forcing myself not to strain to hear something, anything, other than a car driving by every few minutes.

Grabbing my boxers, I threw them on and stared up at

the ceiling trying to figure out if my helmet-to-helmet contact had been too hard. That was the only thing that explained why I wasn't out partying another win right now. Instead, I was...

It was fucking cold and I was a damn moron. I jumped out of bed and wedged my fingers in at the top of my window to slam the damn thing down.

A note drifted in with the cold-as-balls air. I froze. My heart rate spiked like I was back on the field and a play had just been called out. The refrain played again and stopped without the fluidity from the back steps, but it was her. Was she singing too? Even leaning halfway out the window, I strained to make out her voice. My still-wet feet slid on the wood floor and I pitched out the window. The bottom-of-a-rollercoaster feeling did a deep dive into my stomach and my view of the ground was no longer below me, but right in front of my eyes.

My hands shot out. Bracing myself on the side of the house, I caught my feet against the glass. What would the papers write about this when someone found my crumpled corpse in a few days, still in my boxers? Teen sex ritual goes wrong: do you know what your children are doing? I shuddered and walked my hands back toward the windowsill. I'd come inches from killing myself. I flung myself back inside the house after my nearly neck-breaking attempt to hear every note.

What the hell was wrong with me? I shook my head. Falling to my death to hear her voice was a new level of insanity. But I couldn't stop wishing she was playing on her back steps tonight.

∼

The parking lot pageant was a Greenwood Senior High tradition. People with too much money and too much time showing off to the same kids they'd gone to school with since we were five. We all knew Andy Phillips had peed himself in the third grade, so that meant he had to upgrade his Lexus every year. Gary DiNotti was the first to get caught with a boner in eighth grade history class. Mrs. Greene had been hot as hell, but it meant he dedicated himself in the gym to the point where he could barely turn his head.

Everyone cruised into the lot and hung by their cars. Hoods were popped, balls were thrown, and the cheerleader strut would make anyone do a double take. Were we in Pennsylvania or Paris Fashion Week?

"Great game, Dare." One of the senior girls leaned against the hood of my car. Was that a lollipop in her mouth? Her dentist dad had to be pissed about that.

"Hey." A disinterested head nod was all I could muster.

My car rocked. Knox slammed the trunk, retrieving one of the balls stashed there. He chucked it my way and I palmed it, holding it in front of me like a pig-skinned shield between me and a viper.

"I missed you at Bennet's party."

"You'd have had to be looking for me to miss me." I shoved my hand in my pocket, staring over her head. My disinterest didn't seem to register one bit.

She smiled wide and stepped even closer. "I was looking for you."

"Was this before or after you blew Bennet on the deck?" I cocked my head. "You can do whatever the hell you want, I'm not judging, but don't pretend your interest has anything to do with me." This is what I got for getting sucked into the whole football players rule the school bullshit my first two years on the team. It's hard to walk away when you're trying to fit in.

The seniors were gods and I did whatever the hell I needed to in order to stay a member of the team. Bruised, possibly broken bones didn't stop me from showing up every single time—except once, and I'd learned my lesson after that.

They were the closest thing I had to a family, and not making waves was the difference between riding the bench and getting cut. Pretending all the shit they talked about were things I had to deal with too. Not that I fixed dents in people's cars so their parents wouldn't find out, so I could eat and keep the heating on, not for money to score beers from someone's older brother.

Early on, I learned not to talk about what I dealt with at home. It only led to more questions, people snooping around and the threat of being sent away where I wouldn't even have my football family. But with only a little over two months left until graduation, the pretending was getting harder. The cracks between me and them got wider.

Bay zoomed past all the cars on her bike. The bright yellow helmet was unmistakable. She didn't give a shit about all the fakeness. There was no slow roll by to see who was here and who wasn't. If anything, she biked past like it was the last place she wanted to be. I couldn't help envying that sometimes. An escape into anonymity sounded right, but I had to either be a name or make a name for myself to stand out. Otherwise, I'd miss out on what came next, and the final step of going pro.

I flung the ball in my hands to Knox. "Grab my bag from the car. I'll meet you inside."

"Where are you going?" His voice boomed through the rows of cars.

"Lock my car." I shouted over my shoulder, weaving my way past the designated junior parking spots.

I'd been hanging in my garage more than I should, waiting to hear her sing again, but the songbird had stopped.

She threaded the bike rack to the stand beside the side door.

"Bay, hold up."

She whirled around, stumbling and nearly flipping over the thigh-high bike rack.

My hands shot out, steadying her by the shoulders.

She blew her hair out of her face and stared at me with wide eyes before looking over her shoulder.

"I'm fine. You can go talk to whoever you were trying to talk to." She shrugged her shoulders and I let my hands fall back to my sides.

"It was you."

"What was me?" Her gaze dipped and she fidgeted with her backpack straps and clipped her helmet to the carabiner dangling from one side.

"Who I was trying to talking to."

She squinted, peering up at me through one eye. Her nose scrunched up, highlighting the faint freckles across the bridge. "Why?"

"Do I need a reason?"

Her snort told me I did.

"I don't do homework for pay. This is what I look like without these." She pulled off her glasses, batting her eyes at me. They were brown, but not any brown. They reminded me of brownies or chocolate cake. She shoved them back up the bridge of her nose.

"Yes, I'm still a virgin. No, I don't plan on giving it up at prom. No, I'm not a lesbian. That should do it." I was blocking her escape. It took her three half steps in three directions to realize it.

I grinned with my arms crossed over my chest. "Are you done?"

Her eyes were laser sharp. Cool and bright didn't mean she didn't have the confused biting glare down. "Aren't you? Why are you talking to me?"

"I can't talk to you?"

"You never have before." There were crinkles in the middle of her eyebrows from her skeptical look.

I hadn't before, but after hearing her sing, I couldn't stop looking at her and waiting to hear even more.

"Maybe I wanted to try something new."

She squeezed the bridge of her nose. "Who put you up to this?" Her foot tapped like she was dealing with an over-grown child. I mean, sometimes I was, so I couldn't really blame her. And any attention was better than just a head nod or worse, her gaze whipping right past me.

"Why does there have to be an ulterior motive for me to talk to you?"

"Because no one talks to me."

"That can't be true."

She let out a long-suffering sigh that must have tested the edges of her lung capacity. "Fine, there's a small subset of people in this school who speak to me on a regular basis and you're not one of them." Her voice was higher than when she sang. Not as raspy and bold, but no less powerful. My cheeks hurt from trying to keep my smile under wraps.

Maybe I'd like to be. "Have you ever thought it might be a side effect of your glowing personality? With the way you respond to a simple hello, I'm surprised no one else is climbing the walls to get to know you."

Her jaw dropped. "And football fever has gone to your

hadn't just gotten off a twelve-hour shift. "I thought that was you. You're up early."

"I thought I...heard the car." My fingers flew to the hem of my shorts, tugging them down, but that was a losing prospect with the well-worn flannel barely covering my ass. It wasn't my fault my room was an inferno.

"Dare was driving behind me when my car broke down. He pushed it the rest of the way home, so I'm rewarding him with some of these." She added another handful to the top of the pile.

"Some? That looks like most of them." No way in hell was he swooping in and stealing my cookies.

The corner of Dare's mouth quirked up. He fished one out of the massive container filled to the top and took a bite. "Molly, these are outstanding." He used her first name. How frustratingly, annoyingly cocky. "You don't need to call a tow. At least not yet. I can check it out later this afternoon and see if I can fix it."

My gaze narrowed and my hands curled into fists at my sides. Why was he being nice to my mom? What bizarro game was he playing? And why did his tousled hair make me want to run my fingers through it? Was it silky smooth? Was his jaw as sharp as it looked? And what the hell was I thinking? I shook my head to ward off whatever pheromones he was pumping out into the air.

"Let me know how much it would be and I can pay you."

"No payment needed for labor. If I have to order a part, I'll let you know." He grabbed another cookie humming in food induced pleasure. Cinnamon sugar collected on his fingers. He licked it clean as another of my delicious treats disappeared into his face hole.

"So kind." My mom patted his bicep. "Isn't he such a gentleman?" She smiled and made a face at me like 'isn't he adorable?' No, that wasn't exactly the word I'd use to describe him.

"Maybe Bay could make you a few more to thank you."

"That would be outstanding." He grinned wide. A smug smirk while eating my cookies that emboldened me the second my mom left the room.

"What the hell, Dare? Give me my damn cookies." I held out my hand.

"Your mom gave them to me as a gift. What kind of asshole would I be if I turned it down? Are your cookies as good as these?"

"You'll never know." He didn't need to know that I'd planned to finish that batch off when my mom left for work. That was none of his business.

"Oh, I'm sure I will." His grin took shit-eating to a whole other level. I'd never wanted to hit someone before, but he tested my limits of civility and not being an asshole.

"I'll be back later, Molly."

"Thank you so much, Dare," she called from the kitchen.

"Give them to me." I held out my hand, jamming my pointer finger into my extended palm.

He laughed, took two steps backward wearing his smug smile. "Nice PJs."

"I'll—" I looked down at myself. Bare legs, bare arms, and a gap between my top and the waistband of my boxers. My instinct was to yelp and run screaming from the room. Instead, I stood my ground and glared right back at him as he pushed through the screen door.

"Bite me!"

"That can be arranged, Bay. Anytime you'd like." He grinned, laughing as the door closed behind him.

Hanging out in my living room. Stealing my damn cookies. Calling my mom by her first name. Dare might not have

"I can name five other people who can do exactly what I do."

"But they don't look nearly as good when they do it." The line was delivered so smoothly, it nearly rolled straight past me. "Between you and Piper we've probably got the best-looking stage crew in the state."

I stopped, my eyebrows scrunching. A nervous, way-too-loud laugh shot from my mouth, startling us both.

Was this flirting? A day ago, this would've hit me in a much different way. Before I'd been hit with the Dare Effect. Now, this just felt cute and nice, not erupting-volcano over-whelming.

Turning too quickly, I banged my hip against the console and fumbled to the other side, ripping off an extra strip of tape and smoothing down the cables to within an inch of their lives.

Had someone put out flyers or was there a bet going on to see who could get me to go on a date with them? I peered over my shoulder at the auditorium of people. The stage crew roamed around with set pieces, electronics, and micro-phone packs. The actors walked through lines and blocking. No one was looking my way. No furtive glances. I checked the ceiling for a bucket of pig's blood.

I grabbed Piper and headed into the booth with her, closing the door. "Something weird is going on."

"I told them to stick with the hair mics instead of the cheek mics, but you know how Ted can be." She shook her head and stared out the large window in front of us.

"Not that, although yes, we have more hair mics for when something goes wrong and we won't need a full swap out if there's a break down." I shook my head. "That's not what I meant." Tugging on her arm, I leaned in. "I think Jon was flirting with me."

"What?" Her sharp scream turned heads our way even in the soundproof box I'd locked us in.

"It's not that big a deal."

"Are you serious?" She craned her neck searching the rows of seats for an unsuspecting Jon. "Did he ask you on a date? Why didn't you tell me? What exactly did he say?" Her hands wrapped around my arms and she shook me.

The other half of my weird morning has been on the tip of my tongue, but her head would probably explode. I'd be covered in brain matter if I told her Dare had flirted with me. If that was even what he was trying to do, and not playing his part of a school-wide conspiracy to prank The New Girl.

"He said I looked cute at the sound mixing board."

She gasped and clutched her hands to her chest. "What else?"

"That was it."

With her back pressed against the wall in her best Scarlett O'Hara impression, she rested her hand against her forehead. "Why couldn't I be a sound board whiz like you?" She continued to stare at him through the large window separating us from the hustle of the show.

"Do you like Jon?" I stepped in front of her, blocking her view.

"No." She made a dismissive *psh*. "Of course not. I'm not macking on your guy."

"First off, there is no macking. Second, I'd never think you would. And third, if you like him, you should ask him out."

"Not when he's obviously into you."

"He said one nice thing. That hardly qualifies as being into me."

She ran her hand over her shoulder, squeezing it. "I'll think about it."

"The next time I talk to him, I'll steer the conversation in your direction and see how he responds."

She peered at me. "You'd do that for me? You swear you don't like him?"

I crossed my heart and held up my hand. "Swear. Let's get you a date to the prom."

I spent the rest of play practice thanking my lucky stars I hadn't told her about my lemonade encounter with Dare. Piper grilled me on every syllable Jon had uttered, as well as his micro expressions, breathing patterns, and heart rate.

My ride home was blissfully free from a flirtation interrogation. With the sun gone, frigid air made the last hill less horrible than it would be once spring eventually arrived.

"Your chain's loose."

My handlebars wobbled. Straightening them out, I glanced at the car riding beside me. The mussed brown hair made an iconic silhouette. I swear, some girls at school were ready to get it tattooed on their asses. Just great.

"Are you stalking me?"

"Not like I live in the same neighborhood or anything." He grinned, still cruising along beside me.

"Five streets up and take a right, if you're lost."

The slow, gravelly crunch of his tires and mine were the only sounds on the lamp-lit street.

He didn't seem anywhere near as fazed as I was by the awkwardness of this situation. "Thank you for helping my mom."

"You're welcome."

"Is there something else you wanted?"

He propped his arm on the window of his car and rested his head against his hand like he wasn't driving a two-ton machine down the road beside me. "No." He laughed to himself. "Catch you later, Bay."

"Hopefully never, Dare." I called after his muscle car complete with bright red paint.

Once home, I snagged the note off the counter.

I hope you had a good time at practice. Got extra supplies for you. They're already under the sink in the bathroom. There's meatloaf and mashed potatoes in the oven. Go easy on the cookies and save some for me. Be safe and don't forget to lock up!

Love, Mom

I grabbed my plate, soda, ibuprofen and late-night provisions, including a dozen cookies and milk. Tomorrow, my period would be over, but it didn't mean I wouldn't milk the junk-food train for all it was worth, and I wasn't coming back for multiple trips up and down the stairs. Why pretend I wasn't going to eat a dozen cookies tonight? Walking downstairs once the house was silent always freaked me out, not that I could tell Mom that. It was another reason I loved going to the studio. Things were always loud and lively when people were creating. I knew it was time I stopped being afraid of monsters lurking in the shadows. My high steps up the stairs once I turned the lights on, however, said differently.

Without the distractions of my crazy day I could feel the pain killers wearing off. I grabbed the hot water bottle and curled up in my bed, cocooned, and flipped on the TV ready to fall into a sugar-induced coma.

History homework waited for me once I'd finished dinner, but my gaze kept drifting to my dad's guitar. The case had remained closed since the night Dare caught me playing. But notes and a melody formed in my mind. I grabbed my notebook and scribbled down the lines before I forgot them.

Tonight, Freddy would put me to work recording more demos or cleaning out a studio or prepping for sessions tomorrow. He always had room for Miles's daughter. It's how they all knew me. And at school I was The New Girl. Would I ever be me?

I glanced out the window toward the house of the guy slowly filling my mind with bubbling emotions. How did I get rid of these feelings?

DARE

The assistant coach poked his head into the workout room door and rapped his knuckles against the wood. "Dare, Coach wants to see you."

My weight slipped out of my hand and dropped to the floor.

"Ohhhhhhh." Knox added his unhelpful addition to the awkwardly quiet room, where the air tasted like metal and sweat. He'd joined me in my penance workouts, saying he wanted to keep in shape so the pre-season wasn't as brutal. But he didn't need to be here, and both of us knew it.

Over half the rising seniors were in the gym when I walked out. All of their eyes were on me.

I gritted my teeth and clenched my hands at my side.

The walk to Coach's office stretched on longer than any walk to the principal's office. This was serious. This mattered. Playing on the field beside guys I'd grown up with and winning with them was one of the few bright spots in my life. And that was over. Fear gripped me, reverberating down my spine, which ratcheted up the anger monster who lashed out whenever something was threatened to be taken from me.

I dragged the towel across my sweaty face and stepped into the doorway, clearing my throat. "Hey, Coach Greer."

His head popped up and he set down the papers in his hands. "Dare, come in and have a seat."

He motioned to the one filled with stacks of old playbooks.

I moved them to the internal window sill filled with even more notebooks and stacks of paper. The whole place seemed one carelessly flung cigarette butt away from turning the entire school into kindling.

"You wanted to see me?" My nostrils flared and I dug my fingers into my thighs.

Coach rocked back in his chair with his hands braced behind his head, leveling his assessing gaze on me.

The clock over his shoulder ticked louder than any ref's whistle for seconds on end. "I got a call from a scout."

"Do you want me to run more drills at practice for Knox or Bennet? Or for the seven-on-seven Bedlam Bowl two months?" It had been 'requested' I do that for a few practice tapes for the guys when colleges expressed an interest over the past few years.

"Of course."

I nodded, pushing up out of my chair, biting back the anger welling in my chest.

"They want to see you."

I dropped back in the seat, pushing it back a few inches and sending a sharp squeal through the jam-packed office. "Me?"

"You. Did you think I wasn't still trying to get you your spot?"

"It...I didn't know." The hope I'd been clinging to had

been something I thought was only a pipe dream to keep me together, at least through graduation. Most of the guys who'd already signed letters had involved parents who came to the games and rode the coach to make sure their kid had a place in the spotlight. Knox's parents seemed to have monthly meetings, which turned into weekly meetings, on what would be best for him once our season started. Even a few guys had been picked up right after the championship win, but nothing for me.

"I'm giving it to you straight. No one is knocking down my door to grab you, after last season. Even after Ohio State rescinded their offer, there were others interested, but then the fight last year made the paper. Anyone searching for you would pull that up."

The coals I'd long thought were dead were stoked higher by Coach bringing up the fight where I'd narrowly avoided getting arrested last season. I wanted to kick the guy's ass all over again.

"A cheap shot against one of my teammates isn't something I can let slide." I shot forward in my seat.

"And you got his number during the game. That kid was probably crapping turf for a week with how you slammed him to the ground in the next play. And that should've been the end of it. Put it to bed on the field, but you went after him later that night."

"Archer had broken his radius in three places after the illegal hit and they'd only gotten a 15-yard penalty. We lost him for the whole season. That guy could've ended Archer's entire high school career and he laughed."

I'd wiped the punk-ass smile off his face with my fists at their loser celebration the night of the game. Knox backed me up. Well, more like went along to make sure I didn't get myself into too much trouble. If he hadn't been there, I'm

"You're up to something."

"I'm up to nothing."

She glanced down the hall behind me and then over her own shoulder. Her body relaxed a barely perceptible amount. "You're up to something." Peering sideways at me, she closed her locker.

"I could say the same about you. Where were you headed at 2am?"

"How did you..." Her eyes shuttered and she squared her shoulders. "I don't know what you're talking about."

"The green and white Huffy. You were on it in this coat." I ran my fingers over the lapel of the navy pea coat.

Her gaze narrowed before smoothing out and she stepped back. "It must've been someone else."

I wrapped my fingers around the strap of my backpack on my right shoulder. "Maybe it was, but she looked a hell of a lot like you. Maybe you have a long-lost twin."

"Maybe you should mind your own damn business." Her snap was whip-quick.

My lips twitched. "I mean, if there is a twin of yours out there. I'll need to get to the bottom of it. That could be big news. You wouldn't want to meet her?"

A low, simmering growl rumbled in her throat. "Whatever your deal is," she waved her hands in front of her up and down my body, "I don't want any part of it. Leave me and my twin sister alone." She spun on her heel and walked off.

"Does she have a name?"

"Yeah." She raised her hand above her retreating shoulder and lifted her middle finger.

I laughed and called after her. "Real nice, Bay."

"Bye, Dare." Her levels of not giving a fuck were refreshing.

She disappeared through the exit doors at the end of the hallway.

"See you later, Bay." I could catch up to her. It would take her at least a few minutes to unlock her bike. Instead, I headed back to the gym.

Sweaty and smiling for what felt like the first time, I got back to my house. The quiet inside unwound the tension that crept in whenever I stuck my key in the front door. I jogged up the steps and unlocked my bedroom door.

I went straight to the bottom drawer of my desk, flicking the lock and pulling out my newest pad. With aching fingers, I finished my work preserving Bay's back with a raised finger over her shoulder. The flip of her ponytail. The 80s t-shirt. The jeans molded to her legs.

Things were looking up for the senior year I'd thought would be the start of another story of a washed up has-been clinging to the good old days back in high school. Now I had a chance at a scholarship and maybe something else with Bay. What it was or what I wanted it to be I didn't even know, but I knew it felt good. It felt right, and I needed more of that in my life.

Flexing my slowly-numbing fingers, I flipped open my notebook and scanned the page. Words scribbled across the pages spilled into the margins. I hadn't written this much in a long time. And I'd never sung any of these out loud, until now.

But the song clawed at my chest, forceful and inescapable. If I didn't sing the words out loud, my brain might explode. It was too full, too chaotic, and I needed the release valve yanked.

I squeezed the neck of the guitar and tested the lyrics on my tongue. My fingers moved across the strings without hesitation, but my song began thin and reedy. I sucked in a deeper breath and forced it out. No holding back.

By the first few bars of my song, he appeared in the doorway. His arms were braced high over his head, biceps flexing under his black t-shirt.

I wasn't running away. I didn't care what he thought. I sang defiantly, staring right back at him.

Did he think I was scared? Or that I'd run away because he was watching? Not this time, not ever. In the hallways maybe, but here I could channel and funnel the power of my voice into something unstoppable, even for me. With the guitar in my lap and my fingers on the strings, I felt fearless and bold, something I'd never been before.

Our first meeting. The hateful words he spewed at me. The way he'd stared at me.

My stomach burned with a fire recapturing that moment and harnessing all the emotions stirred up by Dare to get it all out.

I don't know how long he watched. But I could feel his gaze on me. Could he hear my words? Did he know what they meant?

Without looking up, I grabbed my guitar and ducked

back inside when my fingers felt seconds from falling off. As much as I wanted to pretend I didn't care, I looked back. Dare left the door open. His body moved across the space, working on the car he'd restored from a rust bucket during junior year. I had a begrudging respect for the bright red Camaro. He hadn't been gifted it by his parents. He'd put in the work over time to make it a beautiful car.

That didn't mean he wasn't still an asshole.

Inside the house, I massaged my fingers to soothe the slicing burn of warmth returning to my hands. I peeked out the back window, making sure I didn't move the blinds.

My phone buzzed in my pocket, scaring me straight out of stalker mode.

"Hey, Bay."

"Freddy, what's up?"

"Can you come in earlier tonight? Our session guitarist can't make it. Do you want to give it a shot?"

I glanced at the instrument resting against the wall. A thrill rushed through me.

My mom would be doing the handover for her shift by now.

"Do you need me to bring my Martin?" I took the steps two at a time back to my room with my fingers wrapped around the guitar neck.

"If you want, but we've got a full set of electric acoustic you can play, if you need to."

I nibbled my lip. Riding my bike with my dad's guitar would be risky.

"How soon can you be here, kid?"

"Half an hour?" I slipped the guitar into the safety of the case and latched it. "I'll use one of your guitars."

"Sounds good. Got to go. See you in a bit."

I changed and layered up. I flexed my fingers in my

gloves and snapped on my helmet. Opening the door, a blast of frigid air pushed me back. Was it ever going to warm up?

The lights were on in the house and I triple checked the locks. I probably looked like I was about to break in from how many times I checked over my shoulder.

Setting off down my street, I pedaled fast, hoping no one would question seeing me out. It was a lot less weird to see someone out on a bike at nine pm as opposed to one am, though. It wasn't like anyone saw me anyway.

I arrived at the studio and Freddy took my bike, stashing it on the bike rack. "You singing today or working?"

"Didn't you call me here to work?" Not to sing. Never to sing. I watched musician after musician waltz in like it was no big deal to sing their heart out week after week, but never me.

"Yeah, but it can't hurt to ask." His shoulders jumped. "We're in here. There's three different acoustics you can choose from. They only need some backing track accompaniment. Can you handle this?"

I nodded. My heart beat rabbit-punch fast and I wiped my hands on my jeans. Unbuttoning my coat, I followed Freddy down the narrow hallways.

"Don't be nervous. You'll kill them, kid." He pushed open the second set of twin doors, the ones that led into the booth side of the studio.

"Here she is."

I froze inside the doorway, my jaw slack. The unmistakable beanie of Logan, worn denim jacket of Vale, Elias's leather pants, and Camden's clear blue eyes that almost made him other worldly. "Holy fuck!"

They all cheered. Big smiles and laughs. Money exchanged hands. Being slapped into the hands of a woman with cascading black hair. "You guys just don't know women." The woman who didn't look much older than me chuckled and pocketed the cash. "I'm Maddy. I'm guessing from the expletive hello, you know who these guys are." She held out her arm in their direction.

"W-without Grey."

She tipped her chin toward me. "Exactly. We need to lay down a track tonight. We could use a little rhythm guitar help."

"Me?" I pointed at my chest and glanced around the room. Lockwood's shredded t-shirt style was missing.

"Only for the test track."

"Where's Lockwood?"

I'd never understood the phrase 'sucked the air out of the room' like I did the second I mentioned his name.

"He couldn't make it today. Freddy said you had history here. Your dad did some great work and you could too. Are you up for it, and can you do us the favor of keeping everything quiet?" Maddy stared at me with a hard edge to drive home the seriousness of the chance I was being given. Not only were they trusting me with this, but so was Freddy.

"I—" It came out like a squeak. I cleared my throat and thumped my chest. "I can do that. Thank you for trusting me."

"Shit, I almost forgot." She shuffled through a stack of papers in a tattered black backpack before pulling out a stack of papers. Flipping through them she mumbled under her breath. "I do, but that doesn't mean I won't still need you to sign this." She slipped a few sheets of paper onto the mixing console with the big bold words 'Non-Disclosure Agreement' at the top. She uncapped a pen with her teeth and held it out. "Being a dick on behalf of these guys comes with the territory."

"I get it. You protect the people you care about."

The corners of her mouth ticked up.

Camden nudged her aside. "Studio time doesn't come cheap. Let's do this. Maddy, stop badgering our new friend." His ice blue eyes twinkled and he nodded toward the door. "Come with me, Miles's daughter. I'll go through the song with you. Can you read music?"

Camden guided me out of the soundboard side of the studio and into the twin door beside the one we'd just left. Freddy followed us into the next room.

"Of course." My stomach was doing a perfect 10 gymnastics routine with each step. Holy shit, I was about to play in front of and maybe with Without Grey—if I didn't crap the bed completely. My fingers tingled, numbness creeping into my hands. I wiped them on my jeans.

"Sorry, didn't mean to offend."

Freddy pointed at the line of six guitars along the wall. "Bay, here are the ones you can choose from. Let me know if there are any issues." He disappeared out the door and back to the other side of the glass, leaving me in the soundproof room where my heart pounded so loudly I wouldn't have been surprised if the mics had picked it up.

Camden flicked his thumb against his teeth. It reminded me of the drama club's production of Romeo and Juliet. *Was he biting his thumb at me?*

"How about singing? Can you sing?"

I jerked like he'd tripped me.

The intercom clicked on and Freddy's voice boomed out the speakers. "She can si—"

I cut Freddy off. "No." More like can't sing, and I wasn't going to face plant in front of Without Grey. Over my shoulder, I shot Freddy a look and walked down the line of guitars.

He backed off.

I swallowed back the nerves and grabbed a guitar, the same Martin model as the one I'd played earlier that day, with trembling fingers. How many times had my dad done the same thing? How many sessions had he played in, but never got to play his own songs? I shoved down those stomach-knotting feelings and took another deep breath.

"A Martin. I'm impressed." Camden picked up his own guitar and sat on the stool beside the piano. "You ready?"

We went over the song twice. The first time, he played it for me with the hand-scribbled sheet music on the keys of the keyboard. The second time, I played along with him, providing the accompaniment.

My fingers flew across the strings, energized by playing with someone. For someone. I was scared as hell, but swallowing that down, I pushed ahead, dropping into the music, doing my best to match Lockwood's style.

The crescendo fell off and my fingers stilled on the strings. Camden plucked the last notes, shaking his finger on the string to draw out the cry of the note. He drummed his fingers on the side of the guitar and tilted his head to the side staring at me with a wide smile. "Damn, Bay. Freddy wasn't kidding. You've got killer chops."

The intercom flicked on. "You guys ready?"

"Hell, yeah. She's got it. Let's go." He swung his hand overhead like he was signaling for a cattle round-up.

"You should hear her sing." Freddy laughed.

My glare shot to him.

"You sing, too?" Camden set down his guitar, resting it against his stool.

"Not really," I mumbled.

His eyes locked in on me with an assessing gaze. "Somehow, I doubt that, but this isn't an interrogation, so I'll let it slide."

"Do you regularly hold interrogations?"

He chuckled. "I've been known to."

The door opened and the rest of the band entered the room. They took their spots and I was seconds from pinching myself. I was sitting in a room with Without Grey about to jam with them. My fingers got all itchy and tingly.

I sucked in a breath. An irrational part of my brain threatened to send me running from the room. They were about to hear me play, although I'd known they were on the other side of the glass the last two times I played this.

A hand dropped to my knee. Camden ducked his head to catch my eye. Kindness and calm radiated through them.

"Deep breaths. Pretend you're sitting in your room, playing the song along to the album. You've got this."

He sat up straight and started off the count.

I closed my eyes and pictured myself sitting on the back steps. All alone, except for his eyes. Why was it so easy to play for him? My fingers flew across the strings, each note memorized and flowed through me. My hand stilled the strings as Camden held the final note.

"Fucking hell!" There was a pile on. Without Grey was tackling me in a hug.

The intercom from the mixing side came on. "Hell of a job, Bay." Maddy stood with her arms folded over her chest and a wide smile on her face. "If you can sing like Freddy says you can and you want a deal, I know some people."

I dropped my head, shaking it. Playing was one thing, but singing? I'd probably hyperventilate and pass out if I tried. "I'll stick to playing."

"Suit yourself."

Freddy barged in on the mic. "We need another take and then you can record the vocals, Camden."

"Sounds good." He rocked back on the stool. "From the top."

I rode home feeling like I could stay awake for days. The energy drummed in my veins like Elias's drum beat. School was in three hours, but I didn't even care. I couldn't sleep. I took the stairs three at a time and tore open my notebook. The words spilled out of me like an overflowing sink. Every single one about him. Maybe I could purge the thoughts of Dare through the written word. Hell if I knew whether it would work, but I'd sure as hell try. Anything else was far too dangerous of a fire to get close to.

9

DARE

The classroom desks shrunk every year. At least the cooler weather meant we weren't all sweating our asses off with the long, narrow windows cracked and giant rotating fans blowing on us every forty-five seconds as we sweltered in the late-spring muggy heat. There had been a reprieve with everyone still in coats, except for the one group of kids who never transitioned out of shorts and flip-flops, even in the dead of winter.

Squeezing myself into a desk and keeping my eyes open throughout the day were the most I could muster at this point. My GPA was fine. I wasn't expecting a Harvard acceptance letter- expectations were lax for athletes. It wasn't that I'd slacked. I'd seen what happened to guys on the bubble with grades and their SAT scores, but between practices, games and recruitment trips, I was over being a senior. Senioritis had hit hard and early, which meant the spaces in my mind previously occupied with turning in mediocre school work were engaged by other thoughts.

Those sleep shorts shouldn't still be flashing through my head. I'd seen women in much less. Much, much less.

But, somehow, Bay standing in her living room, glaring at me with her bed head was one of the hottest things I'd ever seen. The cookies had also hit the right spot. They'd been my breakfast and lunch that day.

Couple that with the song I couldn't drive out of my head, and Bay was becoming a distraction I hadn't anticipated. This year was supposed to be about three things: graduating, finding my way out of town, and never seeing my dad again.

I rocked back in my desk, the front two legs off the floor. Bay was sitting at the front of the classroom. Her seat was always in the first three rows of the three classes we shared. Did she sit in the front rows in the five other classes we didn't share? Where was she going after graduation? Kids in our class were headed all over the country. There were a few Ivy League acceptances, sprinkled in with prestigious state schools, and then all the Division I athletics scholarships. When was she leaving? Or was she staying behind? So many questions and no answers. I hadn't had a chance to ask her, but I needed to change that. The urge to speak to her again rode me hard and was becoming almost unbearable.

She hadn't played the guitar in a while and I'd been longing to hear her voice again. Asking for a serenade didn't exactly fit my image. Watching her sputter and freak when she handed me the glass of lemonade had been worth the slipped wrench and slice to my hand, though.

"Dare?"

"Mrs. Franklin?" I dropped my desk down, and the thud rumbled the windows.

"Can you please let us know the Massachusetts delegate to the Continental Congress?

"Sam Adams." Beer trivia for the win.

Her frown deepened. Revolutionary war questions were

always her go-to whenever she thought someone wasn't paying attention—not that I had been. No, my mind had been on other things. Running through the playbook in my head. Plotting out the seven-state trip my dad was on to anticipate when he'd be back. The melody anchored to the base of my brain stem repeating in my head until the last note finished.

Bay peered back, not even fully over her shoulder. More brushing past her shoulder, maybe thinking she could play it off as grabbing something from her backpack on the floor next to her. Except she never set her backpack so far back, and it was the fourth time she'd done it in twenty minutes. My view was clearer without the need of any pretenses.

She did the same thing every time she glanced back: rolled her pencil three times up and down her desk, picked it up and tapped it on her lips like she was thinking about something, maybe trying to remember something. Then the hesitation, the fake bag search, and a glance in my direction. I was ready this time, not pretending I didn't see her.

Our gazes locked.

Bay's head snapped forward.

I rolled back through my memory to figure out what it was about me that made her so jumpy.

She'd started at our school when she moved to town a few years ago and kept to herself. The girl who'd been beside her at her locker was the only person I'd seen her talking to outside of classes.

Why'd she move to my shitty end of town last year?

"There will be a group project before your exam."

Groans rumbled through the room. No one wanted to be stuck with a group project because Mrs. Franklin didn't feel like grading twenty-five assignments. In every group, there was always someone who didn't give a fuck and another someone who treated each word like it was the difference between life and death.

As seniors who'd all received our college acceptances —or at least already sent them all in and were waiting on last minute financial aid packages—this was one more annoyance before our summer of freedom began. Two months left.

The bell rang and Bay shot out of her seat like she'd been attached to a set of jumper cables. I didn't miss her quick glance back at me before she disappeared through the doorway.

I gathered my crap and stopped at my locker to swap out my books.

"One month until Bedlam." Knox threw his full weight into my back, shoving his hands down on my shoulders.

I grunted and threw him off. "What makes you think any of us need a reminder?" A massive banner stretched across the hallway with tear-off numbers. A big number six had been meticulously painted in navy with a gold outline. People here treated off-season scrimmages like most people treated championship games.

"Has that been here the whole time?" Knox slung his bag over his shoulder and scratched his head.

"Only since post-season began." I tugged the folder and book from last period from my backpack.

"Shit, seriously?"

My laugh rumbled deep in my chest. Knox had many talents, but his keen observation skills weren't on that list.

"What's the deal with next year?"

The flimsy metal of my locker groaned and creaked as I shoved some books crammed in there aside and got out what I needed. Everyone was under the impression that I'd signed on with someone. "One more recruiter's coming. Trying to see if they'll sweeten the deal." My gut knotted.

"Damn, they're taking their fucking time, aren't they?"

"I've got to keep everyone on their toes." I slammed my locker shut.

"I can't believe you're not coming to Alabama with me." There was as close to a pout as possible in his voice.

"You'll find a new guy to snag all his leftovers, don't worry." We got to the next classroom and headed to the back row to our non-assigned assigned seats.

"More like a new guy to be my wing man." He puffed up his chest, wedging himself in the desk, shifting the whole thing back a foot before scooting it forward with an ear-splitting screech.

The hallways were filled with a smattering of people after the last bell rang. In the homestretch of the school year, committees for prom, yearbook and other clubs planned their end-of-year projects. For everyone else it meant freedom. For me, it meant the loss of a refuge I'd had to escape to. And if I didn't get picked up, I'd be another guy at the bar, buried at the bottom of a bottle spewing all about the glory days of high school where I peaked.

The countdown of hours spent within these walls would dwindle to nothing. Throwing my cap in the air wouldn't only end my time at Greenwood Senior High, it would end my time in Greenwood. Or it would end my sanity, if I didn't make it out.

The auditorium doors flew open. Two people came out into the hallway.

Bay was dressed all in black, standing outside the ticket

booth only used on the nights of the fall play and spring musical. Her hair fell in waves cascading down her back. She was with a guy. Their intense expressions and close talking pulled something deep and dark out of me, like a body being dragged down basement stairs.

She popped open the door to the booth and disappeared. Her arm shot out with lengths of coiled cables. The guy with her grabbed them, holding them against his chest. Roll after roll appeared until he balanced them in his arms like an overloaded waiter about to lose the whole thing.

I smacked Knox in the chest. "Who's the guy Bay is talking to?" My chin jutted in their direction.

"Bay?" Knox scanned the few people in the hallway skimming right over her. I knew they didn't have classes together, but did he seriously not know her name? She'd been here three years.

My jaw clenched. "The New Girl." The name never sat right with me. If anyone mentioned her, other than teachers, she was The New Girl, even though there had been new arrivals since she'd started. Hadn't there? Unless it was someone new on the team, I didn't give a shit. But that nickname prickled something I couldn't place. Like a dull throb in the back of my mind clouded by time and haze.

"Oh." Knox looked up like he hadn't noticed two people less than ten feet away from us. He shrugged. "Jon." He snapped his fingers like it took manual effort for the synapses in his brain to fire. "That's Jon...Jon Morgan. Theater nerd. We were in pee wee football together, remember? You laid him out during a scrimmage in fourth grade and he hung up his cleats."

This news wasn't helping. He was still talking to Bay and I wasn't.

She threw her hands up frustrated with whatever he'd

said and stormed into the auditorium. He grabbed the door before it closed and slipped inside shaking his head.

Boyfriend-girlfriend bullshit? Or something else? Either way, the sight of her pissed at him made me happy.

A hefty backpack banged into my back. "Dare, you coming? I'm only doing practices for you and I'm too tired to run extra laps."

"Yeah, I'm coming."

The door opened again and this time Bay returned alone. I guess Knox had better dig deep and find some extra energy for those laps.

She popped the latch on the ticket booth door and walked back in.

I stood in the doorway, leaning to one side. "What are you doing?"

She yelped and banged her head on the counter. A dust avalanche covered her. Rubbing the back of her head, she extracted herself from the spot and stood. Her glare bit as harshly as it had when I teased her eating those phenomenal cookies.

She tapped a roll of Velcro against her palm and stood. Her lips were turned down in a perfectly symmetrical frown. Not a hint of a smile to be found.

"Hacking the Pentagon, what do you think I'm doing?" Half-opened boxes covered most of the floor in the booth, except for one narrow slot she'd slipped into. There were cables, tape and other things stacked in precariously perched boxes. She smelled like raspberry shampoo, or maybe body wash.. The kind Knox's mom used for guests, but I wasn't choosy.

"Do you need help?"

"What's your deal, Dare?" Her arms flailed out at her sides in an abandoned shrug.

"I can't help?"

"First the car, then my locker and now you want to help me lug crap into practice?" She tugged off her glasses, inspecting them. They were coated in dust, same as her hair and shoulders of her shirt. It looked like she had the world's worst case of dandruff. "Excuse me if after three years of being here, I'm a bit thrown by you popping up left and right talking to me." When she whisper-shouted at me, I got a hint of her singing voice. It made me want to keep her talking this way and let it roll over me.

"I'm not allowed to talk to you?"

"You're allowed to do whatever the hell you want, just not near me." She walked like she would barge straight past me, but stopped short inches before running into me. My body filled the doorway.

"You didn't mind being near me with the lemonade or yesterday." My breath ruffled the strands of hair framing her face.

"But I mind now." Her lips pinched together and she swallowed. "Excuse me, Dare."

I backed out of the doorway, giving her barely enough space to squeeze by.

"I'll see you later, Bay."

"Lucky me," she grumbled and disappeared back into the auditorium.

Knox popped around the corner. "What the fuck, dude? Let's go!"

I snatched my bag off the floor and followed Knox out to the field. The three laps went by faster than usual. My thoughts were on Bay, on capturing that frown on paper and hearing her song again.

10

BAY

There were holes in the drop ceiling overhead. This classroom doubled as the detention classroom and most mornings we started the day with a pencil left by a disgruntled detention dweller clattering onto someone's desk.

Mrs. Franklin stood at the front of the class calling ten minutes for us to get started on our group project.

I'd never hated school. It wasn't my favorite place, but I didn't hate learning, stage crew and hanging out with Piper. Some things were unpleasant, like the cold snap that had ripped through town, leaving me nearly frozen to my bike this morning. Wasn't spring supposed to be just around the corner?

The whole being invisible thing got to me initially, but then I got used to it. I faded into the background. Most people didn't care enough to learn my real name—I was The New Girl even though others had joined the school after me.

So, it was decidedly disconcerting to be the center of someone's attention. Dare, in particular. He kept staring.

Third period history had become the most dreaded period of my life. Was he slipping cash under the table to Mrs. Turner?

After going over our final project for the class before our exam, she stood up front and read out the names of our groups. We'd have ten minutes at the end of class to rearrange our desks and go over the paper and presentation work due in two weeks. Which is how I ended up in the unfortunate position of being seated, not ten feet away from Dare, but less than ten inches from him.

In his desk this close, he was larger than life. His jeans hugged his powerful legs. He felt barely contained in the classroom and for the first time I felt a spark of what all those other girls probably felt watching him on the field and in the hallways. My body shifted, leaning in, imperceptibly closer.

I squeezed my hands under my desk and dropped my head, shaking it. No, I wasn't going to become one of those girls. I wasn't going to start fawning and getting tongue-tied around him, blushing and giggling.

Dare, Michelle, Brian and I were stuck working together, and from the faces in our square of silence, no one was happy about it.

Michelle took charge as she always did. It's what valedictorians do.

"We can meet in the library to work together."

"I have play practice."

"Shirking your educational responsibilities." Dare tsked and rocked back in his chair, balancing on the back two legs of the desk. His gaze locked onto me like we were the only two people in the room. This time, though, my stomach wasn't doing the butterfly flutter. It was knotted and tight, a churning volcano pre-eruption.

"We're less than two weeks from opening night and I run the sound board. And I'm pretty sure we've all already gotten our college acceptances." I looked to Brian, our other group member who observed the whole interaction looking like he was pissed he hadn't popped a bag of popcorn before coming to class. But no help from him.

"I have practice, so after school won't work for me," Dare snapped. He turned to Michelle. So, it seemed he did remember there were other people in the room.

"The paper is due next Tuesday and a presentation the Tuesday after. And I'm not getting stuck doing all this myself." Her voice squeaked and she gripped the edges of her paper tight.

"You got that stick up your—"

I railroaded whatever was coming next. "Hey, Michelle, I'm sure we can figure out how to divvy up the work so no one is doing more than their fair share."

"This paper and presentation are five percent of our grade."

Dare stared down at his paper, sketching in the corner of the page. "A whole five percent? Wow, we'd better devote the next month of our senior year of high school to this assignment."

Michelle's fingers tightened around her pencil. "Some of us care about our academics. Some of us stick to our commitments. Some of us aren't self-centered assholes." She came out of her seat with each line, bracing her hands on the front of her desk.

Dare flicked his gaze to her and then me. He followed my gaze, and if I wasn't losing it, a hint of pink colored his cheeks. Turning over his paper, he refocused on Michelle and braced his hands on the back of his head. His elbows out wide and biceps tight under his fitted black t-shirt. "Can the screech volume come down by at least half, Chelle?" His hand twisted in the air like he was turning a knob.

She gripped the front of her desk like she was a second from leaping over it and going straight for his jugular.

"Thanks." He winked and laughed.

Chelle? Did they have a history? I'd kept firmly out of the high school gossip mill, not that anyone was chomping at the bit to add me into the mix.

She sputtered and glared at him, scribbling something down in her notebook.

Picturing Dare and Michelle together was as weird as, well picturing him with me.

My shoulders sagged slightly. And that was why I was a delusional idiot.

Dare plucked the paper with our names written at the top off my desk and scanned it.

I grabbed for it, but he evaded my grasp. "I was reading that."

"This is what he does." Michelle hissed, leaning close to my desk.

"Steals people's papers off their desks?"

"No, whatever the hell he wants." She crossed her arms over her chest.

He turned the paper sideways and ripped it down the middle.

Michelle yelped and grabbed for it, coming out of her seat and nearly toppling her desk.

Brian remained silent.

He ripped the halves in half again and dropped them onto our desks. Michelle's fluttered off the edge and slid three feet away on the floor.

"Now we all know what we need to do. We can add them all to one document or email our parts to you, Michelle. I'm sure your brain couldn't handle not proofing everyone's stuff before we turn it in. For the presentation, we need one person to stand up there and say all the words."

"I can do it." She shot up out of her seat and almost knocked her desk over again.

"We'll all get our work in for the paper by Saturday. It gives us a few days to get it figured out. Then we can move onto the presentation."

"Aren't you doing the Titan Combine in two weeks?" Brian spoke up for the first time since we'd shoved our desks together in the back of the room.

"Maybe." Dare shrugged. "I'll deal."

Michelle re-adjusted her papers, clacking them against the desktop. "Perfect. I can set up the doc and invite everyone to edit."

The bell rang, freeing us.

I swiped everything off my desk and into my bag, abandoning the pencil lost in the great escape. Flinging the bag over my shoulder, I shoved my desk back into place, cutting off Dare's path to me.

I was around the corner before he caught up with me.

"I've never had to work this hard to talk to someone before."

"There's an easy way to solve that. Stop trying to talk to me." I stopped to face him, since whatever was going on with him didn't seem to be wearing off.

"Why won't you talk to me?" With his long legs, it didn't matter how fast I walked—it was a stroll to him.

"Why do you want to talk to me?" I stared at him, trying to ward him off with my blistering gaze, but it only made his smile widen.

"Why are you so defensive?"

"Why are you so evasive?"

His lip quirked up in a way that probably brought most girls to their knees. They'd be a soupy mess of hormones and flustered eye flutters. I'd swerved into that territory for a few minutes here and there, but he wasn't getting the best of me.

"You don't remember, do you?" From the way his pupils dilated, my attempt at a sultry voice had worked.

My breath caught at the intense lick of his gaze. His gray eyes never left mine.

He braced his arm on the wall beside me like he was ready for me to fling myself at him as soon as I stopped playing hard to get. He was all steamy smolder smothered in smirk. "Not in the slightest."

I leaned in closer wanting him to hear every bit of what was coming his way. "Maybe it's because I remember well enough for both of us."

His brow furrowed before he recovered and matched my lean. How many other girls had he done the lean and smirk on?

"It was between third and fourth period on my first day. I was turned around and had no idea where I was going." That I'd held it together that long had been a milestone for me. The spontaneous tears had only happened once, and I'd managed to run to the bathroom, so no one saw. Back then, the waves of grief had been high and crashed into the shore so fast it was hard to catch my breath. But, surrounded by other kids, the waves were more swells that broke rather than slamming into me like a tidal wave. The choice to come to school had felt like a good one—until it hadn't.

"You barreled in through those doors." I pointed over his shoulder. The pretense of my sexy voice dropped. "You must not have zipped your backpack all the way. It caught on the door handle and ripped. Books, pencils, paper flew everywhere. The colorful bouquet of your language turned a few heads, but no one moved to help." They'd known what I hadn't. Everyone else kept their distance and, like an idiot, I hadn't thought I'd need to worry about self-preservation.

"I rushed in to help and crouched down beside you. I picked up a book up against the lockers that slid across the hall and held it out to you."

My bouncy 'let's be friends' naivety curdled my stomach.

"You glared at me like I'd been the one to push you through the door. Heads turned when you barked at me to 'get my fucking hands off your stuff.'" I did my best growly Dare impersonation. The words and tone had been seared into my brain.

His devil may care smile faltered and slid off his face.

"Your lip was bleeding and I remember thinking you must have had a shitty morning. You snatched the book out of my hand and glared. I smiled thinking you might have realized you were being an asshole. The bell rang. Classroom doors flew open and people flooded the hallway." My throat tightened.

"And you said, 'Who the fuck are you, The New Girl? Rule number 1 of Greenwood Senior High is don't touch my fucking shit. It's the tip of the day for The New Girl.'"

His head jerked back. Misery swamped his eyes, but not a flicker of connecting the dots. Dropping his arm from the wall, his Adam's apple bobbed up and down and he stepped back, lowering his gaze.

"You don't remember?"

He raked his fingers through his hair. "No, I don't." A crimson streak raced down his neck and he moved like he was no longer comfortable in his own skin.

"I'm reminded of that day every time someone calls me TNG. Whatever your deal is," I waved my hand in front of me, gesturing to him, "I don't want any part of it." I jerked the zipper of my backpack shut and swung it up onto my back.

"There's no deal." He let out a deep breath like he'd been holding it for days. "I heard you playing your guitar on your back steps. I liked the song, that's all. Your playing..." His fingers gripped his backpack strap even tighter. "It was beautiful."

The words were said nakedly, honestly, and sincerely, and they ripped straight through the armor I'd thought I'd built up when it came to Dare. Turns out those calluses were actually paper maché.

I swallowed, my throat so tight it was like breathing through a reed. Any notion that I hadn't played too loudly went right out the window. "You heard me?"

"Your voice." He didn't smirk or smile. There was no teasing or flirtation. "It—words can't do it justice."

My heart soared, taking flight before dropping back into my chest. Now it was my turn for the lobster impersonation. "It's not a big deal." I shrugged. "You heard me play and now you're, what? You're everywhere whenever I turn around."

"Sorry for trying to make a new friend." He dropped his back against the wall, staring out at the lockers across from us like he believed every word he'd just said.

"It's the last two months of senior year. I've been here for three years, Dare. Why now?" I spread my arms wide at my sides.

"Maybe I didn't see you before."

A sharp sound came from deep in my chest. "You wouldn't be the first one."

He turned his head, his gaze colliding with mine. The gray of his eyes radiated regret.

I couldn't look away.

"I'm sorry for what I did, Bay. I'm sorry I snapped at you like that. It wasn't right. I fucked up and I'll make sure people stop calling you TNG."

And just like that, it evaporated. The weight I'd carried in my chest. The conflict when it came to him was wiped away with a two-sentence declaration. "You're forgiven."

"You don't have to do that."

The grudge I'd held felt silly in the light of day; it was anger I harbored for something he didn't even remember. "We're so close to graduation and I'll leave here and never look back, so it doesn't matter."

"It matters to me." A flash of intensity in his eyes.

My breath came out shaky. "Absolution granted, and I'll be okay. Don't worry."

His lips tightened and he give me a grim nod. With his hands shoved into his pockets, he stared down at the floor. "What about the song?"

"I don't even know if I can finish the song, so you might be waiting on that one for a long time."

"Why not? Why can't you finish?" He said it like he was actually worried I wouldn't finish a song I'd played around with on my back steps.

"Why are you so interested?"

"Why are you evasive?"

Under the Dare spotlight, I squirmed. Why did he have to be the one to see me? Couldn't it have been someone a bit less dangerous to my sanity?

"Is the boredom getting to you? All the easy lays already conquered and now you're looking for a challenge?"

His smile was back now, a cocky set to his jaw. "That's the second time you mentioned sex around me. Why does it keep coming back to that with you? Something tells me you're thinking about sex a whole lot more than I am."

"Weren't you just apologizing for being shitty to me?"

"Pointing out your conversational quirks hardly feels shitty." He leaned against the wall, no longer tense.

"I don't have time for this. Don't you have practice?"

"It can wait."

"Well, mine can't. Thanks for the closure. I'll let you know if I finish the song." Anything to get him off my back and buy me some breathing room. The Dare Effect was back in full swing and my temporary booster shot was wearing off.

"See you later, Bay." He backed away.

The way he said it wasn't a casual goodbye. It was a promise. *Fuck*

11

DARE

I rocked back in the chair with my sketchbook balanced on my lap. The rhythmic scrape of my pencil against the textured paper calmed my nerves. I'd woken early, shooting straight up in bed.

Unbolting my door, I'd checked out the house to make sure I was alone. Early morning wake-up calls were never pleasant for me. But it was just me.

Shutting myself back up in my room, I'd stared at the ceiling for too long before giving in to my need to reach into the padlocked bottom drawer of the desk I'd found on the side of the road and dragged up the steps a couple years ago.

My fingers brushed against the smooth, bright cover of the sketch book I'd driven the next town over to buy. A stack of worn sketchbooks with ratty and weathered edges sat beneath it, bent and curled with time.

My mind blanked and the paper filled with lines and curves joining together, forming a shape. Abstract at first, it came alive with each pass, detail and shading making the picture pop off the page.

Bay's song played in a loop during these quiet times; I was unable to leave it behind until it was finished.

Laughter broke through the driving bass of the music in my head.

I dropped the notepad and pencil on my bed and crossed over to my bedroom window.

Snow blanketed the neighborhood, making everything look like a Christmas card. It was all pristine and untouched, except for Bay's backyard. There were footprints, trails scraped through the snow exposing the fledgling grass underneath.

Molly must have come home from her shift. Bay bounded back and forth, cheeks blazing red, small puffs of breath hung in the air in front of her face. She had on rainbow gloves she used to pack snowballs.

Bay's mom's scrub pants were darker at the bottoms, damp from the loose-packed snow. She rolled some snowballs of her own, flinging them at Bay. They dispersed in the air, showering them both with more flakes. They lobbed misshapen snowballs at one another.

They collapsed in the snow, sliding their arms and legs along the ground to make snow angels. Bay was covered in snow. Her nose was so red, I could see it from here. Snow clung to her coat and hair, dotting it like it had been placed there on a movie set.

Without stopping to think about what I was doing, I fished my boots out of the closet and grabbed my coat. I jumped up and down on the steps, slamming my foot into one warm boot before hopping on the other foot to do the same. My gloves were still in my pockets. I tugged them on using my teeth. I ducked into the garage to get the shovel. Halfway around the block, I repeated the story I'd come up with along the way.

Why was I doing this? Was it better or worse than sitting in my room alone like a stalker watching her run around and play in the backyard? Snow usually meant icicle-cold practices with water-soaked pads, or being blinded on the field during a game, dreading going inside to the warmth —the only thing worse than losing the feeling in your fingers and toes was when it came back.

But there was no practice today. No game. Only Bay laughing and running around, panting and smiling and playing.

I slipped and slid on the sidewalks, rushing to make it around the block. No one was out yet to shovel or salt.

Their peals of laughter got louder the closer I got to the house. They hadn't gone inside yet. I slowed my steps. I hadn't missed them.

Molly's car was parked on the street. The snow had built up on the slope of the driveway, so high she couldn't park it.

I dropped my shovel to the ground, scraping to the concrete and flinging it aside. The two of them rushed around from the back of the house, rosy cheeked and panting.

They spotted me with the shovel and stopped.

"Dare, so nice to see you." Molly pulled off her gloves and shoved them into her pockets.

"Hey, Dare." The no-longer-wary way Bay said my name sent a tingle up my spine. She said it like we were friends, not newly-acquainted, barely-civil neighbors.

"I have a shovel." I cringed and braced my hands around the shovel handle to keep from a full-on face palm. "I can shovel your driveway." I gestured to the pile up of snow and the progress I'd made.

"That's so sweet. Let me just get my bag from the car."

"Let me get it." I waved her off and traversed the slushy

and icy path. My feet slid from under me and I slammed into the side of the car, bracing myself on the roof.

"Dare," Bay called out, concern radiating from the single syllable.

I grinned, my face pressed against the cold metal. Bracing my hands on the roof of the car, I opened the door and fished out Molly's bag.

Navigating the treacherous path up to the house, Bay stared at me with wide eyes like I was crossing a river of lava. Pride swelled in my chest and I stopped myself from spiking the bag when I made it to the steps where they were standing.

"Do you have any salt?"

"In the garage. Thank you, Dare. I hadn't realized how slippery it had gotten."

"The sun's melting it, but the ground is still so cold it's refreezing a bit. I'll get the salt and take care of it for you."

"You're a lifesaver, Dare." Molly headed inside.

Bay lingered on the front steps. A quick nod from her and then she was gone.

I nodded and went back to shoveling.

The door swung gently shut, not a slam like I'd been used to before.

It didn't take much time, but the volume on the song was kicked up a notch this close to her house. Halfway through the last line of the driveway, the screen door squeaked open.

Bay stood in the doorway with her arms folded, rubbing her hands up and down them, doing a dance against the freezing temperatures.

"If you want, my mom made some hot chocolate. It's homemade. You don't have—"

"I'd love to." My stomach rumbled. I hadn't come over

looking to beg for food, but that didn't mean I'd turn it down.

She nodded. "Come in when you're finished."

"Do you guys have more salt?"

"Maybe? Probably not."

"I have some at my place. I can bring some by later, but things are already warming up, it shouldn't be too bad. But I don't want this to refreeze tonight when your mom gets home from work."

"She'd appreciate that."

Bay disappeared back inside, leaving me in the driveway with the puffs of air hanging in front of my face and the early morning quiet. Finishing the last row of snow, I propped the shovel up against the garage.

With numb fingers, I opened the front door. Stomping my boots and kicking them against the top concrete step, I breathed into my hands. The doorknob felt warm after the chill from the shovel.

The cozy heat inside made this feel like so much more of a home in the three minutes I'd been in here than the house I'd lived in had since before I could remember. Puddles formed around my feet. I cursed under my breath.

Molly came out of the kitchen, yawning and covering her mouth with one hand and holding a mug of hot chocolate with the other.

I pressed my back against the door. Shit. "Should I leave these outside?" The dampness spread from my boots.

"Don't worry about that, dear. Take off your boots, we promise we won't steal them."

I toed off my boots and stuck them beside their discarded shoes.

"Come into the kitchen. It'll help you warm up." She waved me forward.

Their kitchen was small like mine, but had been taken care of over the years. The cabinets and countertops were worn, but well maintained. Tucked in the corner was a four-seater table that could only seat three with the limited space. And one of the chairs was occupied.

Bay sat at the table with her hands wrapped around a mug that read 'Yes, you're being billed for this'. She'd changed into a long sleeve Queen shirt and flannel pajama shorts. There were no cartoon characters this time. Her damp hair was piled up on top of her head.

I dragged out the chair opposite her. My mouth watered like my thawing boots at the deep, rich smell filling the room.

She nudged the mug at the center of the table toward me. "There's cinnamon rolls too." Her voice was muffled behind a gulp of her hot chocolate.

I braced my hands on my thighs to not jump up to grab the food. I'd held out for way longer before.

Slowly thawing, I sat watching the easy way the two of them interacted. I'd seen it before, but not this up close.

Molly took the rolls out of the oven and Bay grabbed three plates from the cabinet. She went up onto her tiptoes and the shorts crept up the backs of her thighs showing off the slightest hint of a curve of her ass.

Right about then, I was damn happy to still be partially frozen. Inappropriate boners stopped being excusable probably ten years ago.

"You don't like the hot chocolate?" Molly slipped the hearty cinnamon, sugar, and icing-covered breakfast plate in front of me.

My mouth was a faucet as the warm, delicious smells filled my lungs.

"I love it. I was waiting for the cinnamon roll." I hadn't had the first sip yet. I'd been distracted watching Bay and trying not to go full Neanderthal on the food. The mug was still warm and the rich flavor coated my tongue. The spices in it made me think of a TV Christmas where the family wore matching pajamas and laughed while tearing into wrapping paper in the lit-up backdrop of a perfectly imperfect tree.

"This is delicious." I drained the cup faster than I should with a case of fuzzy tongue as my penance. The taste and my empty stomach had won out over the burn.

"Here, there's more." Molly refilled my mug before yawning again. "I'm headed to catch some shut eye. Thank you again, Dare, and there's some more hot chocolate, if you wanted to take some with you. I'm sure Bay wouldn't mind parting with a couple of her cinnamon rolls." She kissed Bay on the top of her head and the two of us were left alone in the kitchen.

"You baked these." I took another bite of the sugary, sweet roll.

Her cheeks reddened and she shrugged. "I made a bunch a few months ago and froze more of them. They're a pain in the ass to make." She uncurled one strip of the swirl and ripped it apart with her fingers before popping it into her mouth. "But I like to make them for mom when she comes home from work."

I don't think I've ever had anyone do anything that nice for me.

"They're delicious."

"They're a little freezer burned. I need to finish this batch before they're inedible."

"I doubt they could be."

"You can take as many as you want. Let me get you a

container." She popped up and rummaged through the drawers.

One second we were having a nice conversation and the next she's trying to shove me out the front door.

"Can I have another mug of hot chocolate?" I shook it in front of me.

She stopped, standing in front of the stove with a spatula in hand, scooping out three rolls into a plastic container.

"Sure." She held out her hand.

My chair scraped against the linoleum floor and I stood. It took less than two steps to cross the kitchen and stand beside her. The dampness in her hair was gone. Left behind was a messy bun with pieces of hair falling around her ears and neck.

She turned and yelped, nearly running into my chest.

Maybe I was standing a little too close, but I didn't move an inch.

Now she smelled like chocolate-covered raspberries. Was that a thing? If it wasn't, it should be.

"Did you turn in your part of the paper?" She grabbed the mug from my hand and refilled it, using it as a barrier between us. She shoved it into my chest and took her seat on the far end of the table.

"Already done. Michelle screeching at me isn't my idea of fun."

"Me neither."

I slowly sipped my hot chocolate, determined to know more about Bay.

"What's your college plan?"

Her head shot up and she shoved another piece of the roll into her mouth.

"The plan is college."

"I figured, but where?"

She stared at me, her gaze assessing, before dragging another strip of dough through an icing pool on her plate. Whatever the test had been, it seemed I'd passed. "I'm waiting on the scholarship letter from my first choice. It's a school in California."

I let out a low whistle. "That's far."

"It's got everything I want to do, but if the price isn't right, I'll stay in-state. What about you?"

She leveled her gaze like a challenge, like I'd expected her to show me hers, but I wouldn't show her mine. I'd most definitely show her mine. I shook my head because there wasn't anything else to show her. Empty pockets, empty future. There were twelve days until the Titan Combine.

"There's a few more weeks until the decision deadline. I'll have to decide which school will give me the best shot at going pro."

"That's a big decision. I'm not even sure if my degree will help me get a job after."

"What are you studying?"

"Accounting and audio production—music production." She cleared her throat.

"You want to be a singer."

"No—no, I want to produce music. Singing, that's a whole other ballgame and it wouldn't even make sense for me to go to college for that. I'd need a broken-down van to crisscross the country, playing dive bars until my big break where I was chained to a record label for five albums and earned almost no money before suing them and finally breaking out on my own." There was a hint of longing in her voice before she shook her head and laughed.

"You paint such a pretty picture of the music industry."

"Sorry, too many music documentaries for me." Her

phone buzzed on the countertop. "Piper's on her way over." She said it in a pointed, take the hint kind of way.

"I need to head out." I checked at my imaginary watch. "It's already ten."

Another well-earned chuckle. "Eleven actually. Thanks for shoveling."

"I'll bring the salt by later, so everything doesn't freeze up overnight." Sliding my boots on, I balanced against the wall. At least I'd have another excuse to stop by.

"You don't have to. It says after tonight's cold snap, tomorrow things will be in the 60s, so everything will melt. You probably didn't even have to shovel today. We could've just waited it out."

Here I was trying to find reasons to see her, and she was looking for reasons to shove me out the door. What was I doing, and why was I torturing myself?

12

BAY

The brass instruments blared in the enclosed gym. Deafening noise rumbled the wooden seat under my ass, inching me to the right. If they played for much longer, I might slide right off the edge onto the worn gym floor. The basketball court didn't get the kind of love the football field got, but the rain had shunted our school-wide pep rally inside.

"There isn't a game for another six months."

Piper sat beside me, waving her cheerleader issued pom-pom with the energy of a tranquilized turtle. "You're forgetting about the Bedlam Bowl. Four juniors signed their commitment letters after that game last year."

I squinted peering over at her.

She shrugged. "What? I hear things. And you should know by now that introducing the starting line-up for the next season has taken on as much fanfare as homecoming or any other football-based activity." The pep in her voice was as fake as half the tans in the overly-loud, echo-y gym.

"Stage crew tech was held together with literal electrical tape." She tucked the pom-pom under her arm.

"No shit, I got zapped at least five times helping you guys set up, but there never seems to be a dip in funding for events like these." I could barely keep my eyes open. I'd gotten less than three hours of sleep last night.

"At least we don't have to change for gym today?"

"Always looking on the bright side." I laughed and scribbled down one of the answers on the last row of my homework assignment. Yesterday might have left a little less time for finishing it than normal with the snowball fight and two cups of hot cocoa with Dare.

"I need you to play it cool." Her fingers tightened on my forearm.

"Death grip much, Piper?" I stared at her.

"Be cool! Dare is looking at you."

My fingers tightened on the highlighter, sending my line graph off the edge of my notebook. I flipped the page, not looking up. The last thing I needed was for Piper to sniff out that something was up even more than she already had. She was a bloodhound for any shifts in the high school hierarchy, and there had been a serious disturbance in the force.

"He's not." Please let him not be staring at me. Maybe there was someone else behind me.

"He definitely is." She kept staring at the gym floor. "Is something going on? He hasn't looked at anyone else as long as he's looked at you."

"Piper." I stuck the highlighter in the center of my notebook, letting the pages flop over. "He's not—"

Our spot on the bleachers was the perfect spot for late arrivals and early escapees from the mandatory pep rallies. In the center of the court, the entire team was lined up, and behind them was the coach, who looked three seconds from an aneurism. His face was beet red, with veins raised on his neck and forehead like a topographical map of the Rockies.

He introduced the starting lineup and played up the tradition of the junior vs senior game, the Bedlam Bowl, and how at least eight of their rising seniors signed commitment letters within a week of the game every year.

With his hands clasped behind his back and the most 'over it' look on his face, Dare stared right at me.

My stomach flipped, cartwheeling around inside my body. Senior year just got a hell of a lot longer with the required crash course in Dare Diversion.

The train wreck of a pep rally continued with cartwheels, and an ear-splitting rendition of 'Hey, Look Ma I Made It' by Panic! At The Disco blared by the marching band. Did no one ever listen to the lyrics in the verses instead of the chorus? The football coach brought up how this team would go down in Greenwood Senior High history at least ten times in his ten-minute speech.

He mentioned that in a little over a week, more than half the team would be going to a skills combine to show off their athleticism for recruiters. Dare's gaze snapped to the coach. Was he going to that? Where would he be going to college next year? He'd been evasive when I'd asked him on Saturday.

"How many more of these self-congratulatory sessions do they need before we're all put out of our misery?"

"The official trophy hasn't even arrived yet. We've got at least two more of these to go," Piper responded unhelpfully.

We stood, not because we were driven to our feet by the excitement of the atmosphere, but because we needed to get out of here before we were gridlocked in the hallways.

Leaping—well, more like tumbling—from our spot on the bleachers, Piper and I evaded the crush of people waving plastic pom poms and pennants and rushed out of the gym. Flyers for the talent show fluttered off the bulletin board beside the doors as people rushed to freedom.

Ducking and dodging, we made our way through the sea of people who would hang out at school until the championship trophy bonfire caravan out to the clearing in the woods in three hours.

I needed to get the soundboard set up for the dress rehearsal and get to the studio by nine. Leaving closer and closer to when my mom left upped the risk factor, but playing beside musicians, not just watching them through glass, had stirred something in me I hadn't felt before. The songs were coming fast and furious. I hadn't had the courage to sing them in front of anyone else, but every day it felt like more of a possibility.

Singing in front of Dare got easier every time. I didn't have to pretend he wasn't there or that I didn't care what he wanted to hear. I needed him to hear. He was the only person I'd been able to sing in front of since my dad died. Out on my back steps I was supposed to be alone. All the houses were dark, but he'd been there, and he'd listened, and I'd kept going. My throat hadn't closed up. My vocal chords hadn't frozen. I'd kept going for a few more notes, and I'd do even more now.

He wanted to talk to me and play whatever game he was playing, but I wasn't taking the bait. I'd let him know he wasn't scaring me off, but part of me knew there was something he'd unlocked. I didn't like it one bit.

I needed him near me to burst through the block on my fingers on the strings and wrench the words from my chest.

We burst through the auditorium doors and others from the cast and crew flew in through the other doors to our soundproofed refuge.

"People." Our director, Mrs. Tripp, clapped to get

everyone's attention. "There's a lot happening out there, but we need to focus on what's happening in here." She took a deep breath, clasping the clipboard to her chest.

"There are less than ten days until our first performance. Our first full dress rehearsal will be in a week and the orchestra will be here then. Everyone, we need you on your queues. Andrea, I can tell you're not wearing stockings. Please, we need those on or it looks like you're walking on uncooked chicken legs up there."

"Stage crew. We need those set piece transitions tightened up." She squeezed her fists and her whole body, maintaining her bright-red lipsticked smile. Mrs. Tripp rarely yelled, but it didn't mean we weren't all waiting for the inevitable blow up where she'd storm out of a rehearsal announcing the whole thing had been cancelled before being cajoled into returning by the assistant director, Mr. Rourke, and the stage crew wrangler.

I walked out my back door, but didn't stop even though I could feel his eyes on me from the second I'd opened it. He wasn't even pretending he hadn't been waiting to hear me as much as I'd been waiting to play. A private concert was much easier when I didn't have to look him in the eye.

He disappeared from view once I got closer to the fence that separated our yards. With every step, I was equal parts wanting to break out into a sprint or turn back around. There was no coming back from this or pretending I wasn't playing for him anymore. He'd know.

I leaned against the fence. It shook and shuddered, steadied by the weight of my back against it. The ground was still cold and wet, but I played. My fingers moving kept the numbness from creeping in too deeply.

My fingers flew across the strings. A new melody unfolded. I had my notebook beside me and scribbled down words and phrases, erasing and rearranging them until I could sing the whole chorus.

The fence shuddered and I knew he was there too. Whether it was all in my head or not, I could feel his back against mine, the heat of his body, and the thumping of his heart. A new rhythm took over and the words poured out of me, flowing over the notepad and out my fingertips.

I stopped to scribble down a whole verse, pinning the guitar against my side and the fence and using my thigh as a makeshift desk. Singing other people's words spurred my own thoughts and opened up avenues that had once been dark and blocked off.

"Don't stop now, Bay."

The way he said my name, I couldn't move from this spot. My body swayed with the fence when a weight was added from the other side.

"Any requests?" My voice was whisper quiet.

"Play the one you played the first night you sat down."

A simple enough request. But I couldn't choke out the words.

"I forgot it."

"You forgot it? It went like this." He hummed the melody back to me.

Whether because he remembered it or the smooth cadence of his voice, my heart and stomach were in a tug-of-war for which was about to be ejected from my body first.

I swallowed, my throat coffee-straw tight. "I'll try to remember it. The bonfire's going on right now." I dropped my head against the fence. It shuddered gently.

"I know."

Fighting the face palm, I searched for something more to say. Of course he knew.

"Shouldn't you be out partying in the woods with everyone else or something?"

"More like 'or something.' I'd rather not drive out to the woods where drunk people fuck with my car. I usually only go because Knox needs me to keep him out of trouble."

"Is he going to shave half his head and dye the other half blue again?" Knox was hard to miss. He was Dare's wingman, never too far away. He had a nose that looked like it had been a casualty of a bad tackle, but he'd preferred to leave it that way instead of getting it fixed. His rough-and-tumble had smooth, polished edges, unlike Dare's, which were ragged and cutting.

"You remember that?"

"He doesn't exactly blend in."

"With the blue hair, he would've. Half the school did it."

"You didn't."

"Blue isn't my color."

I laughed. Dare's dry humor surprised me. "I'm sure you could wear anything you want."

The fence shifted like the compliment made him uncomfortable. "Why aren't you at the bonfire?"

"It's not my scene." I brushed my fingers over the strings. The metal was cold after only a few minutes. Was this damaging my dad's guitar? The cold might be shocking the wood, maybe warping it. I looked to the back steps and chewed on my lip.

"Same with football games." His voice pulled me back from my worries.

"Especially football games." I chuckled. I'd made it a point of pride to not have been to any.

"What do you have against them?" The fence rocked.

I shrugged even though he couldn't see me. "They're not my thing."

"Why not?"

I peered over my shoulder. The flannel of his shirt and a bit of his neck and hair peeked through the gap. "Why do you care? There aren't enough adoring fans screaming your name?"

"Not all screams are created equal." He huffed out a laugh.

"You wouldn't even notice mine added in."

"I would." Through the gap, he caught my eye. His gaze, intense and direct locked onto mine.

"Dare, we've been in school together for years. All the sudden you're interested. I'll come right out and say it. It feels like I'm setting myself up for something." I tore my gaze away and back to the instrument in my lap.

"What's that supposed to mean?"

"It doesn't make sense why you keep doing this. Why now am I suddenly the most interesting person alive, to the point that you're missing Greenwood Senior High traditions to come hang out with me?"

"Maybe they never interested me to begin with."

I ran my fingers over the strings.

A voice broke through the silence between us. "Dare, what the fuck? I was about to leave your ass."

The fence rumbled, his weight shifting off it. "Why didn't you call me?"

"I did. Bonfire waits for no man. What the hell were you doing out here?"

My back shot off the fence, rattling the loose planks of wood.

There was a beat and I held my breath.

"Nothing, man. Let's get the hell out of here."

Why did that hurt? What had I expected him to say? Just out here hanging with my weirdo neighbor while I waited for you to go to the bonfire even though I said I wasn't going.

I stayed by the fence until the rumble of Knox's engine disappeared in the distance, then carried my guitar into my bedroom and flopped onto the bed, staring up at the ceiling. The itch tickled my fingers, traveling up my arms to my chest. The pulse grew faster and louder until I couldn't block it out anymore. I snatched my notebook off my desk and ripped it open to the first blank page, immortalizing this moment—at least until I decided to shred the page.

Maybe tomorrow.

Maybe I'd show up at school and sing this song in front of everyone.

Maybe I could force him to feel the way he made me feel.

13

BAY

After tech rehearsal wrapped up, I hopped on my bike for the sludgy, salt-lick ride home. Most of the snow had already melted, but the gray and brown monstrosities on the sides of the road looked like the world's worst snow cone. I felt like an owl who'd been given too much coffee to make it through the day.

Halfway up the hill, my feet moved on the pedals, but the bike went nowhere. I pitched over before I could get my feet down. The concrete came up fast. My hands shot out, taking the brunt of my fall and most of the gravelly scrapes.

The chain snapped. I kicked my bike, cradling my hands against my chest. Shit! A sharp burn spiked through my palms. The adrenaline pumped through me, turning the pain into a throb. But it was only a matter of time before the sting came rushing back in.

Papers from my backpack were stuck to the wet grass, having made a safe and gentle landing, while I'd ended up on the dirty side of the road. That seemed about right for my life.

Grabbing the papers, I winced. Pain shot down my leg.

My jeans were ripped at the knee, and a bloom of red stained the denim. Dammit, I loved this pair. I took a deep breath, not wanting to look at what was underneath. The pain hadn't hit me yet, but walking my bike home was going to suck.

A car door opened. "You okay?"

"Yeah, I'm—" I shoved the papers into my backpack, sucking a sharp breath in through my teeth at the lick of pain radiating from my palms.

"Shit, you're hurt." His voice sent goosebumps down my arms.

I shielded my eyes from the afternoon sun.

Dare rushed around the front of his car and crouched down in front of me. "Those look nasty."

"They're not so bad. I'm fine." I tugged my hands from his grasp and pushed myself up with my fingertips, careful of my cuts.

His hands wrapped around my waist, hefting me off the ground like a weightless sack of potatoes.

My nudges and not-so-subtle elbows to his side were ignored or unnoticed. I looked everywhere but at him. "Thanks." It came out sharp and biting.

He cocked his head to the side and stared at me.

My body throbbed in time to the cuts and scrapes on my skin. But anger simmered in my chest.

He picked up my bike and dumped it into his trunk, which I hadn't seen him open.

"What are you doing?"

"Were you planning on walking your bike home? You're hurt. I'll drop you off." He closed the trunk halfway and came around the passenger side. "You coming or what? "

"No, I'm not coming. Give me my bike."

"I'm not giving you your bike. It's busted. Get in the car."

"Screw you."

"Language, Bay. What's your problem? I thought we'd come to a truce yesterday."

"You mean right before you went to the bonfire after telling me you weren't into it? Right before you told Knox you were outside doing nothing?" The words turned in my mouth like it was full of old pennies. Bitter and petty. What did he owe me? Nothing. The same as I owed him.

He stared up at the sky with his lips moving like he was asking some higher power to give him strength to deal with me. Welcome to the club.

His gaze leveled at me. "I never said I wasn't going to the bonfire, only that I wasn't there. And I figured you wouldn't want me to broadcast to Knox that you were singing for me. It doesn't seem like something many people know about you."

The asphalt was interesting at that moment. "You were right."

"I know." With a flick of his wrist, he popped open the passenger side door and held it open. "And I'd much rather have stayed listening to you play than gone with him, but he tends to get into trouble."

My feet moved before my brain could reason my way out of it. Letting him off the hook shouldn't have been this quick and easy.

His arm dropped across the open doorway like a toll bridge barrier. And I was fresh out of coins.

I unclipped my helmet and held it in my hands, nudging him with it to give me a bit more space.

"Don't worry, Bay. I'll take care of you." The whisper across my ear started that chemical reaction that only occurred in his presence.

He closed the door once I was in the seat and jogged around to the driver's side.

A few silent minutes later, we sat in the driveway of my house.

"You can drop my bike in front of the garage. I'll fix it tomorrow."

"No." He turned off the ignition.

"Fine, I'll take it out of the trunk myself." I flung his door open. This game we were playing was driving me crazy.

His door popped open and he held down the partially-open trunk.

"What the hell, Dare? Let me get my bike." My attempts at lifting it were thwarted by his nonchalant hand on the top of the hood and the extra eighty pounds of muscle he had on me.

"No."

"Are we playing the one-word game?"

He laughed. "No."

"Would you say something else then?"

His smile widened. "No."

Those butterfly wings were dangerous. They threatened to lift me off the ground straight over a cliff with the way he smiled at me. Like we had been friends for ages and had our own inside jokes.

"Has anyone ever told you they hated you?"

A chuckle. "No."

"I highly doubt that. Give me my bike and you can be on your merry way. Your good deed for the day is completed."

He rounded the trunk and took my hands in his, flipping them over palm up.

My heart shot into overdrive.

His face turned serious and his gaze dropped to my hands. "No."

His fingers traced the roadkill side of my palm.

I winced. The cut on my hand had partially dried giving me a nice moist patch of gravel and blood.

"Let's get inside." He said it like we were at his house, not mine, but I followed him anyway, handing over my key and letting him open the door.

"Where's your first aid kit?"

I pointed toward the cabinet beside the sink.

He opened the cabinet and produced the box. Rummaging through the contents, he found what he needed.

"Sonofabitch." I hissed. The burning alcohol prep pad sear brought tears to my eyes.

"There she is." He ran the acid-soaked evil over my skin.

"There who is?" I gritted my teeth, forcing my fingers from curling.

He cupped the backs of my hands, holding them steady.

"Your inner badass." Dare blew on my palms. It evaporated the stinging antiseptic and distracted me by how close his lips were to my hands.

My smartass reply froze in my throat.

He peered up at me and my heart stalled.

"Is that better?" His eyes were filled with concern and laughter, like he couldn't fully relax until he had my answer.

It would take jumper cables to restart my brain. I nodded and tried to tug my hands out of his grip before he felt my skyrocketing heart rate.

"Yeah, it's okay now." The cuts throbbed, but the sting was gone. I pulled my hands free from his grasp and dropped them into my lap.

"I'll get you some Band-Aids." He rummaged through our white metal first aid kit. "Perfect." He waved two still wrapped oversized bandages at me.

"These are in shitty spots, so they'll come off easily, but if I use this, they'll stay for a bit longer." He held up the easy tear medical tape my mom always had in her scrub pockets when she came home from work. Ninety percent of the tape in our house was from those rolls.

I opened and closed my hands. The palms smarted, but at least I didn't have to worry about a nice slushy-snow infection. "You're pretty good at bandaging. "

His smile faltered. "Football isn't exactly ballroom dancing." He ducked his head and cleaned up the wrappers and blood-tinged cleaning supplies.

"Do you usually use SpongeBob Band-Aids to patch yourself up?"

He laughed. "No, my first aid kit is nowhere near as colorful. I could've used the Disney princess ones, so count yourself lucky."

"My dad was under the perpetual impression that I was still eight years old and bought Band-Aids like he was preparing for the apocalypse. Did you know Band-Aids expire? They do."

Dare's throat worked up and down. "When did he die?"

"Right before I started at Greenwood Senior High. We'd moved to town two weeks after."

"What happened?" His knee brushed against mine. "Sorry, you don't have to answer that."

He shuffled back and did the awkward 'sorry for bringing up your dead parent, please don't burst into tears' sputter.

I dropped my hand onto his knee.

His muscles tightened and I jerked it back.

Taking a deep breath, I ran my fingers over the neat bandages. "It was an aneurism." I snapped. "One second he was in his office at work and the next, they were calling an ambulance. The doctors said it was quick, like flicking a light switch. He was here and then he was gone. No pain though." I shrugged, trying to keep the welling emotions at bay. My throat was tight and my nostrils flared. This was my new normal. A life without him. Even three years later, sometimes it still felt raw.

"That's good for him, and you two didn't have to deal with watching him go. Apparently, my mom was in a lot of pain for a few days after she had me. Then she was gone."

My head snapped up. "I didn't know your mom died." Why hadn't I pieced that together? I didn't think of Dare as anything more than sprung from the ground fully grown, but of course he had a family. A mom and a dad.

"It's not a big deal." He shrugged. "I don't remember anything differently, so it's not like I can even miss her."

My heart ached. What was worse? Losing a parent you loved or never even getting to meet them?

"What a pair." I reached for his hand and hesitated, but the sadness rippling off him wouldn't let me not hold his hand.

I slid mine under his, our thumbs hooking. "I'm sorry you didn't get to meet her."

"I'm sorry your dad's gone." He tightened his grip on my hand, keeping clear of my shredded palm. "He taught you to play the guitar?"

"He used to play me to sleep every night, until I hit twelve and thought I was too cool for it." The look in my dad's eyes when I shook my head as he sat behind my bed —at the time, I hadn't paid attention, but now I'd give anything for one more bedtime lullaby.

"Then he taught me how to play."

He lifted his chin. "You should take your jeans off."

I shot up, sputtering. "Forward much?"

He laughed. "Peeling the jeans off your cut once the blood has dried will suck. Trust me." A sadness flickered in his eyes.

I looked down at my leg. The area around the rip was red. It looked sticky and angry. My cheeks and neck were hot with embarrassment. "Right, I'll be back."

Taking the steps one at a time, I changed out of my ripped jeans. Maybe I could patch them later. Instead of my pajama shorts, I grabbed long loose pants where I could roll up the leg. Back downstairs, Dare patched me up again.

"So you've been playing the guitar since you were twelve?" He looked up at me with gentle eyes, the grays bright and deep, melded together into a tapestry of mystery.

"You think I'd be better at it."

His fingers brushed over the sides of my knee.

My pulse rampaged in my chest like a stampede.

I saw my chance at escape and popped up. "Do you want to see it?"

"Of course."

I rushed back to my room, trying to keep my head clear. Whenever I was close to Dare, let alone touching him, the neurons didn't fire properly and I couldn't stop myself from leaning in closer, staring longer, wanting more. I retrieved the case from my bedroom closet and hurried back downstairs.

Dare tucked the first aid kit back into the cabinet and closed the door. His gaze dropped to the case clutched in my hand.

"Come into the living room." The kitchen was too tight, there wasn't enough room for me to put space between us.

In the living room, I sat on the love seat with the case in the empty spot beside me. I unlatched the case and pulled the shiny, smooth body from the velvet lining.

Instead of taking the seat on the other couch, Dare gently slid the case off the cushion and deposited it on the floor.

My seat jumped beneath me as he settled his large frame beside me.

I turned, angling my body so my back rested against the arm rest and my bent knee supported the body of the guitar.

"He loved playing. He played standing under my mom's window when they were in college to get her to agree to go out with him."

"Sounds like he loved your mom, too."

"He did. They were always so happy together. Laughing, never afraid of being silly, especially when they saw how much it embarrassed me."

"Sing me something." He leaned back with his arm propped up along the back of the couch. His fingertips were inches from my arm.

Why hadn't I seen this coming? Not *play* me something, but *sing* me something. No one busts out a guitar just to look at it. Of course he'd want me to sing something. My balloon animal stomach had two extra knots added to the poodle tail.

"No, you don't want to hear me play." My escape to the case on the other couch was thwarted by his hand on my shoulder. It wasn't restraining or hard, only a gentle pressure.

"Please, Bay." His eyes sparked with encouragement —and something more.

My fingers trembled against the smooth wood in my lap. I cleared my throat. "Sure."

My smile was thin and shaky. "What would you like to hear?"

"Anything you want to play for me."

I licked my lips. At this point, I'd be more comfortable doing a striptease for him. My boobs would be a welcome distraction from the flustering cave of bats losing their shit in my chest. Clearing my throat, I ripped my gaze away from Dare and focused on the cool metal pressing into the pads of my fingers.

My pulse thudded, warming the strings.

I closed my eyes, pulling together the frayed edges of the blanket of my mind and cocooning myself in the musical beauty, blocking out everything except for the music and Dare.

14

DARE

She sang for me. I'd thought she'd bolt from the living room, possibly locking herself in her room rather than play on the couch beside me, but she closed her eyes, took a deep breath, and played.

I made no sudden movements, and barely a breath escaped my lips as I watched her.

With her eyes closed, she rocked and shook her foot hanging off the edge of the couch to the percussive beat, woven into the melody. She sang an acoustic version of "Use Somebody" by Kings of Leon that made the original look like the cover. Hers was slower, sadder, more powerful. I heard the words for the first time, and they didn't need the full accompaniment playing behind them. They deserved Bay's voice and nothing less.

Her fingers moved across the strings with dropped notes and squealed from the metal on metal.

My hands itched for my sketch pad. It never left my room, always locked up in my drawer. But right now, I wanted a life-sized canvas to capture this moment. As I basked in the afterglow of her holding the last note and throwing on a little vibrato on the last string pluck, the need to hear her original song burned even deeper in me.

I wanted to hear her words. Know her feelings. Know her heart.

Suddenly, the thing I'd been searching for was sitting beside me, the girl next door. That scared the shit out of me. So much to lose. So much to screw up.

I jumped up from the couch.

Bay's smile faltered and her expression dulled before going blank.

"I need to go. I'm supposed to meet Knox in a bit and it slipped my mind."

She stood and she nodded before turning her face away and sticking the guitar back in the case. "Right. Well, thanks for helping me with my bike. You don't have to fix it. I can fix it."

I backed up, racking the back of my calf on the coffee table and almost toppling over.

Her hand shot out to steady me. The barest scrape against my skin sent a jolt ricocheting down my arm.

I vaulted over the table to avoid her touch. "No, I can fix it. I'll get it back to you by seven am. Maybe drop it off later or early tomorrow morning."

She curled her fingers back and tucked her hands under her arms.

I was messing this up, but she was too much. In this quiet house, she was ripping me open with a damn pop song. I needed to get outside so I could breathe. Bursting through the front door, I raced down the path to the driveway.

"Okay. See you later." The question in her voice was a lance to my side. She peered out the screen door.

I ran to my car, throwing myself inside like I'd stolen

something. Without looking up, I peeled out of the driveway, my heart jammed up against my ribs and I took the long way to my house.

Sitting in the driveway, I slammed my hand against the steering wheel before dropping my head to the smooth, hard surface.

This whole time I'd been trying to get her to open up to me. I'd been nudging and prodding, getting in her space to hear the song again and get to know her. The second she shared a piece of herself with me by showing me her dad's guitar and singing, actually singing for me, I rushed out of there leaving her confused and hurt.

Why was I such a screw up? Why did Bay make it impossible for me to act like anything other than an idiot?

"Fuck!" I screamed at the top of my lungs, hoping my voice didn't travel far enough for her to hear, muzzled by the interior of my car.

≈

"What's up with you, man?" Knox jogged beside me during our warm up. The combine was in eight days. I'd scraped enough money together to pay my way on the team bus.

"Nothing." The clusterfuck of my solo concert with Bay had been replaying in my head in skin-peeling, excruciating detail. I'd run from her house like she'd threatened to jam bamboo shoots under my nails and returned her bike at two am, under the cover of darkness a solid four hours after her bedroom light had shut off.

She'd kept her curtains drawn. Her shadow moved back and forth in front of it in a silent taunt.

It hadn't helped that once I'd paid for the Chicago trip I was scraping together pennies for food. School lunch wasn't enough with all these work outs. I gulped down even more water trying to fill my stomach.

"You're being weird as hell."

"We're all weird as hell."

"True." He nodded like my advice had been sage, not me covering for the shit storm raging in my head that had nothing to do with all the fears bearing down on me about my future.

The game I'd hung every hope on was days away. The room for error was razor thin and I wasn't going to be the guy who screwed over the entire team and flushed their college ball chances down the drain. The thought of my old man's sloppy, slurred joy at seeing me crash and burn pushed me forward.

But Bay...she'd looked for me during the morning hallway rush. How the tables had turned. Now I was the one ducking down hallways to take the long route to class and keeping my gaze locked onto the board in every class. What was I doing? Why had I decided to chance a tightrope walk like this when I needed to focus on getting the hell out of town by whatever means necessary?

Because I hadn't had a choice. From the first note, she'd wound herself around a part of my soul. She'd brought me out of the haze and into the light.

What happened in less than two months when we graduated and she ripped my heart out by moving across the country? Of course she'd get the scholarship. Who wouldn't want her at their school?

"Dare. Do you need a special invitation?" Coach shouted from the team kneeling in a circle around him.

"Sorry, Coach." I jogged to the spot left between Knox and Bennet.

Helmets cracked against helmets and we ran the plays

from this season that were etched into our brains, putting the rising seniors through their paces before we kicked their asses in a few days at the seven-on-seven. Every pass, every fake, every throw was choreographed until we could all run them in our sleep.

With practice pads covered in grass, dirt, and sweat, we left the field. I grabbed my gear and shoved it into my locker. My usual rush to shower and get home was stalled knowing Bay would be home. Or was she at play practice? With Jon?

I gripped the edge of my locker. It squealed, bending in my grasp. I jerked my hand back, checking over my shoulder. Closing it, I rocked my shoulder against it to flatten it back out.

"Bennet's looking for you." Knox ducked his head and yanked off his cleats.

I tugged my shirt over my head. My clothes were rank. They could probably play a defensive position all on their own. Grueling workouts were part of the deal, but damn if I wouldn't soak up as much of the off season as possible, relaxing before the real work started.

"Now is not the time for me to play party host." I grabbed my towel and soap and walked to the shower. My stomach was beyond growling; it was freaking the fuck out for some damn food.

"Who's hosting the final party?" Bennet called out rubbing a towel over his head.

Slipping past him, I cranked on the shower and stepped under the spray.

The party place wouldn't be my house this time, but I had no doubt I'd be forced to host a celebratory party or an everyone's-getting-shit-faced-to-drown-our-sorrows   party before graduation.

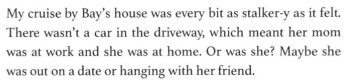

My cruise by Bay's house was every bit as stalker-y as it felt. There wasn't a car in the driveway, which meant her mom was at work and she was at home. Or was she? Maybe she was out on a date or hanging with her friend.

I pulled to the end of my street, and the truck parked in my driveway sent my stomach plummeting straight through the floorboards.

He was back early. Why the fuck was he back early? How long had he been back? The case of beer was probably halfway finished now. I could either walk in there now and hope he'd passed out or wait until later and hope he passed out then so I could be in and out before workouts tomorrow. Fuck, I didn't feel like dealing with this now and the possibility of showing up for a two-hour gym session bruised wasn't my idea of a good time. I couldn't even go into my own damn house.

My fingers gripped the steering wheel so hard they ached. Every heartbeat reverberated through my palms. I wanted to burst in there, knock him the hell out. But I had a workout and a practice. I wasn't going to let him screw it up for me again. I wasn't going to let him take anything else from me.

Getting arrested or breaking or bruising something before we played would only be a win for him. Something else in my life for him to ruin. I pulled a U-turn and headed to the only other quiet place I had.

I drove the winding back road past the abandoned excavation and construction equipment. In the middle of the week, no one was here, but on the weekend it would be filled with cars, cases of contraband beer, and even worse decisions. My headlights flashed over the dirt mounds until they were lost in the dark expanse of nothingness past the sheer drop.

The cops had stopped even trying to put up fences before I could drive.

I cut the engine and clicked off my headlights, bathing everything in darkness other than the moonlight above.

The full moon hung in the sky like a searchlight that had lost its way.

Gravel crunched under my feet as I walked to the edge.

Cranes hung over the edge of the quarry pit, over the water down below. No one knew exactly how deep it was. Twenty feet? Fifty feet? A hundred feet? Or maybe it was bottomless.

All the hope and plans I had for the future had been shoved straight out of my head by a busted-up semi parked at the end of my street. Even though I'd be gone in a few months, sometimes it felt like he'd haunt me forever, standing over me with a drunken smile, telling me to stop my bitching.

At least I was still breathing. The stillness of the night roared in my ears.

I walked to the edge of the rusted, formerly-yellow crane most people jumped from. The paint was reduced to flecks that would disappear within a year. With my arms out at my sides, I stepped onto the metal. The twang of metal on metal rubbing reminded me of Bay sitting on her couch, playing for me.

I froze one step from crossing from the safe ground to the precipice of darkness.

Headlights flooded over me. I glanced over my shoulder.

A beat-up ride pulled up next to my car.

Knox popped out of his window, sitting on the door through the window opening. He drummed on his roof. "I knew I'd find you here. Have you lost your mind? Do that shit after next week. Get your ass in your fucking car."

A laugh broke free from my chest. Leave it to Knox not to let me get away with losing my mind.

I got in my car and followed him to his place.

Both his parents' cars were parked out front. They were pristine S-Class Mercedes, which looked even more untouchable next to Knox's car. They'd made him work for his car, and that was what he could afford.

Knox's parents were probably some of the nicest people there were, but I wasn't up for being on my best behavior tonight.

"Not feeling up to playing, Mr. Polite?"

I shoved my hands into my pockets and lifted my chin.

"It's cool. Let's go." We went around the side of the house and took the stairs down to the basement. He ran up the basement steps and his feet thudded overhead like he was trying to jump through the floor.

The smells of cheese, tomato, oregano and spicy meat wafted down the stairs before he even opened the basement door.

He slid the oversized pizza onto the table. "It's Antonio's. They ordered an extra pie." Had this asshole called them on the drive over? He was the best kind of pain in the ass.

It could've been ripped from a dumpster and I wouldn't have cared. I inhaled two slices. My fingers were greasy, and my stomach was finally not nearly as pissed off at me.

A cold can tapped against my shoulder. He shrugged. "It looked like you could use it."

I glanced up at the ceiling like they could see me through the floor and rolled the can between my hands.

The hiss and spray of the can opening was followed by his first gulp. "Don't make me drink alone."

There was a Knight family rule. If you drank in the house, you couldn't drive anywhere until the next morning. What waited for me at home? Did I even want to know? Playing with bruised ribs or a fucked-up hand or worse. My stomach threatened revolt.

I tapped the top of the beer. The cold metal against my palm slowed the steep race of my pulse.

Even though he wasn't looking my way, Knox was watching me. He didn't know the dirty details, but he knew I didn't have the warm and fuzzy relationship with my dad that he had with his parents. And I didn't want him to know any more about it. I'd made it almost this far without being that kid at our school, I wasn't going to start now.

I pulled the tab on my beer and downed it in one go.

We played video games until midnight. The TV cast a glow of nostalgia over us as we played, and I felt like we were twelve again over the summer, trying to stay awake as late as possible.

Knox's mom brought down the Dare Bundle filled with oversized pillows and extra-long blankets. Their basement sofa was ten times nicer than my actual bed.

We cleaned everything up and he headed for the stairs.

"Thanks, man."

"Anytime." He flipped off the light and headed up the basement stairs.

Alone in the dark, not worried about keeping my guard up, my thoughts drifted back to Bay. Maybe not dragging her into my fucked-up life was for the best. Not having to deal with my bullshit with less than two months until graduation was a gift I could give her.

It was the only gift I had to give anyone—staying away.

15

BAY

The pages in my notebook were filling up.

He'd backed out of my house like I was a newly-turned zombie. After all the poking and prodding to get me to sing for him, he'd bailed the first time I did. What the hell? Dare would give any girl a complex, and I wasn't one of those girls who'd built up a strong skin over time, knowing exactly the games to play to get a guy to pay attention to them.

Almost all the attention I'd been paid had been accidental. Like someone tripping over me or knocking into me. It was mainly due to people not being aware enough of their surroundings and me not registering on anyone's 'pay attention' meter.

But Dare had me thinking maybe that was changing, and then he'd run screaming from my house. Okay, maybe not full-out screaming, but it might as well have been. I wasn't letting him get away with it.

I stormed around the corner and out the school doors, fury pouring off me in waves. He'd skipped history where our group project was due at the end of next week. This sent

Michelle into a near-convulsive state and I'd had to be the one to talk her down. At least he'd added his part of the assignment, but he hadn't had the courtesy to let anyone know.

The humidity prickled my skin. We'd gone from winter to a swampy, murky mess in a matter of days. Overcast and dreary, the day was headed from bad to worse. A dot of rain hit my cheek. I'd better make this fast before I was caught in a downpour. Storming off didn't have the same panache when you ended up looking like a drowned rat on the way back home, but the angry clouds served as the perfect backdrop to the chewing out I was prepared to give him. It was like I was using my superhero powers to sway Mother Nature.

This morning I'd waved, and he walked right past me like I was invisible again. Screw that. I'd gone over the whole thing multiple times playing both our parts, and there was no good explanation.

A huge semi sat at the end of the cul de sac. Was that always here? I'd never even been down Dare's street, let alone gone to his house.

The lawn was overgrown and the screen door hung off at an angle. Our rental wasn't palatial, but the landlord had given my mom a great deal on the rent. My mom had helped coach his wife through her labor after his head had whacked off the floor of the delivery room and he'd had to be awakened with smelling salts.

Steeling myself, I banged on the door. Silence. I shifted from foot to foot. I raised my hand again and the door flew open.

Dare's expression shifted from anger to confusion and shock before sliding straight back into anger. "What are you doing here?" He closed the door behind him and stepped out onto the top step, crowding me.

"That's all you have to say to me?"

"What the hell else am I supposed to say to you?"

"You ran from my house, dropped my bike off when you knew I wasn't awake, and then you ignored me at school."

"Now's not a great time." His body was tense with his hands clenched at his sides.

I peered around him and through the crack in the door before he blocked my view.

He had on jeans and a t-shirt, so it wasn't like I'd caught him in the middle of Bang Town with someone else. He didn't have anything on his feet, though.

No shoes, which wouldn't have been possible only a week ago with the cold snap, when he'd shoveled our driveway and we'd shared a moment in my kitchen. And now he was staring at me with his arms folded over his chest like I was trying to sell him meat from my trunk.

"Too bad. You don't get to weasel your way into my life one second and then sprint from my house at lightning speed the next."

"What do you want me to say?" He stared down, his eyes boring into mine.

"I want the truth."

"There is no truth. I wanted to talk to you and I did." His gaze swapped from fiery to bored like an internal switch had been flipped.

And that pissed me off. Burning, fire-and-brimstone rage bubbled up inside me. I jabbed my finger into the center of his chest.

"You don't get to decide if this is over. You spend all this time trying to talk to me and get me to open up, and then, when I finally do, you're done? Just like that?" I snapped in front of his face. "Well, screw you."

His head shot up and snapped to the side. "You need to go, Bay." He edged further away from the door, closing it behind him.

"No, I'm not moving until you talk to me." I planted my hands on my hips. "You'll have to tackle me to get me to move."

He let out a long, low hiss. "Fuck." His shoulder dropped and my eyebrows dipped.

My yelp was loud, probably reverberating through the whole neighborhood when his shoulder planted in my stomach. Not hard and heavy—other than the surprise it didn't hurt at all, but I was upside down. His bare feet were silent rushing down the uneven paved walkway to his house.

The stun wore off and I pushed off his back, brushing my hair out of my face. "Put me down."

A set of keys jingled and he shifted my weight. I was dumped in the front passenger seat of his car.

He looked back at the house and threw himself into the driver's side before throwing his arm over my seat back and careening out of the driveway, bottoming out at the dip to the road and taking the turn before rocketing down his street like he was an F1 driver.

"Where are we going?"

"I'm taking you home." He cut his gaze in my direction, leaning forward in his seat, hands tight around the steering wheel.

"Nope, not happening." I clicked my seatbelt in and crossed my arms over my chest. "I'm not getting out of this car until you talk to me."

"Would you stop—"

"Being so frustrating and difficult? Welcome to the club. You'll have to drag me from this car and peel my fingers off the door frame to get me to leave."

He let out a low growl and blew straight past my house.

"You don't have any shoes on."

He lifted his left foot and glanced down at it. The edges of his mouth turned down.

"You didn't notice before now?"

"I had more important things to worry about."

"Like what?"

"Getting you the hell away from my house."

I shrank back into the seat. This wasn't how the scenarios had run in my head. They'd all ended with him apologizing and kissing the hell out of me. Right now, I'd be lucky if he didn't drop me off on the side of the road and force me to walk back to my house.

"If you need some quiet time or something, I can leave you be."

He shook his head. "Now you're ready to leave me alone? What happened to me having to peel your fingers from the door frame?"

"Maybe you driving like a maniac through town has showed me the error of my ways."

His leg jerked up off the accelerator and the odometer dropped by at least twenty miles per hour.

"Dare..." I rested my hand on his bicep. It bunched under my hold. "You can talk to me. Let me help."

His gaze didn't flash 'back the hell off' like it did when he'd first stepped out of the house. Now it was more lost, as if the situation with me in front of him was something hopeless.

"Or not." I sank back into my seat and stared at the window. The trees whipped by, and he didn't show any signs of slowing down. Dots of rain splattered the windshield, but not enough to need wipers.

"When you played..."

He licked his lips and pressed them together. "When you played it shook me, Bay." His gaze cut to mine.

I sucked in a sharp breath. My mouth opened and closed, but no sound came out. I gathered up my courage to ask, "Shook you? Shook you how?"

"I don't let many people close to me. I just don't. But you walked straight into my life like it was no big deal."

"You had a part in that, I think."

He let out a huffy laugh. "True. When you sang that first night, I was dealing with some stuff."

"What kind—"

"It doesn't matter, but your voice pulled me back from a bad place and I needed to hear it again."

I turned in my seat angling myself toward him. "And when I played, I took you back to that bad place?" My stomach knotted and clenched that my playing had made him feel bad, so he ran from my house.

"No." He shook his head and pulled off to the side of the road. Although he wasn't driving anymore, he wasn't looking at me. "It didn't." He flung open his door and stood on the side of the road with his fingers interlocked behind his head, staring up at the sky.

Clouds gathered, wanting front row seats to my confusion. The spitting rain had turned into a drizzle, drumming on the car roof.

I threw my door open, tired of this dance of miscommunication we were doing. "It took you to a good place. Don't we all want to be happy? Why is that a bad thing?"

"Because you're like an unpredictable opponent out on the field and I've got no idea how to cover you."

As if him saying the words opened the literal flood gates, the skies opened and the drizzle turned into a downpour. I shielded my eyes and charged ahead.

"I'm someone you need protecting from?"

He jerked his arms from behind his head and spun to face me. "Probably the only one."

"Stop talking in circles. Stop talking around me." The water slammed into me. Fat, heavy droplets soaked through my shirt.

"Let's get back in the car."

I planted my feet. "No, not until we get this all out. One second you're following me everywhere, popping up in places I don't want to see you, and the next, you're avoiding me like a psycho ex-girlfriend. I'm not getting into the car until you tell me everything." He was a hazy figure in front of me. My glasses were streaky and wet.

"What's there to tell? Do you want to know how you made me feel?" He stepped closer, rounding the front of his car. The street was empty, deserted except for me and him, finally ready to bare everything to one another. Water trailed down his strong, straight nose dripping off the end in a steady stream.

"How it was like you reached down deep into my soul and started planting your mark without me even knowing it?"

His hair was plastered to his forehead.

My chest squeezed tight. I didn't breathe. I couldn't make a single move that might stop Dare from telling me what I needed to hear. Screw the consequences.

"How it makes me crazy knowing you're going to California in a few months and I don't even know where I'll end up? Is that what you want to hear?" He stood in front of me, staring down at me, panting. Like this exertion matched what he did in practices or during every game.

I nodded. Water poured down my face, trailing off the bottom of my chin continuing to soak my shirt. "Yes. Do you think I haven't thought those same things? I've stared at my ceiling, looked out my window trying to figure out how my excitement at going away to college in a few months now has a bittersweet tinge to it because you won't be there."

He moved so fast I had no doubt there wasn't an opponent he'd gone up against on the field who could stop him, only I didn't want to.

His lips were on mine, fierce, hungry and unyielding.

My chest pressed against his, my softness crushed against the hard set of his body and his determined mouth.

His hand was on the side of my face, his fingers cupping the back of my neck and his thumb along my jaw, keeping me where he wanted me. Keeping me where I wanted to be.

The storm raged around us, showering us as our unquenchable thirst for one another overwhelmed every other sense.

A horn honk and a car blazing down the road broke us apart.

I stared at him, panting, trying to remember if I'd ever felt more alive before. Every cell in my body yearned for his touch again.

He shielded my body from the road and ushered me back to his car.

"I'm soaked."

"It'll dry. Let's get you home." He opened my door and held my hand when I sat inside. I cringed, the wetness seeping through the seat.

He closed the door and walked around the back.

I checked on him in the mirror.

He raked his fingers through his hair and paused before coming around to his side of the car and climbing inside.

We drove back to my house in silence, but our fingers were interlocked the whole ride.

I was The New Girl. No one saw me. I didn't even know if I wanted them to. Except that sometimes, when he stared at me, he saw through the shields I'd worn since I'd arrived in this town. And I'd done the same to him.

But these feelings churning inside me worried me. When I left him, I wasn't sure I'd survive.

16

DARE

My heart kept trying to leap from my chest straight out my window, ready to become roadkill.

Kissing her was a mistake. It was supposed to be the period at the end of the sentence, closing the book on this attraction between us. I'd thought maybe she'd slap me or shove me away.

Instead, she'd met my lips with her own uncontainable desire. I'd pressed my hand against the small of her back and held her face to mine. Staring into her eyes, I knew it wasn't the end of anything.

I'd dropped a lit match into a warehouse of fireworks, and all I had was a garden hose to fight this fire.

I parked out front of her house. Instead of letting go of my hand, she climbed over the center console like letting go was as hard for her as it would've been for me.

We walked up the straight and tidy path to her house. The weather had shifted again. The downpour had stopped, but the drizzle added to our drenched clothes.

Her white t-shirt clung to her chest, outlining her

silhouette perfectly. Her pants stuck to her legs and her shoes squished on the walk to the front door.

My bare feet were a reminder of how going home wasn't an option, of why this had happened in the first place. When she'd shown up on my doorstep, my first and only objective had been to get her to go.

Sure, my dad was passed out drunk, but I'd let my guard down one time too many, and I knew that didn't mean he wouldn't wake from his stupor enraged and ready to take down anything in his path.

Getting Bay to safety had blocked out everything else until she was beyond the property line of my house. Throwing her in my car hadn't been part of the plan, but when had I ever been great at making those?

She hadn't freaked out, demanded I take her home, or tried to jump from the car. Instead, she hadn't let me escape with the dodge I'd attempted.

Her keys jingled in the lock. She opened the front door and looked at me over her shoulder. Her hair was plastered to her face and down her back.

The soaking wet pants stuck to her, showing the outline of her underwear cutting straight across her ass. This was what I'd been reduced to? Ogling Bay's fully clothed ass? No one had come close to holding my interest for more than a glance since her night on the back steps. She'd mounted an emotional and sexual ambush on me without a single weapon raised—only her voice, her words, and her body.

The weight of my soaked sweats and boxers provided the only protection I had from the growing erection primed for action by the look in her eyes. I was seconds from punching myself in the dick to keep from stepping out of line.

"Come with me." She nodded toward the stairs like now would be when I'd finally let go of her hand.

It felt like stepping onto hallowed ground. Climbing the steps, my pulse throbbed in my veins.

She pushed open the first door on the left. Her room. There were no posters on the wall, only pictures. Notebooks and textbooks were strewn all over the desk and bed.

"You can wait here. I'll get you a towel and something to wear."

We stared down at our hands. We'd have to let go at some point. But here, surrounded by Bay's things, it didn't feel half as wrong as it would've felt in my car. I released my grip and she released hers.

"Two seconds." And she was gone. Doors opened and closed in the hallway and I looked around the room. With a shy smile, she came back in with a stack of towels.

I trailed my finger along the edge of her desk, careful not to wet anything more than I needed to. There was a puddle around my feet.

She crossed in front of me to her dresser and tugged out the drawers. Slipping her hand inside, she grabbed a shirt and shorts.

My Adam's apple bobbed as I caught a flash of Bay peeling her sopping clothes off her body, revealing wide, smooth, perfect expanses of skin to my hungry gaze.

She turned to face me with her clothes clutched to her chest.

"Did you want to rinse off? I'm feeling kind of grody." She tugged her shirt away from her chest. "Obviously, you don't have to do that here. You can go home." Her voice trailed off, quieter with each word.

A pang slammed into my chest. The warmth spread. She wanted me to stay and I didn't want to leave.

"I'll take a shower."

"I'll get you a change of clothes while you're in there." She laid the soft, fluffy towels—softer than any I'd used before—in my arms.

"Thanks."

"It's the first door on the other side of the hallway."

I set out on my adventure to use another person's bathroom. And not just any person. Bay. The expedition I'd been unprepared for was underway.

The house was a mirror of my house. Configuration aside, nothing felt the same. The tiles were bright and white. No cracks, discolored grout, or missing medicine cabinet. Everything inside screamed nice family home filled with people who gave a damn about one another.

A quiet knock on the door broke through my exploration.

"Is everything okay?"

"Yup, I'm good." I set down the towels and cranked on the shower. "I'll be out in a couple minutes." I peeled off my clothes and jumped into the shower, cleaning myself as efficiently as I did after practices. The addition of my semi hadn't escaped me, but I hoped it would escape Bay. Her raspberry body wash sat on a shelf in the shower.

Her scent enveloped me, and my blood went rushing straight from my head to my dick. Now wasn't the time. I cranked it to cold and gritted my teeth until the inopportune erection went away.

Standing in the doorway to her bedroom with a towel wrapped around my waist, I was acutely aware of how bare I was. Locker rooms had desensitized me to nudity in general, but she had never been in a locker room with me before.

She spotted me and stood, her own towel wrapped around her chest and tucked in neatly over her left breast.

The swell and curve of her breasts kept the terrycloth around her, and I'd never been more pissed at a set of breasts in my life.

"I got you some clothes." She patted the small stack on the edge of her bed. "They were my dad's, but they should fit you." Her bottom lip disappeared into her mouth as she nibbled it.

"I...I'll be right back." She gathered up the clothes on top of her dresser and jerked her thumb over her shoulder and rushed from the room. The bathroom door closed.

I stared down at the shirt and shorts she'd left for me. Her dad's clothes. From the way she talked about him, it meant a lot that she'd entrust these to me, even if it was only for a few hours.

Putting them on, I folded the towel and sat on the edge of her bed with my forearms resting on my thighs. The t-shirt was tight, but the shorts had fit.

Everything here—even me—smelled like her. I must've grabbed her shower soap.

Standing, I wandered her room again. The Bay expedition continued.

The guitar case sat propped up against the wall beside the closet. Clothes were shoved in the hamper by the door. It was lived in, but not messy. She made her bed. Her backpack hung on the back of her desk chair. A basket of clothes lay beside her door.

There were notebooks and textbooks on her desk. Which classes was she in that we weren't in together? I lifted a notebook without a subject written neatly on the front.

A hand slammed down on it, knocking it back down to the desk. "Don't look at that."

Bay gathered up the notebook and shoved it into her top desk drawer.

"Sorry." She bent to pick up her abandoned towel and ran it over her hair.

"No, it's what I get for snooping. I wasn't thinking. I'm sorry." What was wrong with me?

She peeked at me. "It was an overreaction. I've never shown anyone this before."

"You don't have to show me if you don't want to." I turned away from the desk, giving her space. I sat on the edge of the bed farthest from the desk trying to think of something witty or at least not completely stupid to say, but the memory bank was filled with cobwebs. Right about now would be a great time for me to take my sorry ass home.

The wet towel gently thudded in the hamper. She tugged open the drawer and took out the notebook. With the pages gripped in her hand, she sat on the bed beside me. The mattress dipped.

My muscles tensed in nervous, twitchy anticipation of her letting me see something no one else had.

"Try not to laugh too hard." She shoved it in my direction without looking at me.

"Bay..." I caught her turning head with a gentle touch of the back of my hand against her cheek. Holding her gaze, I didn't let her escape into the rabbit hole of doubt.

She stared into my eyes. Her gaze shrouded in uncertainty.

"Nothing I see in here will change what I think of you."

A nod.

I flipped open the cover. A rainbow of scribbles filled the first page. Bay's designated does-this-pen-fucking-work page.

She shot up, tidying the room as I turned to the next page.

Some of the pages had a title at the top and others didn't.

Some filled only a few lines and others took up multiple pages.

Each told me a little more about her, uncovering those secrets I'd been dying to learn.

Songs filled page after page of the notebook. Older ones where the handwriting was loopier and sloppier and in bright and bold colors. That's where I learned she loved My Little Pony and hated a boy named Anthony O'Connell in the fifth grade.

The ink had faded in some, but there were others that were newer, even recent, from the brightness of the pen strokes and the change in the emotional charge. These were no longer about recess and water balloon fights. They were about the struggles of finding herself and what her family was with her dad gone.

Grappling with finding her place in a town where no one knew her name. My heart sunk. That had been my doing. I'd made that time in her life even harder than it needed to be, and I couldn't even remember it.

The next song was one of confusion and searching for a reason a quasi-enemy was now trying to play nice. The last page detailed the chaos in her head trying to sort through the feelings that brought up. The feelings I brought up in her. Each one painted a picture so bright and clear it was like being inside her head.

To see myself how she saw me as a one-time villain who'd transformed, although she fought it hard, fortified my resolve. I wouldn't hurt her again. I closed the notebook and sat it on the bed beside me.

"What did you think?" She peered over at me from the basket of clothes she folded.

"You have a gift."

A huffy laugh burst from her lips. "I'm not that on edge, you can tell me what you think." She shook out a t-shirt five times before folding it against her chest.

"You think I'd lie?" I turned the page of lyrics primed to cut out a piece of my heart if she sang them to me.

"You'd do your best not to hurt my feelings. Especially after reading 'Wrong'." The drawer rattled as she opened it and shoved in a stack of shirts.

"If I ripped everything you write down to shreds, would you believe me?"

Another laugh. "Probably. It's always easier to believe the bad." She picked a piece of real or imaginary lint off the shirt in her hands.

"Maybe you need to be the one to stop judging what you've written. Can you sing one for me?"

"Which one?" She shoved her t-shirt into her open drawer.

"'Found.'"

"Out of all the songs in there you want me to play 'Found'." Her eyebrow lifted.

"What's wrong with 'Found'? Don't judge my song choice."

She shook her head and picked up her guitar. Sitting on her desk, she checked the tuning and opened and closed her hand.

"You don't know it by heart."

"The song I wrote in sixth grade about losing my retainer and having to sort through three lunch periods of cafeteria food? No, sorry, I haven't committed that one to memory."

"I'd have thought it would've left a permanent mark on your mind." I handed over the notebook.

She shuddered. "So much ketchup. I can't eat it to this day."

I pushed myself back on her bed until my back pressed against the wall.

By the end of the song, tears of laughter rolled down my face. I'd never look at French fries and green beans the same way again.

I stood, cupping my hands around my mouth, pumping my one-man crowd roar as she sang the last syllable of 'corn dog' before taking a seated bow.

She flung a balled-up sock at me, hitting me in the chest. "Does anyone else know you're such a goofball?"

"No one but you, Bay."

17

BAY

My neck ached. Eraser shavings covered my bedspread. The words on the index cards blurred. But I'd finally made it. I'd crossed the bio practice final finish line.

"How can you stand it?"

"Stand what?" I kicked my feet and scribbled in my notebook. Words flowed, filling line after line, page after page. My bio textbook and notebook had been abandoned. The first part of the practice test with a giant 92 in Piper's bubbly, flowing handwriting covering the entire first page meant it was time for a reward. I'd gone downstairs and retrieved the container of goodness and two glasses of milk. Chocolate chip and peanut butter cookies.

"Being this close to Dare." She sighed, a legit hand-to-chest, staring-out-the-window-longingly sigh.

My hackles raised before I tamped them down. Of course she was interested in Dare. Who wasn't interested in Dare?

"He's at least a hundred feet away. You've sat closer to him in class."

"He's not shirtless in class."

I dropped my pencil and scrambled across my bed to her sentry station in front of my window. After our shower and my impromptu concert, he'd come over to watch a movie the next night. He'd practically lived at my house through the weekend of our relationship reckoning, only leaving when I went to the final tech rehearsals before the musical performances this week. Whether that would go beyond staring at him, shirtless and glistening after a post-downpour shower, remained to be seen.

We'd shared our explosive kiss during a downpour, but he hadn't made a move since. Sitting on my bed in a towel, I'd expected him to whip it off before kissing me again, instead he'd averted his eyes and let me leave. When I got back, I thought okay, now I'm not coated in roadside grime, maybe this will be when it happened, instead he'd asked for a solo concert.

"Are you going to go to prom?"

I scoffed. "It's too much money for pigs in a blanket and sparkling apple juice and wearing uncomfortable shoes."

"I'm sure if Dare asked you, you'd go," she sing-songed.

"Not even if he asked. He'd have to kidnap me and throw me in the trunk of his car for that to happen."

"Now you're just talking dirty."

I flung a pillow at her head.

"Jeez, you hit hard." She blew her hair out of her face. "I'm not going either. Unless a certain stage crew guy asks me."

"Why don't you ask him?"

She gasped and pressed her palm to her chest, fanning her face with the other hand. "And what kind of lady would do such a thing?"

"One who wants to go to prom."

"It's a rite of passage."

"I'm sure I'll get over it."

"You're no fun at all."

I pictured Dare showing up to my house in a tux with a corsage and matching boutonniere. I shook my head. Maybe it was a convincing-as-hell hallucination and he'd never kissed me at all. My first kiss. Well, my first non-playground-behind-the-jungle-gym kiss. A kiss while soaking wet on the side of the road, one so explosive I'd have been happy to never leave that spot. But how many other lips had he tasted? How many other tongues had danced against his, knowing all the right steps and not fumbling around in the dark trying to figure out what room they were in. It had been face palm territory for sure.

He didn't need to know it was my first real kiss. I'd remember it forever, though.

From the way he jerked his hand back when our fingers brushed, I expected to get the letting you down easy talk any day now. At least he wasn't avoiding me. Not my calls or my texts or even in the hallways. Not that making eye contact shouted we were in a non-relationship relationship, but at least I wasn't back to being invisible.

So, a shirtless Dare might not be something I saw again.

Peering around the edge of my curtain, I stared at him in all his rippling-muscled glory. Shiny with sweat and laughing, throwing a ball to Knox. He looked so carefree. Not like he did at pep rallies or pretty much any other time I'd seen him with other people. There was always an intensity in his gaze, like he was going to flay anyone who got in the way. It was at odds with our popcorn fight during the end credits of Goonies, and I was having trouble reconciling both sides of him.

But playing with Knox, he looked like him. The same

guy who'd made me trip over my own feet with a sip of lemonade. Was that how his charm worked? Could he just turn it on to get women to drop to their knees in front of him?

A foreign flutter rippled through my stomach. I dropped my hands across it and couldn't take my eyes off him.

I got it now. The Dare Destruction. It wasn't just on the field. He'd streaked a path through the town with that damn smolder. How many other girls had experienced those lips?

"You've never even thought of leaving the lights on when you change at night?" Piper held onto the curtains, throwing model poses, and talking in a way that let me know I'd missed a few minutes of her monologue on how I could seduce him through my bedroom window.

"I'm not doing a striptease for him." He'd already seen me in a towel.

She looked at me with disbelief written all over her face. "Why the hell not?"

"My cheerleader body upgrade got lost in the mail." A red splotchy neck and chest to match my t-shirt had been another reason I wasn't sure him dropping my towel wouldn't have ended with me yelping and running for cover. All those other women he'd kissed—how many looked like me?

"Dudes don't care."

"I care. Can we get back to work?"

She flung the curtains open wider. "Oh my god, he's looking up here. Shielding his eyes to see."

"What? No!" I grabbed her around the waist, wrestling her away from the window.

"He's going to think it's me perving on him."

Her grip on the curtains was tight.

"Piper, stop it!"

"He wants a show, I'll give him a show."

I braced my feet against the bed and tugged her, wrapping my arms tight around her. The fabric and cross bar popped out of the brackets and fell on top of us. She fell on top of me, our foreheads collided.

Dots of light swam in front of my eyes.

"Bay!"

"Piper! What the hell?"

"You're no fun." She pouted, rubbing her forehead.

"I could kill you." I shoved her off me and stared at the flooding light pouring in through my window and the dismantled curtains laying on my bed. I had to get those up before my mom came home, but no way was I struggling with them in front of the window with him down there.

"Then you'd have no one to help you through bio." She grinned.

"It's the only reason you're still alive." I leveled my pencil at her like a weapon.

～

There was a thud at the front door.

I peered out the window and Dare's car was parked in the driveway. He passed by the window and I jerked open the door.

"Wait."

He skidded to a stop and half turned. "Your mom let me borrow that a little while ago. Mine broke and I didn't have a chance to replace it." He gestured to the wrench sitting on the top step with a note.

Mom hadn't gotten rid of Dad's tools even after three moves since he died. And she'd also freak out a bit if she found out my entire curtain rod was leaning against the wall, probably losing us a chunk of the security deposit.

"Thanks for returning it." I grabbed it and set it beside the door. "Why haven't--Do you think you could help me with something?" I half squinted and winced bracing for him to run away again, but there weren't many options at this point.

He looked back to his car like he might dive through the open window and peel off down my street to escape.

"Sure, what do you need?" He turned around and headed back to the front door.

I brought him upstairs. The butterfly colony going crazy that he was now standing in my room. I went to get the tools he needed to put it back up.

"So this just fell down on its own?" Dare stood on the step ladder and smiled down at me over his shoulder. His words were muffled around the screws held between his lips.

"Piper was here. It got tangled when she grabbed her books."

"So that wasn't you watching?" Even through the screws there was an intensity to his words. Did he want me to be watching?

"She was trying to determine the velocity of your throw." Of all the excuses...but I kept my hands folded across my chest, instead of smacking myself in the forehead.

"Seems legit." He hammered in the plastic plugs to fill the holes where the screws had been ripped out. "Just so you know, you're a terrible liar."

"She was spying on you. Checking you out when you were playing with Knox." I spilled like he'd threatened to pull out my toenails.

"And here I thought that was you." He ran one finger

under my chin from the hollow of my throat out to the edge of my chin. "Or maybe I just hoped it was."

A sputtering reply was all I could muster. "I wasn't sure if you would or not. You've been quiet lately."

He turned to face the wall and held out his hand. "Can you hand me the drill?"

I scooped it up off the bed and offered it up for him.

Our fingers brushed and he took it, going back to his work.

"I didn't want to suffocate you. My dad left, so I didn't want to be in your hair all the time."

"What does your dad leaving have to do with us hanging out?"

He shook his head. "It doesn't. I just...I figured you'd be sick of having me around."

"Do you have big plans this week?" I dragged my finger over my bedspread.

"Other than the Titan Combine in Chicago on Thursday? No."

"Oh, I forgot about that. Never mind."

"Tell me. What's going on?" He looked over his shoulder.

"It's the last night of the show. Sometimes people go out to celebrate after."

"You're inviting me to a stage crew party?"

He'd probably rather rip his own eyeballs out.

"No, definitely not. But maybe we could get some burgers or something."

His jaw clenched and he faced the wall.

"Is this straight?" He tilted the rod.

Did he not want to hang out with me? Why did I feel like I was getting whiplash? We'd kissed. He hung out with me for nearly 48 hours straight, then disappears and was now pissed I wasn't inviting him to a stage crew snoozefest?

"A little higher on the left."

"Can you hand me the level?" He held out his hand.

"After the Combine thing are you finished working out?"

"There's the Bedlam Bowl in 3 weeks."

"Oh, those banners." They all ran together at a certain point. A football, bubble lettering and a date. How did anyone keep them all straight? "I forgot about that."

"Only you, Bay."

My cheeks turned molten.

"With all the senior year madness who has time to notice anything?"

His gaze snapped to mine. "I notice."

My heart leapt.

He balanced the curtain rod in one hand and the drill whirred as he fastened the last three screws.

The frames on my dressers shook when he dropped down off the ladder.

"And it's done." He pointed with the drill at the perfectly straight curtain rail and green and blue mosaic patterned fabric hanging down.

"My mom didn't come in my room yesterday, but it was only a matter of time before she did." Nerves bubbled in my stomach and I tugged at the hem of my shirt. Why did it feel like it was shrinking by the second and a quarter of an inch away from choking me? "Sorry if I made you late to something, or you had other, better things to do."

"Bay..." His voice trailed off and he stepped closer. Almost like he was being pulled along against his will. Stilted, hesitant steps.

The spark had caught the kindling and the flames were slowly creeping higher up my body.

His head dipped and I prepared myself for the same fierce possession of my lips he'd taken in the rain.

Bang, the door downstairs opened, hitting the wall. "Bay, can you help me with this?"

I stared at him, stunned. Dropping back onto my heels, I dropped my head. I hadn't even realized I'd gone up onto my toes to meet him halfway.

"Bay?"

"Coming, Mom." I skirted around him.

"Let me help." Dare followed me down the stairs. His shadow falling over my body.

I peeked over my shoulder.

"There you are." Mom came in the front door with a massive box in her hands. "Oh Dare. I didn't know you were here." Her gaze swept over us both. No disheveled clothes, speedy exit from my bedroom, only mildly panting.

"We had a father drop off twenty fruit bouquets and dozens of boxes of donuts. I think he thought he was bringing donuts for the whole hospital. We needed to get it out of there before it all spoiled."

"I can take some off your hands, if you want. Is the rest in the car? I can go get it." Dare set down the drill and ducked out the front door before either of us could respond.

I walked into the kitchen behind my mom.

"How long's Dare been over?" She wasn't looking at me, but I could tell her mom radar was pinging like crazy.

"Not long. He dropped off the wrench he borrowed." I unfolded the top of the chin-height box she'd slid onto the counter.

"And returned it to your room." She laughed.

"Mom, come on. We were just talking about a group presentation we have on Tuesday. He's one of the most popular guys in school." I glanced over my shoulder. "It's not like that. Dare's being nice."

She made a disbelieving sound and turned to me. Her hands dropped to the tops of my shoulders. "You're eighteen. In a few months, you'll be away at college. I know what young adults your age do. I want you to be safe and happy. I love you."

I hugged her tight around her waist. Leaving would be hard for so many reasons.

She kissed the top of my head and squeezed me.

"I figured you could take a lot of this to the theater club tonight. You've been putting in a lot of long hours there. You look so sleepy all the time." She brushed my hair back from my forehead.

I kept the smile balanced on my face.

"You're always hard up for snacks and performance fuel."

Peering into the box, a bouquet of pineapple, green apples, strawberries, chocolate covered strawberries, berries of all kinds and marshmallows poked up on skewers from a green Styrofoam base, barely visible through the fruit avalanche.

"I picked up an extra shift for tonight. Maybe I could drop you off early. You can't carry this on your bike."

A throat cleared behind us. "I can take Bay back to school."

I froze with my back to him. Oh god, how long had he been standing there. Had he heard the 'did he like me' chat?

"You're always such a gentleman, Dare."

I covered my laugh with a cough at her not-so-subtle 'don't dick my daughter around' tone.

He slid the boxes of donuts and even more chocolate covered strawberries onto the counter.

"Can I have one of these now, Mom?"

"Please, they're getting more stale by the minute. I'm heading up for my shower. You kids be good." She patted the doorway before her footsteps padded up the stairs and across the floor above my head.

"Do you want a donut?" I flipped open the lid on the box, my shoulder nudging into Dare's chest.

He didn't step back and neither did I.

I was playing with fire and the giant bucket of ice water teetering on the ledge was right upstairs.

The box held a dozen donuts with so many flavors and colors. I grabbed the glazed rainbow sprinkle one with chocolate frosting and bit into it. It was a sugar rush explosion in my mouth.

"Hey, that was the one I wanted."

I covered my full mouth with at least a quarter of the donut rammed inside, with my hand. "Sorry."

"How about we share it?"

I held up the donut. Instead of taking it from my hand, he wrapped his fingers around my wrist and brought it to his mouth.

He watched me as he took a bite.

I'd forgotten how to chew, nearly choking on my donut. My heart did double back handsprings in my chest. My pulse throbbed.

It probably felt like a jumping bean rumbling under his fingertips.

He moved the donut back toward my mouth and I took another bite.

His nostrils flared, and the hungry look had nothing to do with the delicious pastries filling the countertop.

And I was supposed to ride in a car with him later tonight? I was a dead woman. Death by hand-fed dessert.

18

DARE

"Where the fuck are you going?" Knox barreled out of the bus along with everyone else, coated in dried sweat and grime, but grinning from ear to ear.

My grin had nothing to do with the Titan Combine, though. I'd never sprinted faster, tackled harder or had stickier hands than I'd had in Chicago. But I had one singular thought: getting back here to get Bay.

Donuts had never been sweeter than off her lips. We might have steamed up the windows in the parking lot when I dropped her off. Sure, she'd run in with the bags instead of letting me help, but today's performance coupled with seeing her again for the first time in thirty-six hours meant that no amount of dried stinging sweat all over my body mattered.

"Dare." Coach Greer called after me.

I skidded to a stop after grabbing my bag and jogged back to him. The play would be over by now. Had she already left to go hang out with the other stage crew people? With that guy, Jon? "Coach."

"You had a hell of a performance out there today."

I shifted from foot to foot. "Yeah, I felt good."

"And that run-in with the kid from Pennsylvania."

My hands clenched around my duffle. The cloudy haze of the cheap shot almost dragged me back into the fog of rage. I closed my eyes.

"I didn't hit him."

"Only because someone got between you two."

I gritted my teeth. "He could've broken my leg with the shit he pulled."

Coach sighed, long and troubled.

The hairs on the back of my neck stood up.

"We can talk about this later." He shook his head. "Get a shower and get some sleep."

I nodded and headed toward my car. The other guys were grabbing their bags. They were my soon-to-be former teammates, but now they were in my way to my goal.

If anyone thought my skills at making a path through opponents ended on the field they were dead wrong. Right now, these were opponents in the way of getting to my true celebration tonight.

I rushed home and back to school. Sweat poured down my back. Even showering and changing clothes hadn't stopped the pounding in my chest or the sweat jumping from my pores like it was abandoning ship after an iceberg collision.

I sniffed my pits, hopped in my car and drove around to the auditorium doors on the other side of the school.

Knox: Overlook

Me: Not tonight

Knox: Where have you been going?

Me: None of your business

Knox: I tell you everything going on with me

Me: Against my will
Knox: You're an asshole
Me: I know

There would be droves of people at the Overlook excited to stand on the empty quarry edge singing team fight songs, talking shit about the Bedlam Bowl, and drinking until midnight.

I parked a row back where there was only one other car parked. Nerves ping-ponged inside my chest. Winning a state championship had felt a lot less scary than standing out here.

Hers was the lone bike locked to the rack. I hadn't missed her.

I leaned against my car with my hands shoved in my pockets, waiting. A wordless song hummed in my chest, washing away some of the jumpy feelings.

The side door flew open and she walked out with a couple other people. She waved to them and headed to the lone bike locked to the bike rack with a lone bike still locked up. Dressed all in black with her hair in two braids, she looked like a badass cat burglar.

I wouldn't have minded waking up to her climbing in my window.

She unlocked her bike and strapped on her helmet. At someone's honk, her head popped up and she waved. Her gaze skated across the emptying lot, sweeping over me and back to her bike.

The front wheel *thunked* as she pushed it out of the rack and she froze.

My smile widened.

Her spin was so fast, she whipped herself in the face with one of her braids.

My smile could've been seen from the space shuttle.

"What are you doing here?"

She dropped her bike and unclipped her helmet, dropping it to the ground and rushing over to me.

"This is a nice look." I toyed with the end of her braid, holding it between two fingers.

Her breath came out in small pants. She stared at me like I'd shown up with a wreath of flowers.

Shit, I should've gotten flowers.

Her gaze sparkled with amazement and happiness, and I forgot all about the wilted grocery store flowers I'd thought about giving her.

The same feelings rumbled in my chest. No one was here. In an empty parking lot after winning the Combine to decide my fate, she made me feel like I'd never been luckier, all because she was happy to see me.

She swallowed and placed a hesitant hand on my chest. "How'd your football drill trip go?"

"You didn't check the score?"

"Two of the stage crew dropped out at the last minute, which meant I had to run the board and move set pieces during the intermission. It's been a busy night, but I guess the same goes for you, huh?"

"Three years."

Her eyebrows dipped and she tilted her head.

"It's how long I wasted not being able to do this." I wrapped my arm around her back and another at her waist, pressing her against me. Our lips met in a heated, hungry collision. Every time was explosive with her, overwhelming and too little all at once.

She squeaked, falling against my chest, her kiss matching mine. Her arms wriggled out from under mine and wrapped around my neck.

A car pulled into the lot and she tensed.

I palmed her ass and she yelped, pressing her palms against my chest. Intensity overdrive and I'd scared her. I let her go, allowing her to drop down from her tippy-toes and stared into her eyes.

She wore a lopsided smile and her chest heaved in pants like the ones I'd breathed racing to get over here. The car parked and someone hopped out.

Bay took a step back and cut her gaze in their direction.

"Sorry." I dropped my arms.

She released her lip from between her teeth, but she watched the car idling in the parking lot. "No need to apologize. I was caught off guard is all." Taking my hands in hers, she wrapped them around her back, letting me hold her close again.

Not until the car pulled out of the lot did she turn back to face me completely.

"This was me showing up to give you a ride home and nothing more. I don't expect anything from you, Bay."

Every part of me wanted to throw open my car door and lay her down in the back seat, but I reigned in those thoughts with a crack of my mental whip. Bay wasn't a back-seat kind of girl. The anvil of information she'd dropped on me about being a virgin hadn't been forgotten.

"Shouldn't you be out celebrating? It seems that's all anyone's doing through the end of the year."

"Not until next weekend when the trophy finally gets here. They don't put the order in until tomorrow morning."

Her jaw hung open and she laughed. "I was joking."

"Oh. You've never paid attention to all the shit they do when we win?"

"It's more than they normally do? I can't say I've paid much attention to football until now. Until you."

Why did that make me feel this way? Tethered and free

all at once. Grounded by the way she looked into my eyes and flying when her lips touched mine.

"After four it's more of the same. Mainly a chance for Coach and the mayor to get up and talk until everyone gets restless and then our QB lifts the trophy over his head and pretends he did it all himself. You didn't miss much."

"If you're there, I'll watch from the crowd."

"Why don't you watch as my date?"

Silence. She stared up at me with a stunned expression.

"After all this, do you think I'm not into you, Bay?" I brushed the back of my fingers along her cheek.

"I had a feeling, but..." She stepped back.

A bit more pressure from her and I dropped my arms.

She glanced around the now vacant parking lot. "I wasn't sure." Peeking up at me, she ran her hands over her face like this had turned into an ordeal. "I wasn't sure what you wanted or even what this was." Her eyelashes fluttered, framing champagne eyes highlighted with deep caramel inlays, perfectly lit up by the street lights.

My gaze traced every line of her eye before I snapped myself out of it and replayed what she'd said. *What this was.*

I shoved my hands into my pockets. That flying feeling changed to free falling. "What do you think I want?"

She shrugged.

"If you've been thinking about it, you obviously have some idea."

"They're thoughts, and I don't even know if they make sense to me, so they're not going to make sense to you."

"Try talking to me and find out." I walked past her and picked up her bike and helmet from the grass. Passing her, I popped the trunk of my car and stashed her bike inside.

"Is this our thing? You stealing my bike?" She planted a hand on her hip.

She was as frustrating as she was beautiful.

"Sometimes it's the only way I can get you to listen." I opened the passenger side door.

Her gaze narrowed and she exhaled long and deep before coming around to the other side of the car.

I didn't move, taking up most of the doorway. A tempting test.

Her lips pursed, but I caught the twitch of a smile. "Am I supposed to sit on your lap? It might make it hard to drive."

"No, but I want you to know you're not pushing me away." I hadn't meant to say it. The feelings inside me were hard to contain when she was around. Brimming to the top of a cup ready to overflow and drown us both.

"Oh, how our roles have reversed." She ducked her head and squeezed against me before climbing into the passenger seat.

"Maybe that's our thing." I closed the door and jogged to my side, trying not to think of how good it felt to have her sitting in my car. I pulled out of the lot.

The streets were deserted. Everyone was already in bed or at their designated parties and wouldn't be on the road until morning. One car's headlights flashed over us on the way to Bay's house.

She perched her chin on her hand and stared out the window.

A question had been rolling around in my head. "Why do you think I wouldn't want you to be at the parade?" I glanced over at her.

"Then everyone would know we're doing whatever this is." She gestured between us.

I didn't try to hide my smile. "You've been doing a lot of thinking when it comes to me and you, but you're not willing to share anything with me."

"Why put a label on it?" She propped up her elbow against the window frame and put on her best I-don't-give-a-fuck look.

I'd never wanted labels before. Never wanted to be anyone's. Never tied down and never looking back, but with her, different feelings were trying to railroad their way inside my chest.

She flicked me a look. "Besides, I heard you don't like to date."

"Who said that?"

"Every girl who's talked about your ass in football pants, including some of the moms."

"Maybe no one's asked me on a date before."

Her eyebrow arched sky high. She shook her head and sank back into her seat. "Welcome to the party, pal."

"You've never been on a date?"

"I'm 'The New Girl'." She put it in air quotes. "And I do stage crew. What was your first clue?"

"That people are damn stupid."

"Including you." Her head tilted. "I've been here all this time." The tease in her voice wasn't enough to cover the hurt. The hurt I'd put there.

A pit in my stomach twisted. Three wasted years. "There's not a day that goes by that I'm not kicking my own ass knowing that."

She cracked a smile. "Okay, that makes me feel a little better."

"So, when's our date?" I pulled the car into her driveway, put it in park, but let the engine idle. Her mom was working. She was home alone, but after her caution in the parking lot, I wasn't pushing things any further until she was ready.

"I didn't agree to a date."

"Sorry to do this then, but I'm going to have to lay down

the law. No more kisses from these lips until I get a date." I dragged my fingers across my lips and threw the imaginary key over my shoulder. She wasn't ready and I wasn't ready to be the guy who pushed her faster and further than she should be going. But the thought of someone else fumbling all her firsts made me want to punch something. It made me want to burn everything down to think she wouldn't have the best, and while she deserved a hell of a lot more than me, my selfishness won out on this one. I couldn't help myself anymore. I'd do whatever I damn well needed to be that guy for her, even when I was finding my way through a forest with a match in the dead of night.

"You're going to not make out with me again until I agree to go out on a date with you?" She shot up straight, her voice jumping two octaves.

"I said kiss. We've yet to make out."

A small sound escaped her open mouth and I ran my finger under her chin closing it. "We haven't?" Her words were a rushed whisper.

I shook my head.

"Not even a little bit." My cocky grin was back in full force.

"But..." She sputtered. Her eyes widened. "What's making out like then?"

"I'm going to need the date details first."

She licked her lips. "Isn't that a little old fashioned? Are you going to grow a handlebar mustache and pick me up in your penny farthing?"

I laughed. "Out of my car, Bay. You've been banished."

"You're going to kick me out onto the streets."

"The driveway, actually. The one right in front of your face. And kick out is a bit strong. More like assist out of my car and into your house."

"My mom's working tonight." She tried to put on a sexy, sultry look, but it was undone by the nervousness flickering in her eyes.

Now that I'd said I wouldn't push things further her courage was showing, but I wasn't backing down.

"Good night, Bay." I popped open my door and grabbed her bike from the trunk.

She flung open the door and stared at me as I kicked out the kickstand and set her bike down at the end of the garage.

"Seriously." Her hands were on her hips.

I hopped back in my car and leaned out my window. "Seriously, Bay. Trust me, I want to go in there with you right now, but not as much as I want a date with you."

She relaxed her stance some, uncertainty flickered in her gaze.

"Good night, Bay."

I pulled out of the driveway, but didn't leave until she was safely inside. Doing a bit of mental math, I could figure out a date with Bay. Somewhere nice—I could call in a favor or two. As the weather warmed up, more people would be out joyriding and need their cars fixed. Maybe I could help business along with a few well-placed ball tosses in the morning. I shook my head. Now I was trying to fuck people's cars up, just to take her out? No, I'd do this right and find a way.

Back home, I tried to keep myself from watching her window, but I did give it a peek. She pulled her shirt up over her head with the curtains wide open.

My heart raced and I palmed my dick, feeling like an asshole for watching her until she glanced over and smiled. She unbuttoned her jeans and stood in the open window.

My erection was no longer a question. I pawed at the

drawer to get my sketch pad. Her body deserved to be memorialized.

She turned and unhooked her bra before pulling the curtains closed and ending the show.

I choked out a laugh and took deep breaths to calm my dick trying to keep myself from jumping the fence separating our yards and doing something monumentally stupid.

She was absolute trouble. Who'd have known my late-night bike riding, guitar playing, stage crew maven neighbor could be so dangerous to my sanity? But here I was, and I wouldn't change a thing.

19

BAY

I sat in the kitchen, leaning against the counter in front of the slatted blinds, the only thing shrouding me from view. Outside, the whir of the lawn mower turned into a rumble doing things to me I'd never thought a lawn mower sound could do. It might have had something to do with the sweaty guy pushing it up and down our front yard, maintaining meticulously neat rows.

He squared off the last row and I rushed to the living room, holding my now cold mug of coffee. I'd pretended to be sipping it earlier, but I'd given up all pretenses at this point.

His mouth twitched every time he mowed facing my house. He knew I was watching him. And I knew he knew I was watching him, but we both pretended he'd decided to come over to mow out of the goodness of his heart and I was also terrible at efficiently drinking a beverage.

With his shirt off and a towel thrown over his right shoulder, I wasn't the only one enjoying the spring afternoon view.

"Bay?"

I screamed, drenching my shirt in cold coffee.

"What is going on?"

Mom peered out the blinds and turned to me with a knowing look.

"I came down to grab a cup." I walked into the kitchen after her and set my now empty mug in the sink.

"Sure. And your distraction has nothing to do with the neighbor of ours out there mowing?" She poured her own cup of coffee, smirking.

"It might a little."

"He certainly seems to be showing up here a lot more."

"He's helpful."

"I only hope you're being safe."

"Mom." An exasperated shout.

"I'm working nights. You think I don't know what can go on while I'm away?"

"No one other than Piper has been in this house when you're at work."

"Does that mean you go to his house then?"

"I've never been to his house. Mom, stop it." I clapped my hands over my ears.

"Your dad and I raised you, but I know you're not a kid anymore. College is a few months away. You forget who I see at the hospital every day."

"I haven't—We haven't—We're not even—I'm still..." I dragged my hands down my face. "Dare and I are friends. That's all."

"Something tells me he'd like that to change."

"What makes you think that?"

"He's looked up at least twenty times since I've come down here." She walked past and squeezed my arm. "Be safe."

"You gave me The Talk in sixth grade."

"I meant with your heart." She pressed her hand against the center of my chest. There was a flicker of sadness in her eyes before she left the room. Her footsteps trod overhead.

Staring out the window, I couldn't help the stuttering heartbeat that overcame me every time he looked up and smiled at me. I grabbed ingredients from the cabinets and whipped up a batter I knew without needing a recipe. A splash of vanilla and some chocolate chips took my buttermilk pancakes from not bad to damn good.

With three pans going, I doled out the batter and stacked them high on a plate.

The drone of the lawn mower cut off, bathing the house in an absolute silence.

He pulled the mower behind him toward the garage.

I set down the spatula and rushed out the front door. The freshly mowed grass wet between my toes. "There's extra pancakes, if you wanted some." I shrugged, failing miserably at playing it cool.

"Of course." He parked the mower and followed me inside, wiping his neck with the towel. His body glistened in the early morning sun. Unfortunately, he pulled the t-shirt hanging from his back pocket on instead of staying shirtless. It had been on the tip of my tongue to tell him I didn't mind. My gaze roamed his body like a hungry wolf. So much temptation in such a large package.

I held open the door for him.

He stepped in, his nostrils flaring before alarm filled his eyes.

My head whipped around. Smoke wafted from the kitchen. "Shit." I rushed in and dumped the charred and smoking pancake into the sink, cranking on the water. Even more smoke billowed from the metal basin. I shoved at the window, cracking it open.

I grabbed a towel and swung it around overhead to keep the smoke away from the detector on the ceiling.

Dare rushed past me. "I'll take care of the other pancakes."

More smoke billowed from the pans. He turned off the flames and dumped the rest of the burnt pancake remnants into the sink. Coughing, I kept up my fanning.

He ran them under the running water, so they didn't become charred messes.

My eyes watered, prickling from the burnt butter and batter-turned-smoke-bomb.

Fresh air flowed into the room. Now the smell wasn't solely charred breakfast fumes, but also freshly-cut grass. He'd opened two other windows and the front door, leaving the screen closed.

"Thanks."

"It's the least I could do after you made these for me."

"What? No, I didn't. I'd made them already."

He got even closer. He smelled like grass and sweat. I'd never thought it would appeal to me, but I wanted to grab him and pull him against me.

Our bodies brushed against one another with each breath. "When are you going to learn, I'm always watching you, Bay?" He stared into my eyes with a fire that required at least three towns worth of fire departments to put out.

I locked my knees, trying to keep myself upright. If I fell to the floor, I wouldn't be as close as possible to his lips. The ones getting closer at an excruciatingly painful pace.

I sucked in a shuddering breath and stared into his eyes. "You are?"

He nodded like it was a solemn admission. "I saw you grab the vanilla and the chocolate chips. The little dance you did when you flipped each pancake." His finger skimmed down my arm.

Goosebumps accompanied the pounding of my heart. I swallowed like I'd never done it before. "I thought you might be hungry." My voice was breathy.

"I'm always hungry." His lips crashed down onto mine. Both of his hands wrapped around my arms, anchoring me to him.

Everything froze before roaring forward like a speeding train. I fisted his sweaty damp shirt in my hands, pulling him closer although we were interlocked.

The backs of my legs, banged against the table toppling the cups and banging it against the wall.

"Everything okay, Bay?"

We broke apart. Panting. My heart leapt doing crazy flips in my chest.

He grinned at me, a winning-the-big-game kind of smile that had me searching for pom-poms.

My mom's footsteps hit the stairs.

He backed up, putting some space between us.

"Wow, what happened in here? Was something on fire?" My mom walked in, waving her hand in front of her face.

I ducked my head and tucked my hair behind my ear.

"Bay let my try my hand at a round of pancakes and I screwed it up. Sorry, Molly."

"Don't worry one bit. Did you two already eat?"

"Only a nibble for me, so I'm starving now." Dare took the plate my mom held out to him and peered over at me.

Rippling waves of yearning rushed through me. What would've happened if my mom hadn't come down?

Our feet brushed against each other's under the table. Each time, my gaze shot to my mom.

Dare finished at least eight pancakes before heading home.

I walked him out to the end of my driveway. Our hands brushed with each step that was beyond an accident. I wanted to reach out and grab his, interlacing my fingers with his, but I kept them at my side, not bold enough even after the blistering kiss that still lingered on my lips.

"Where do you go at night, Bay?" He rested his arm on the top of his car.

"You want to know?"

"I want to know everything about you." His fingers grazed the front of my t-shirt so the fabric barely brushed my skin.

"Come here at ten and I'll show you."

His nostrils flared and his gaze intensified.

I ducked my head and tucked my hair behind my ear. "You can drive me there and see for yourself."

He nodded, letting his hand drop away from me. Even the absence of the barest of touches hit me like a loss. His gaze flickered to my house. He dipped his head, bringing it closer to mine. "I'll be here at ten."

I stood outside until his figure retreated around the corner.

My afternoon turned to evening. Schoolwork finished, I picked up the guitar and gently strummed the strings, scribbling down the words that poured out of me whenever my pen got close to paper.

Mom stopped in the doorway in her scrubs.

"Mail for you." Mom slid the letter onto the bed beside me.

Under her watchful eye—even though she was pretending to look elsewhere—I ripped open the envelope with the UCLA logo in the top left-hand corner.

My hands shook, making the lines difficult to follow, and my eyes could barely track each sentence. The dollar sign in the break between the paragraphs sent my head swimming.

I held the paper out to her.

Her eyes scanned the paper and a huge grin broke out across her face. "You did it!" She squeezed me tight, rocking me back and forth. "You're sure?" Her gaze was riveted to mine. Pride and happiness brimming from the corners of her eyes.

"Yes." My mouth was dry. "Of course. UCLA here I come."

"You'll love it there. The way your dad talked about the campus—I wish he could be there with us when you move in."

My throat tightened. "Me too. Accounting just like him, too. You know how much I love spreadsheets." I could crank them out with ease, unlike when I tried to squeeze out a note and my throat was like a rusty gate. Singing for Dare gave me hope, though. Maybe I could do it. Maybe in my time in LA, I'd be able to turn my minor into something else. Intern at a studio. Maybe Freddy had a few contacts.

She laughed like I should take my comedy show on the road and rethink college all together. "He always said it grew on him. I'm heading—" She stood and froze spotting the guitar out of its case and resting against my desk.

"Is that your dad's?"

I nodded.

"He loved to play with you." Her voice was wistful and sad. "But that world was never kind to him. So many false starts and broken promises. Every time he'd come back from a studio session or giving someone his demo and nothing came of it, it crushed his spirit a little more."

"He loved it anyway."

"Maybe he shouldn't have." She shook her head. "All those late nights in the studio. If he'd been resting and sleeping, not spreading himself so thin..."

"The doctors said it could've happened at any time. And he loved the studio. He loved being there with Freddy."

"Freddy." She made a dismissive huff before closing her eyes and shaking her head. "What are your plans tonight?"

"Finishing up schoolwork." I gestured to the books on my desk. "I also need to go over the tech crew notes for the senior awards ceremony on Wednesday."

"You're always so busy." She came into my room and kissed me on the forehead. "Be good and lock up when I'm gone." She paused at the doorway and tapped her hand against the door jamb. Her mouth opened and she closed it again before waving and heading downstairs.

After a few more minutes, the front door closed.

I sat on my bed in silence, waiting for any indication that she was coming back. There were still two hours until I needed to meet Dare.

I grabbed the guitar and let those feelings flow through me. The anticipation. The feel of his lips on mine. Every second his eyes are on me.

At five minutes to ten, I gathered everything I'd need tonight.

I opened the front door and yelped, nearly walking into Dare's outstretched arm, mid-knock.

"Dare." I didn't mean it to come out as breathy.

"Hey, Bay." He wore that lazy smile like a perfectly-fitting pair of Vans.

I stepped outside, locking the door.

Dare didn't back up, so my back pressed against his chest. "Where are we going?"

I peeked at him over my shoulder and shoved my keys into my bag.

He closed the door to my side of the car and climbed in. The engine roared to life and I ducked my head, hoping no one on the street was paying attention.

I gave Dare directions and soon we pulled up to the studio. "You've got to be fucking kidding me. You've been coming here every night by yourself? On your bike? What the hell is so important you'd risk that, Bay!" There was a ripple of anger through his words.

20

DARE

She stared back at me with disbelief, a hint of fear flashing in her eyes lit up by the flickering overhead street light.

I took a deep breath. "Bay. This isn't a place you should be hanging out this late at night."

"Then you can go home. I have work to do." She flung open the door and slammed it shut, rocking the chassis of my car.

I jumped out and followed her. The wet pavement was slick under my feet, and I caught up to her and stepped in her path.

"What are we doing here?" The street was vacant. I expected a tumbleweed to roll by. This was a shitty part of town, and my car wasn't exactly inconspicuous.

Her lips pinched and she glanced up at the pitch-black sky with her hands on her hips. "None of your business. If you're too scared or whatever, just go home."

"I'm not leaving you here. How would you get home?"

"I don't want you here now."

"Too bad. I'm not leaving." I glanced over her shoulder

at my car sitting under the street light, the pristine paint job a beacon for someone to come and fuck with it.

She stepped around me. "The protective shtick is already old. Go back to the car, then."

"What are you into, Bay?"

She stopped.

I nearly ran into her and braced my hands on her shoulders to keep us both from pitching forward.

"Do you think I'm a weekend stripper or something?"

"Is this guy giving you trouble?" A huge guy who looked half Santa, half Hell's Angel stood on the sidewalk, smacking a bat against his palm. Just great, now I was going to have to beat up MC Santa to get Bay out of here.

"It's okay, Freddy. He was just leaving."

I hooked my hand around her arm as she tried to pass by, not taking my eyes off the guy who had to be at least six-three. "You know him?"

"No." Her voice dripped with sarcasm. She shook off my hold and headed toward the building.

Breaking out of my stunned stance, I rushed after her.

She jogged down the stairs behind Freddy, the MC Santa, without a backward look.

He blocked my path with his arms folded over his chest.

My nostrils flared and I clenched my fists at my sides. "She didn't tell me where we were going, and I was giving her a hard time for coming here late at night all by herself."

His stance relaxed and he uncrossed his arms. "I've been telling her the same thing for years." He shook his head and held out his hand. "Fredrick Isaac, but everyone calls me Freddy."

The name jingled something in the back of my head, but right now I was worried about Bay disappearing down the dark stairwell leading to who knows where.

Bracing myself for I-didn't-even-know-what, I stared, barely keeping myself from wiping at my eyes when we walked through the doorway at the bottom of the stairs. The walls were red and covered with pictures of musicians, and gold and silver albums. Hardwood floors flowed through the area, and there were dim lights around the exterior making the whole room feel like a club.

"What is this place?" I followed Freddy.

Bay was nowhere in sight.

"Only the best damn recording studio in Chicago." He rattled off the names of musical acts over the past five decades that had passed through these halls.

Was Bay secretly recording an album? Part of me was torn with wanting those songs to be something only we shared, but also something no one else should be deprived of.

He stopped outside a doorway down a hallway filled with other doors. "What are your intentions with Bay?"

My mouth opened and closed. "We're—she's—my intentions are not to do anything that would ever hurt her."

His gaze narrowed and he looked me up and down.

"She's got an amazing voice."

His eyebrows jumped. "She's sung for you?"

"A few times."

"Then I guess I can't kick you out, if you mean that much to her. I haven't heard her sing a note since her dad died." A sadness clouded his eyes, but then was gone like a summer storm.

His words were like a dart thrown straight through my chest. 'If you mean that much to her.' The phrase rang in my ears as he pushed the door open.

Bay sat behind a huge board with buttons, levers, sliders, and a computer monitor. Her legs were tucked up under her in a rolling chair. Her gaze turned to the door before snapping straight ahead when she spotted me over Freddy's shoulder.

"I'll let Bay give you the studio tour." He clapped me on the shoulder. "They're riding through on their way to Chicago, so they won't be here for another hour, Bay. I'll check with their manager to see if it's okay if he stays."

"He's leaving." She rolled to the computer screen.

"I'll check just in case he decides to stay." His grin widened. "Good luck," he muttered under his breath on the way out the door.

I took a deep breath and grabbed the chair by the door, flipping it backward and parking it beside her. "You've been sneaking out to work at a music studio."

"Gee, how'd you piece together that mystery?" She didn't look at me, only continued to tweak knobs and levels.

"It scared the shit out of me to think about you riding your bike on a dark, deserted street to get here every night."

"I've been doing it for a year and a half now. I don't need your protection."

"You act like I have a choice. I can't stop myself from being worried about you."

She scoffed. "Three kisses and you're already playing the overprotective boyfriend."

I sucked in a sharp breath. Boyfriend. I rolled the word around in my head.

"I didn't mean that you were my boyfriend—I only meant—it's nothing, never mind." Even in the dim light of the studio, the flush of her cheeks glowed.

Gripping both arm rests of her chair, I wheeled her around to face me.

"You're under my skin, Bay. Ever since that kiss and those pancakes, I've wanted more. And knowing you've been doing this most nights, putting yourself at risk, makes me a little crazy and it scares me."

"But Dare—"

"I know, you've been doing this on your own. And I know in a few months you're going away to college and we'll be maybe thousands of miles apart." My knees hit the front edge of her chair.

"And I know a few months ago, I wouldn't have even noticed, but I was a fucking moron and I notice now. I can't help myself. It's an involuntary reaction when you're around, and even when you aren't." Her legs settled against the inside of mine, some of the tension fading from her posture.

Leaning in closer, I held onto her chair to keep her from rolling away. The brush of her legs against the inside seam of my jeans and the thump of my pulse in my grip on the seat narrowed everything in my world down to the connection tethering us together like a live wire.

Since the last time I'd tasted her lips, it had been all I could to do to keep my mind focused on my workout this afternoon and the Bedlam Bowl coming up in two weeks. Everything else paled in comparison to the full curve of her lips and the way she'd batted her eyelashes as she met my gaze, like the kiss had shocked her just as much as it had me.

"Dare?" There was a question in her tone like she didn't understand what was happening either. The magnetic pull wasn't one I wanted to be free from.

A bang behind us had us both shooting apart. The room was bathed in relative brightness from the dim hallway into the even dimmer studio.

"Is this where I record?" A guy stood in the doorway in shadow with a guitar case in hand.

"The other—" Her voice was croaky. She cleared it. "The next set of doors down." She shook her head. "I'll show you."

The escape route I'd denied her before was wide open. Hopping up, she glanced down at me before scurrying away.

I dragged my hands down my face. Pushing her wasn't what I wanted to do.

The seconds ticked away and I stared at the other side of the wall-wide glass window. A piano, guitars and a full drum kit filled the space. All the buttons and knobs on the sound board were labeled and the computer screen filled the space with a blue glow. Even my own thoughts seemed muted in the soundproofed space. The blood rushing through my veins was muffled and quieted, and a calm stole over me. I got why she liked this place.

Sometimes everything inside my head felt too loud, but in here it all mellowed out.

The door swung open. Bay rushed in with a piece of paper in hand. "The good news is you can stay. The bad news is you need to sign this. I remembered off the bat this time." She pumped her arms in self-congratulation.

She shoved a thick document and pen into my hand. "A non-disclosure agreement? Who the hell is coming?"

"When you sign it, I can tell you." Curiosity made it impossible to walk away. I scribbled my name across the bottom of the packet where the little labels told me to. The last time I'd done that had been at the signing ceremony for my recruitment. A sourness swamped some of the intrigue coursing through my veins.

The door opened again. This time a woman with long black hair up in a high ponytail stood in the way. "Did he sign?"

Bay nodded.

The woman held out her hand palm up and motioned to hand it over.

Bay gave her the papers and she flipped through them, eyeing me in between each signature check like she could somehow tell if I'd used invisible ink or a fake name.

"Cool, I'll go get the guys." The door closed with a muted whoosh.

"The guys?"

Bay grinned.

And that was how I spent until five am hanging out with the guys from Without Grey.

Money exchanged hands after the door opened and I shouted like a clown with a butcher's knife was chasing me.

Freddy moved across the wide board of sliders and knobs doing who knows what. But I was riveted by Bay on the other side of the glass, sitting with Camden for one of the songs Lockwood bowed out of playing.

She bounded out of the studio and grabbed onto my arm, nearly ripping it from the socket. "They want to use my backing guitar to fill out the sound on the album." Happiness poured off her in waves. An infectious happiness I couldn't stop myself from absorbing.

"That's amazing." I ran my hand along the side of her cheek, her hair brushed against the back of my hand tickling me.

The rest of the guys poured into the studio.

"Have they heard you sing?"

All eyes swung to us.

"You sing too?" Camden rested his arm on the back of Freddy's chair and looked her up and down.

For a split second I wanted to leap over the two people between us and break his damn jaw. My arm tightened around her waist. "She does."

"Dare." Through gritted teeth, she whispered at me.

"Just try." I kissed the side of her head.

I held onto her hand and stepped behind her. Her pulse jackhammered against my hold or maybe it was because of how tight I was holding her right back.

She opened her mouth and sang the first verse and chorus of Emotional Gridlock.

The guys stared at her slack jawed. "Why the hell didn't you tell us?" Camden jumped up from his lean against the board.

She ducked her head, her cheeks beyond tomato-red, and shrugged.

"That was killer, Bay." He grinned at her and she grinned right back.

The fucking monster in my chest got shoved deep down. She deserved her chance to shine.

"Guys, did you get it?"

"We got it, Maddy, and you won't believe who can sing."

Maddy's head tilted and she nodded and scribbled on her tablet with her stylus. "Filing that away. Since you guys are done, we need to head out. We'll be back tomorrow. Freddy, thank you as always."

"Anytime, Madison."

"And, Bay, we'll see you tomorrow?"

Bay looked to me with her mouth hung open. "Of course."

On the drive back, I was more amped than she was.

She sat angled in her seat watching me.

"You're not freaking out about this? You played with Without Grey! You sat next to Camden Holmes and played a new song no one else has ever heard before. And you sang for them."

"Trust me, the singing has me flying high, but playing

with them? It feels more natural now. I was definitely freaking out the first time."

I nearly swerved off the road. "You've done this more than once?"

"A month ago. We had a few sessions in between their tour dates."

"Fucking hell, Bay." How had I ever not seen her? As in, really seen her. There were people who walked the halls like they were gods because they'd gotten third row tickets to see them on their last tour and Bay sat beside them in a room playing along like she belonged. And she did. She was that good.

"It's pretty cool." She was trying to downplay the whole night.

"That doesn't even begin to cover it."

The morning sun hinted at its approaching arrival.

She covered her mouth with one hand, capturing her yawn.

"Are you going to be able to stay awake in school?"

Her shoulder jumped. "I've been doing it since junior year. No reason to think I can't now."

"I'll bring you a coffee and give you a ride to school." I had enough to swing by 7-Eleven and get us both a coffee. She'd love a mocha.

"You don't have to. I'll ride my bike."

"Bay, come on. Let me drive you." Walking into school with my arm around Bay's shoulder, everyone would know we were together.

We pulled into her driveway. She flung open the door and hopped out of my car like it had suddenly become electrified.

"It's okay. I'll be fine. I have to meet Piper early to go

over the notes for the bio exam." She poked her head in the open door.

"I can go early."

"Really, Dare. It's no big deal." She bit her lip and it hit me.

She didn't want anyone to know we were together. It's why she didn't wave to me when I was playing ball with Knox in the back yard or ever talk to me in school unless it was required, like for our group project. A few times I'd hung by her locker and sworn I'd seen her, only for her to disappear.

"Maybe we could—"

"Thanks for coming tonight. I'll see you in class." She closed the door before I could respond.

I drove back home to the silent house like I was sitting under my own personal dark cloud. Pouring myself a bowl of cereal and skipping the milk that had gone bad, I crunched through it, trying not to dissect all the feelings rushing through me. The high of Bay finally telling me where she was going. How pissed I was when we got there. How good it felt for her to turn to me when it was time to sing and then how it felt like I'd been kicked in the teeth with a newly-opened pair of cleats at her nearly jumping from my moving car at the thought of being seen with me at school.

The churn in my gut was ugly and angry. And it made me want to throw on my sneakers and run until I passed out.

21

DARE

My time had come—again. The blow-out celebration to cap off our season of crowning achievements was here. This was the fifth hosted at my house this year.

It hadn't been my idea to have the party tonight, but when Knox and Bennet suggested it, I hadn't said no. I'd let the party planning committee take over, giving them access to my house like I always did.

One perk of having a house people flocked to for parties was that I never had to buy my own booze. But he would be back soon. The cloud always hanging off in the distance waiting to rumble into my life and rip it to shreds again. Every day he was away made breathing easier, but the longer he was away the heavier the weight got, because it was only a matter of time before he was back.

Tonight was the night to forget all that, though—at least for a little while. This was the senior year party to end all parties. Why they didn't want to have it at one of the swanky houses with a pool, I'd never know.

I leaned on the kitchen counter with a beer in my hand.

The cracked and warped linoleum counter was the perfect place for more cases of beer and a few bottles of liquor someone had scored. I rolled the bottle between my hands, pretending I was paying attention to whatever recruiting trip story Bennet was recounting. With my head down, I stared into the open mouth of my beer. The same beer I'd had since they wheeled in the kegs three hours ago.

Parties were easy to get away with when your parent didn't give a shit about you and was on the road 300 days a year. It was still 65 days too short for me. Another factor was not having anything worth a damn in the whole place. It was bare bones, which made it perfect for rowdy high schoolers' underage drinking and playing loud music into the night.

From the kitchen window, I could see straight out back to Bay's house. The light was off in her bedroom. Relief washed through me. She'd mentioned going to the studio tonight after stage crew, which meant she wouldn't be home until just before dawn.

I didn't want her anywhere near these assholes. Other than Knox, I'd never want any of these guys breathing the same air as her. But a part of me had let this party happen even when I didn't want it out of anger. When Bennet sent the text, I could've said no. I could've told him I'd take a rain check, but I hadn't.

She'd blown me off. The day after our night in the studio, somehow, wherever I was, she wasn't. In the hallways, her locker remained unopened. In class, she always kept her gaze locked on the front of the classroom, scribbling down notes even though everyone else had long settled into their senioritis holding pattern.

I downed my warm beer, flinging the bottle onto the stack of cans and plastic cups overflowing from the trashcan. Freshmen were tasked with cleaning shit up after team parties. I grabbed another beer, cracking open the tab and finishing it before I could stop myself. Someone handed out red plastic cups of punch, and instead of waving them off like I had at every other pass, I took one and gulped down half of it.

The hard liquor buzzed in my veins, going in straight for the kill.

It was a salve to the burn from her running from my car. Running from me. Maybe in the early morning light, whatever she felt for me paled in comparison to spending late nights with Without Grey.

And they'd heard her sing. Their manager made a note of it. What would happen when she got her big break? She was already playing in the studio with one of the biggest bands to explode to the top of the charts. Her life had a trajectory rocketing her toward things I couldn't even imagine.

Right now, all I could hope for was a back-up spot on a college team to fill a gap in their roster in the hopes of still turning pro. If I did that, would I be worthy of her then?

People around me laughed and screamed, flinging ice at one another, sliding around in beer and water from the coolers soaking the floors. Off-key singing accompanied the music rumbling the counter against my back.

Now, surrounded by all these people, I wanted out. Out of my own house and out of this life I'd been living for so long. I couldn't even begin to figure out how to start something new, how to break away from where I'd been placed.

I couldn't tell why I sent the text—maybe I'd bumped myself down to lightweight status after not partying much after Bay and I started hanging out. Or maybe it was something else, something I didn't want to face.

Me: What are you up to?

How stupid was I? Was I trying to screw myself over tonight? In the wait for a response, I drank the other half of the punch, wincing at the sharp and pungent burn. If someone had dumped rubbing alcohol into the garbage can serving as a punch bowl, I wouldn't have been surprised.

My phone buzzed, vibrating my cup. Her name flashed up on the screen, quelling some of the thoughts racing through my brain like a kick return.

Bay: I'm about to leave the board and go into the studio. What's up with you?

Me: Are you coming home straight after you're finished?

Or would one of the guys, blown away by her talent, try to get in a bit more than musical mentorship during their last night in town?

Bay: Where else would I go? Are you home?

Someone ran past with a water gun, spraying it as they rushed out the back door into the yard. I scrubbed my hand down over my face.

Me: No, I'm out. Wanted to make sure you got home safe.

Bay: The worry is cute. You can come pick me up, if you're still worried.

I stared at the cup in my hand. Fuck. Regret cratered even harder in my chest.

Me: I can't. I already had a beer.

Or five.

Bay: No problem. Tell Knox I said hi.

Bile that had nothing to do with the battery acid I'd just chugged came racing for my throat.

Me: I will. Have a good night and be safe.

Bay: You too. See you tomorrow.

I leaned against the window facing my back yard and

squeezed my eyes shut, banging my phone against my fore-head. What an idiot. If I hadn't gone along with this, I'd be in my car in a few hours on the way to pick up Bay.

Someone cranked the music, and girls were sitting on guys' shoulders, although there was no pool in sight, to do their beer-induced singalong wobbling in the air. At least there wasn't any shit to break at my place. Nothing that wasn't already broken or easily replaceable. How did people like Knox or Bennet let people into their houses? All my stuff sucked. Like hell would I let anyone near things I cared about.

My bedroom door was locked. No one was getting in there.

Fear crept up my spine, slow and low at first. People swamped my place, in every chair, couch, counter, every-where. What happened when Bay got home?

Knox rammed into my back, draping his arm over my shoulder. "I need a favor."

"You're not using my room."

His cold beer can pressed against my neck. "I told Rebecca I didn't believe her bra matched her panties and she wants to show me." He shook my shoulders, rocking my head back.

"You're not having sex in my bed."

"The floor?" He cocked his head in negotiation.

"Take her to your car."

"People are still showing up, and if we try anywhere else, someone might see. Please, man." He pressed his palms together. "How many times have I bailed you out? It's one of my last chances before graduation. You know I've had a thing for her since freshman year."

He'd been my best friend, and his house had been a refuge for me. But everyone partying needed to be gone.

These things normally wrapped up by four, but I needed things shut down by two at the latest. It would give me time to get rid of any stragglers and make sure Bay came back to the quiet, normal neighborhood she expected.

Trying to break up a party in full swing was an invitation for fights and people taking things to the streets. The last thing I needed was her coming home to a parade of cars rounding the block.

"I'll make you a deal. Help me get everyone out of here by two. Make sure all the stragglers are in taxis or their parents have them or whatever. I don't care. If you help me with that, you can use my room."

"I swear. Hell, I'll have them out by one." He stared back at me with determination. I wasn't sure if that was to help me or to get laid. Probably ninety percent getting laid, but I'd take what help I could get.

I nodded and slapped my hand into my pocket.

"Don't touch anything and don't have sex on my sheets." I dangled the key in front of his face.

He snatched it out of my hand. "I promise. I'll order you new sheets." His head bobbed and weaved through the crowd, only to reappear seconds later leading Rebecca upstairs with his hand high in the air holding hers like they were in an extended ballroom dancing spin.

"Dare, why aren't you dancing?" A junior wrapped her arms around my shoulder, her drink sloshing onto the floor.

"Not my scene." I unlooped her arms and turned her toward one of the rising juniors.

I rode out the rest of the night teetering on the razor's edge of calling the cops myself and shoving people out the door.

True to his word, Knox emerged from the bedroom and helped me corral everyone out of the house.

I directed the freshmen to start in the backyard to clean things up, including their own puke.

By dawn, everything looked normal, at least from the outside. Inside, the house was still a disaster zone, but at least, my room was relatively untouched. Whatever Knox had done, he'd left my bed as he'd found it.

Turning off the light Knox must've turned on, I collapsed in my bed in my boxers. The shades were drawn or I'd have had a perfect view to Bay's house. The lights were still off when I'd come upstairs. Crisis averted.

Lying in bed, I vowed not to let the stupid shit going on in my head screw things up with Bay. But the clock ticking down to graduation only a few weeks away sat like a weight on my chest. Striking the balance between not screwing this up and not losing what little time we had left sent an uneasiness creeping through my body.

Was I trying to fuck this up with her?

Tomorrow, it would be like this had never happened. Bay never needed to know.

My handlebars wobbled as my eyelids drooped. I held onto the rubberized grips tighter.

A ride from Dare would've been great tonight. But if he'd had a drink, I didn't want to be responsible for him getting behind the wheel of his car.

We'd finished early, getting the songs done in only one or two takes. Lockwood had joined them in the studio, and riffs they'd struggled with fell into place like magic.

There was a little quirk of doubt at whether I'd actually been a help. These long nights and jam-packed days were catching up to me. Wasn't senior year supposed to be when you slacked off and did nothing?

As energized as I'd been in the studio, I had to dig deep for every drop of energy to make it to my house.

Parking my bike, I yawned, my jaw popping. My feet shuffled against the pavement and concrete steps leading to the front door. It only took me three tries to get the key into the lock.

The house was quiet. Coming home to an empty house

sent a ripple of panicky, uneasy feelings shooting through me.

Before, I'd walk in and mom and dad would be watching TV, or dad would be watching sports and mom might be out. Coming home to an empty house was a new part of my changed reality, and I hated it. It wasn't like things would be different when I went to college, but I'd be choosing that.

Having something ripped away is a lot different than leaving it behind.

At the bottom of the steps, I stopped.

Music rumbled the back windows.

I froze with my hand on the railing not wanting to look. He wasn't. He wouldn't.

Up in my room I changed into my pajamas, trying and failing to keep my attention from his house. It was probably another neighbor, or sounds carrying from a different street. Only I hadn't heard anything coming up to my house.

Instead of turning on my light, I left it off. An act of cowardice. I should've flung the window open and screamed across our yards for him to keep it down, glaring at all the partygoers.

His questions about where I'd be tonight made it even worse. Had he been checking to make sure I wouldn't be there and wouldn't want an invite? What if I'd said I'd be home early? Would he have invited me, or had the party moved? Maybe this was his way of seeing if I'd be up for the party, but not wanting me to feel bad since I couldn't make it?

I opened my window, letting the cool spring air fill my room, and looked out. The wall of music was even louder, rumbling the floorboards under my toes. Laughter and screaming came from every direction. Headlights flashed between the houses, all headed straight for Dare's.

Up in his bedroom, a pair of shadows moved across his drawn curtains. A guy and a girl. Her curvy silhouette doing a dance for him sitting on the edge of the bed, ready and waiting for her show to end. The special feeling I'd had after all his assertions about never letting anyone into his room and how big of a deal that was curdled in my stomach. It seemed I wasn't the only one.

Unable to look away, everything played out for me across our back yards. Him reaching for her. Her sitting on his lap. The reach across the bed until the entire room was bathed in darkness.

My stomach knotted, like a sandbag had dropped on my chest. Keeping my lights off, I curled up in bed and hugged my pillow to my chest. I buried my face in the soft, floral-scented fabric, tears falling from my eyes no matter how hard I squeezed my eyelids shut.

The hammering bass of the music didn't stop until two am.

Was this what it felt like to have your heart ripped out? Like someone had sawed into your chest and escaped with your still-beating heart? I'd always imagined it was a figure of speech, but this didn't feel imaginary at all. It was raw, searing, and I couldn't catch my breath through the tears as pain coursed through my body. Recovery? How was I even supposed to open my eyes tomorrow?

The rawness of my throat and eyes blared like a throbbing wound, and I was walking through a salt mine. I had one goal: make it through the day without a run-in with Dare. I grabbed books from my locker before Piper got there. More time in the open meant more chances of running into him.

Calls and texts had been blocked. What did I say to him? I know you fucked someone on Saturday night, get lost? What were we even? Neighbors. Friends? Something more? Obviously not.

"Bay." I slammed my locker closed and rushed down the hall with my notebooks and books balanced in my hands.

I brushed past people. Their heads turned, not to acknowledge me in any way, but at the owner of the voice shouting behind me.

Seriously, were they jumping into my way to slow me down? I plowed through them to escape the six-foot-three tight end hot on my heels.

"I know you can hear me."

"And I obviously don't want to talk to you." My voice barely carried over the before-the-bell scramble to homeroom.

The beacon of safe harbor flashed up ahead. The skirted silhouette and a door to put between us.

I shoved open the door, letting it slam in his face. He wasn't an asset to the team for nothing. He wove his way through the crowd with no issue. Everyone moved out of the way for The Great Dare, but they flung their bodies into my path like I wasn't even there.

Running my wrists under the cold water, I closed my eyes. The bathroom door opened.

"Why are you avoiding me?"

I squeezed my eyes shut harder before turning off the faucet. "I'm not avoiding you." Three cranks of the paper towel dispenser and the most fascinating hand drying known to man completely occupied my attention—at least I hoped it looked that way.

"Yesterday, once you were home, I texted you and stopped by the house."

"I wasn't home yesterday." I tossed the crumpled-up paper towels into the trash can and turned to face him. "I came home early on Saturday night."

It would've been comical, if it weren't so tragic. His face morphed from confusion to shock to caught-red-handed guilt. "You saw the party."

"Saw, heard, and felt it shaking my windows. I'm surprised you're not still nursing your hangover after how late things went."

"I only had a couple, but I didn't want to drink and drive."

"Good to know you won't be using the 'I was drunk and didn't know what I was doing' defense." My notebooks were clutched against my chest like that would protect me. All the swirling in my head and stewing over being cheated on —ha! Was it even cheating? Were we even dating? I'd been hinting at something more and he'd kept me at arm's length, never taking any of my hints. Maybe it wasn't that he was oblivious, maybe it was that his fascination with me had nothing to do with getting in my pants. Which meant those red-blooded football player oat-sewing engines were in overload.

"It was shitty to have the party and not invite you." He looked at me like I should jump with joy over his admission.

"No shit." I trained my gaze on the door over his shoulder. My escape and the only way to preserve my sanity. Being this close to him meant trouble.

"Those parties aren't a place I'd want you to be." He lifted his hand and I took a step back avoiding his touch.

"Got that loud and clear." I saluted and tried to get by.

He blocked my path. "People get trashed. Bombed out of their minds. Puking. Fighting sometimes. Last year at our after-championship celebration two people were sent to the hospital for broken arms after jumping from the roof into the pool and missing. After the first guy got taken to the hospital, some idiot did it again. It's insanity."

"And people having sex."

A sharp exhale and nod. "Yes, and sex."

"People like you." It was pointed, knowing, angry. I peered up at him, trying to keep my gaze steely and my words forceful.

Inside, I was coming unglued. The edges I'd barely threaded together were already fraying and the last thing I wanted to do was dissolve into a puddle at his feet.

"No." His eyes widened and he swiped his hands in front of him like he was clearing a path for more lies. "I didn't have sex."

I tightened my hold on my backpack straps with my elbows locked in at my sides almost like I was protecting myself from an emotional blow with my body. "Why not leave here with a clear conscience?"

The bathroom door was pushed open.

His voice boomed in the three-stall bathroom. "Out. We're having a discussion."

There was a yelp and whoever it was thought better of confronting Dare on the fact that he absolutely didn't belong in here.

"We're not." I tried to get around him again.

He braced his arms in the gap between the tiled wall and the first stall, blocking my exit. "I didn't sleep with anyone, Bay."

My laugh was hollow and angry. "I'm sure there wasn't any sleeping involved. I saw you. Up in your room. You know, the one you keep padlocked."

"If I'd invited you, would you have even come?'" My gaze darted away. Walking into his parties would've invited all kinds of questions and looks, laughter, and flat-out ridicule.

The bell blared in the tiled confines of the bathroom.

"Well, we'll never know, will we?" I crossed my arms over my chest. "If it wasn't you, then who was it?" I glared up at him. All that talk about letting it roll off my back was total bullshit. I was pissed, and more than that, hurt. A raw, deep, slicing pain at the center of my chest.

"Knox. He took a girl up there that he's been crushing on since sophomore year." His jaw clenched.

"And you let him into your room."

"He's my best friend. It's senior year. His last shot and he promised he wouldn't have sex on my bed."

I crossed my arms over my chest. It killed me how much I wanted to believe him. My guidebook on dating a bad boy had been lost in the mail.

"You still lied to me about the party."

His shoulders sagged, whether it was with relief or defeat, I couldn't tell. He nodded. "I know."

My head dropped and I picked at the frayed edges of my backpack. "Did you not want to invite me? Did you not want people to know—do you not want people to know we're —whatever we are?"

He dipped his knees to hold my gaze, rising slowly so I'd raise mine. "I'll scream it out from the rooftops of the school. I haven't said anything because you've been the one ignoring me in the halls. Have you even told Piper yet?"

I bit my lip and my gaze darted away. "No."

"If anyone's acting ashamed, it's you. We go to the studio and you tell everyone I'm your friend. Your best friend doesn't even know about us."

"I didn't even know if you did girlfriends. There's an us?"

"Of course there's an us. And, no, I didn't do girlfriends, but with you, I'm all in. Now there's the question of whether you want everyone else to know there's an us. I'm one hundred percent on board with everyone knowing.

"That lip nibble is getting pretty intense." He held onto my chin and ran his finger along the underside of my bottom lip until I freed it from my teeth.

"We—what we do isn't anyone else's business."

He sighed and tilted his head back.

"I just don't want people staring." And pointing and laughing.

"So what if they stare?" He held his arms out at his sides.

"You're used to it. The only time people are doing it to you is when they're in awe. I had all their eyes on me that day in the hallway and at the talent show. It's only ever been bad and I can already hear all the things that will be going through their heads."

"Screw them. You're going to UCLA in a few months."

"In a month."

He sucked in a breath like I'd hit him in the stomach with a bowling ball.

"There's a pre-session I was invited to with my scholarship."

"A month." It came out almost like a wheeze. He stepped in close, his hand on the side of my neck. I leaned into his hold.

"I'd rather spend the next month with you, and not worrying about what other people are saying or thinking. It'll freak me out." I wished I were stronger. I wished I were braver. I wished I weren't so afraid of what happened when we walked across the stage with diplomas in hand.

And then my face was buried in his chest as he wrapped his arms around me, holding me tight. "You freaked me out,

Bay. If there's something wrong, please talk to me. I can only fix what's wrong, if I know how I screwed up." His face was buried in my neck.

"You didn't screw up."

He looked down at me.

"Okay, we both screwed up. But what if you can't fix it?" Some things were unfixable.

He pulled back, staring into my eyes with his hands on either side of my face, his thumbs brushing soft strokes across my cheeks. "I'll fix anything for you." A fierce sharp kiss was interrupted by the door banging open.

We jumped apart.

A voice bounced off the tiled walls. "Dare. Ms. Bishop."

"Sorry, Mrs. Turner. We'll be on our way."

Mrs. Turner stood with her arms crossed, but stepped out of the way for us to leave the bathroom. The hallway was empty.

"There are going to be questions when we both show up late." The idea of everyone knowing about me and Dare was a lot easier to handle than the reality of snide looks and whispered speculation.

"I'll skip. I need to talk to Coach Greer anyway." He backed away down the hallway, watching me until I ducked into the classroom.

"Ms. Bishop, you're late." Mr. Mercanti glanced at me as the door closed behind me.

"Theater club emergency."

He gave me a dismissive huff. "Take your seat."

I slid into my desk and pulled out my notebook and textbook. The rest of the day dragged on, so slowly I swore the second hand on the wall clock in seventh period ticked backward at least a few times.

After school, I looked for Dare, but didn't see him.

Asking people where he was would only have drawn some serious stares, so I headed home after stage crew, unsure of what, exactly, this newness between us meant.

And the surprise in my driveway kept the questions bubbling.

23

DARE

I popped up off the steps when her squeaky bike brakes sounded at the end of her block.

She froze at the end of her driveway when she spotted me, then walked her bike up to the garage with a tentative smile on her face.

Erasing any flicker of doubt she still harbored had been about the only thing on my mind since our moment in the bathroom. I didn't want even the tiniest bit hanging out in the back of her head.

"What are you doing here?" She slung her backpack up onto her shoulder.

"I wanted you to see something."

"What is it?" She approached cautiously and tilted to the side like she was trying to see behind my back.

"It's at my house."

Her eyebrows scrunched down. "Are you going to bring it over?"

"You have to come to my place to see it."

Her eyebrows dipped, but she nodded. "Give me a second."

She ran into her house, the screen door slamming behind her. It swung back open and she joined me on the walkway.

"I had to leave a note for my mom that I was going back out. I'll need to take the bike, in case we're not back by the time she's back from the store and heads out to work."

"Let me push it." I grabbed for the handle bars.

"I can do it." She pushed the bike. We walked in silence back around the block.

My body had suddenly created ten times the normal amount of pores, each working overtime to crank out the sweat like I was walking through Death Valley.

We walked into my house. I hurried her up the stairs, not wanting the stench of stale beer and cigarettes and the outdated and shitty—well, everything—to steal anything away from this moment. Also, the rush helped to keep me from losing my nerve.

The padlocks on my bedroom door clicked, the only sound other than the muted creak of the floorboards under the worn and ripped carpet.

"You weren't kidding," she whispered behind me.

I grimaced and shoved open the door, closing it behind us to block out all the shiftiness outside my refuge. The space seemed so much smaller with someone else in it. I opened the window to push back against the walls closing in, and to let some of the fear about what I was about to do out.

Crouching down in front of my desk, I grabbed the padlock. My hands were clammy and sweaty. I could taste the metal through my skin.

Bay looked around my room, soaking it in. Seeing it from her point of view, I winced. Hand-me-down, side-of-the-road furniture was all I had, and even that was only a dresser, a desk, and my bed. The edges of everything were busted and barely hanging on. Her room fit her...and I guessed mine fit me too.

I wiped one hand on my jeans and unlocked the padlock. The body of the lock scraped against the chipped particle board drawer.

Clenching my chest, I took a deep breath. My blood felt like sludge in my veins, and also like someone had jammed a needle of adrenaline straight into it. My body hummed with dread.

Refusing to let my hands shake, I pulled the top sketchpad out of the drawer and stood.

My fingers tightened around it. "I wanted you to see something."

She blew out a long, low breath. "You're freaking me out a little bit, if I'm being honest, but I'm happy to see it's just a notebook you pulled out of there, and not a severed hand. I was getting worried that you needed me to help you bury the rest of the body." Her smile wilted as I swallowed, forcing myself to step closer to her holding out the weapon of my demise.

I gripped my offering so tightly my pulse rocked it in my hold, causing the pages to flutter in the breeze through the open window. "You can go afterwards, but I want you to see my world the way I see it."

Her head jerked back and her eyebrows dipped. She unfolded her arms and held out her hand.

I slipped the sketchpad into her grasp and waited. My stomach churned and bile raced for my throat. Handing her the stack of papers felt like sawing open my chest and handing over my heart, serving it up on a silver platter with a set of razor blades and telling her to have at it.

My throat was tight, choking me like it wanted to put me out of my misery before she eviscerated me.

With a skeptical look, she flipped open the cover, not taking her eyes from my face. The corners of her mouth turned down and she dropped her gaze to the first picture.

She gasped, her eyes searching the page like she couldn't believe what she was seeing.

A car door slammed in the distance, and birds chirped, but every turn of the page rumbled in my ears like a hornet's nest. Everything else was lost in the *whoosh* of blood rushing through my veins.

My palms were clammy and it was hard to catch my breath, like I'd been running laps for an hour. The sweat on my forehead and upper lip had come along for the anxiety slam. I wanted to break something and run and hide. I braced my hands on the back of my neck and breathed through the freak-out.

She was the first person to ever see this, and probably the only person who ever would.

Her head snapped up and she looked from me to the notepad again before moving onto the next page. A flicker in her gaze and another turn.

"Dare."

She stepped away from me and lowered herself to my bed. The old springs creaked. "You drew all of these?"

I nodded, keeping my gaze trained on the room-wide slit in the carpet running between my feet. I'd never wished harder for a portal to another dimension in my life. The pounding in my chest was harder, like fists against a locked closet door. Was I trying to get in or get out? I wasn't sure. The closed door to my bedroom made me cagey, but I stopped myself from pacing.

She hadn't gotten there yet. I braced myself for impact.

This was a new sketchbook. It had only taken me a month or so to fill it. Most were scenes stored in my head like snapshots to recreate in the silence of my bedroom, but after the first few pages there was only one subject that had filled my head with images I itched to commit to paper.

"Of me?"

I should've chosen a different notebook. This one would only freak her out. "There're not all of you."

"Don't dodge." There was an intensity to her words.

"Yes."

She held it up. "This is in Mrs. Turner's class?"

I didn't need to look. Although I'd drawn it to preserve those memories, her face flashed behind my eyelids whenever I closed my eyes. I nodded, tipping the top edge back toward her and glancing over my shoulder like someone had focused on us with a telephoto lens.

With my stomach churning, I sat on the bed beside her. This time the creak was more of a groan.

Her knee brushed against mine. "You never look like you're drawing in class."

"This sketchbook has never left my bedroom."

"But you're showing me." Her eyes glistened, a sheen coating them.

"I needed you to know." A faint sheen of sweat broke out all over my body.

Her throat tightened and her fingers shook. "To know what?"

"How you're all I can think about." I squeezed my thighs right above my knees, trying to channel this nervousness, bracing myself for a hit-to-the-chest feeling.

"You've been on my mind a lot too. All my songs are about you now." She ducked her head and tucked the strands that had fallen free from her ponytail behind her ear, showing off the curve of her jaw and the shell of her ear.

My fingers itched to grab any scrap of paper and capture all her lines and curves against the backdrop of the light streaming in through my window.

"It seems like we're both dealing with the same problem."

The corner of her mouth quirked up and she shot me a sidelong glance. "And what's that?"

"Needing to know this is real. I need this to be real. And I feel like if someone other than us doesn't know, I might forget what it's like to touch you and worry I made it all up. And all I'll have left are my sketches and the fear that this was never real."

She dropped the notebook to the bed and turned, angling herself toward me. Her hand cupped my jaw. "No matter what happens this will always be real. California is on the other side of the country, but you don't know where you'll end up for college yet, right? And even if you end up on the East Coast, it's not like we're living in the 1800s and I'll only be able to write you letters." She put on a Southern Belle accent. "My dearest Dare, your most welcome letter has arrived by the postman today."

"My Dearest Bay, my train journey has speedily taken me as far as Philadelphia. It has only taken three weeks."

"Oh Beauregard." She slapped the back of her hand over her forehead, and laughter overtook us both. "Email, video chat. I've been saving up for a car. We can figure it out."

"Are you serious?"

Hesitation flickered in her eyes. "If you want to." She tried to slip her hand from resting on my leg.

I grabbed her and pulled her close, crushing her against my chest. "Of course, I do. As soon as I figure out where I'll end up, we'll figure it out." Even staying in town didn't feel as scary anymore. If I had Bay, the void of my life after Greenwood High wasn't a pit of despair, but a tunnel I'd come out on the other side of.

Catching her chin with my fingers, I tilted her head up and captured her lips with mine. The electricity I'd only ever felt seconds before the first play on the field ricocheted through my body.

The hum of her soft moan pinballed its way through my body, revving up every engine.

I broke the kiss first, when her fingers snaked their way under my t-shirt. Staring into her eyes, fear grabbed me in a chokehold, slamming me against the wall so hard my ears rang.

This was too good. She was too sweet. When did this all get ripped away from me?

She ran her fingers along the side of my face and stared into my eyes like I held the keys to the universe, like I was someone who could do anything. Holding her against me with her sugary-sweet taste lingering on my lips, I believed her.

With her in my arms, the unknown wasn't some monster lurking in the dark, threatening to leave me battered and bruised. It was a place I could finally let my guard down completely.

But what happened when we graduated? When her California adventure changed what she thought of me? We were new. This was new, and as much as I wanted to leave an everlasting mark on her soul and in her heart, could we withstand the end of this chapter of our lives?

Jumping straight into college with a fresh-minted relationship seemed like a recipe for disaster.

I dropped my hand to the back of her neck and dove

back into her kiss, desperate to widen the gap in her heart and wedge myself in before she was too far away.

A train was hurtling toward a ravine, and I was laying the track as quickly as I could, but what happened if I wasn't fast enough?

He broke off his kiss and stared at me with worry clouding his gaze. The desperate edge of his lips and teeth against mine was still there as we panted, laying down on his bed.

I wrapped my arms tight around him, squeezing him as hard as I could. The solid mass of muscle barely moved, but I wanted him to feel my arms even after I left. Why hadn't I taken my guitar outside the day I moved in? Hell, why hadn't I taken it the first day of school and played it in front of everyone? With his chin rested on top of my head and his heart pounding against my cheek, playing and singing in front of the entire school didn't make me want to puke. Not that I'd do it, but the thought didn't send panic chills racing down my spine.

But Dare seemed on edge. All the panic and uncertainty flowed off him in waves. The sketchbook pages rustled under my leg, and I got it. To my core, I understood how scary it was to show someone a piece of yourself you kept locked away. My football player who could beat the crap out of anyone on the field was afraid of what I'd think about something that obviously meant a lot to him. My football player. My Dare.

After I'd taken him to the studio, he finally felt he could show me this. I looked up at him and brushed the hair back from his forehead. "They're incredible. Thank you for showing me."

His eyes slammed shut and he leaned back, pulling me with him. A shudder rippled through his chest. His blankets smelled just like him: a hint of the mint of muscle relief ointment and freshly folded laundry. Most guys probably didn't change their sheets more than once a month, but his smelled like they'd come straight out of the dryer.

Our legs were still dangling off the side of his bed. My shoes were still on, but the nakedness of this moment and the vulnerability brought a tear to my eye. I ducked my head.

Resting my cheek against his chest, listening to his heart with his arms wrapped around me, I wanted to know this was real too. I squeezed him harder and snuggled in deep against his side.

He let out a contented sigh, his fingers tightening like a cuff around my arm to hold me closer.

'Next' was a scary word now.

Next had always been an escape to something bigger and better.

Now, next meant the loss of something I didn't even fully comprehend.

The emotional overload took its toll, and my eyelids drifted shut. Only a few minutes. That's all I needed.

I jolted awake.

Dare's room was dark and filled with backyard sounds coming through his open window. Only it wasn't sunset, it was nearly dawn.

I jumped up, running my fingers through my hair and scrambling for my phone. "Shit! Shit! Shit."

Dare yawned and stretched like an oversized cat, rubbing his eyes. The sexy guy routine was blocked out by intense dread.

The screen only had one notification.

Mom: Saw your note. Be safe. See you in the morning.

I clutched the front of my chest and braced my arm on Dare's wall to keep myself from falling over.

With adrenaline injected, trembling fingers, I sent my mom a quick message.

Her reply, filled with relief and letting me know she'd be home from work in a couple hours, shot a bolt of guilt through my chest.

Lies were stacking up on top of lies. It came so naturally now and that scared me. How long before I believed the lies I told myself?

Now that I wasn't anticipating my own death at the hands of my enraged and worried mom, I took in the room and the bed. The one I'd slept in all night with Dare. His lips on mine had been hungry and demanding as ever, but also gentle and sweet.

He slid off the bed and wrapped his arms around me, staring down at me. "Is everything okay?"

I nodded and tucked my hair behind my ear. "My mom's going to be home in a little while. I have to get back."

His nod was somber and jerky. He held me close and we rocked from side to side in the early morning sun.

He walked me outside and I was still so lost in the battle between dream and reality that I wasn't sure which side of that wall I was leaning toward.

"Let me walk you home."

I shook my head. "Don't worry. I won't get lost. I don't

want to risk her seeing us, if traffic was light on the way back."

"I don't want you to go." He laced his fingers through mine.

My heart skipped into triple time. "You should come to my place for dinner. My mom's working tonight, but I was going to make shrimp risotto for her before she left, and there'll be a lot left over. I know it's nothing too exciting like beef wellington or lobster thermidor or anything like that, but…"

His eyes widened.

Flames licked along my jawline. Did that sound like a proposition? Did I want it to be? "I-I figured there would be a lot left over and you'd be hungry." I ducked my head feeling idiotic about springing a dinner on him like he was my boyfriend or something. "Not like a date or anything. Not like we're seeing each other."

"What side of town do you think I've lived on my whole life, Bay? I don't even know what those meals are, but whatever you make sounds like the best thing I'll ever have." He lifted my chin and pressed his lips against mine, saying the words against them. "I'd take you on a date right now, but I don't think you're ready for that. But make no mistake about it, Bay. We are seeing each other."

I tried to pull my face away. My splotchy, embarrassed, probably still sleep-creased face.

He held on for a second before letting me go. "I'm serious." The intensity of his gaze melted away some of my worry.

The lump in my throat choked me. All I could manage was a nod. A stunned, stuttering nod.

He kissed me again, strong, deep and over too quickly, before letting me walk away. Our fingers stayed intertwined until they slipped free, and we brushed fingertips before losing the connection.

I looked back over my shoulder at least twenty times before I finally rounded the corner of his block and rushed home.

I showered and changed into my pajamas, messed up my bed like I'd been there all night, and came downstairs to cook sausage and put together the breakfast enchiladas. Sausage, cheese, bacon and eggs with tortillas—it was hard to go wrong, and so much better than when we used to have pot roast or chicken alfredo for breakfast. I'd learned to cook early, and found ways to compromise between me not wanting a steak at eight am and my mom not feeling like French toast for her dinner. Really, though, who'd have a problem with that?

My mom got home and we had our dinner/breakfast before she went back upstairs, like nothing was off in the slightest.

The whole time, I felt like the telltale heart of my lies was thudding under my feet. She was back out again for our afternoon of browsing for everything I'd need for my dorm. Move-in checklists and questionnaires arrived every day, filling up both our inboxes and sharpening the reality of me leaving.

The white-knuckle grip in my chest loosened by the time we pushed the cart back to the car. Back at home, I finished up some research on my final paper for English. The ticking clock began again. Dare was coming over in less than 2 hours.

I started the risotto, ready for the torture. He'd be sitting in my house. At the table behind me. We'd be alone. Again. This time both of us completely awake. My head was spinning just like my wooden spoon around the bottom of the pan. I added more broth, hoping to drown out the thundering in my head.

The door closed after my mom left, and I hurried washing her dishes and getting everything ready. When everything was dried and back into the cabinets, I took the stairs three at a time and changed.

I settled on my green-and-white polka dot skirt and a white t-shirt. It was a little nicer than usual, but not like I was trying too hard. Not like I'd prepared a meal just for him, and made sure to buy extra shrimp, and cycled through five outfits to get to this easy casual look.

Checking the time again, I grabbed two plates and turned the stove back on, hoping reheating didn't ruin the risotto. Dare choking down a plate of glue-like food wasn't how I wanted this evening to go. The little voice piped up asking me how exactly I did want it to go, but I locked that voice in my mental closet and jammed a chair under the door to keep it there.

I added butter and garlic to the shrimp pan. Sizzles and pops accompanied the extra boost of good smells filling the kitchen.

The solid knock on the front door whipped me out of the frenzy in my head. I wiped my hands on the dish towel hanging from the oven door and rushed out of the kitchen.

Taking a deep breath in front of the closed door, I smoothed my hands down the front of my skirt. Expectation and anticipation hurtled through my veins like someone had signed me up for the track and field team without letting me know.

Another knock.

Oh, yeah, I actually needed to open it to let him into the house. With another glance behind me, I grabbed the door knob and tried to look as casual as possible, but my heart vaulted straight for my throat when I saw him.

His hair was slicked back on the sides, giving him a slight pompadour at the top. It wasn't overdone, though, not caked with product. He was in a button-down shirt and jeans. The fabric stretched over his chest and arms. His smile and the single daisy he held out to me made me feel like I should be standing on a balcony, not at the top of my three front steps.

A giddy, completely inappropriate laugh burst free from my lips.

His smile faltered.

"Sorry. Come in. Come in." I waved him in and stepped out of the way.

He took a hesitant step forward over the threshold. "This —this is for you." His lips tightened like he was handing me a fish head.

Checking up and down the quiet street, I closed the door behind him.

He stood less than a half step behind me looking on edge and nervous, completely unlike how he'd shown up on my front steps in full teen-movie-hero style.

"It's cute." I took it from his outstretched hand and cupped the back of his hand with mine. "Thank you. And I wasn't laughing at you. I was laughing because this is the closest I've ever come to a first date."

He pulled me closer, the flower trapped between our two bodies. "If I thought you'd let me take you out, I'd bring my car around in a heartbeat." His fingers looped around my hair sending sparks along my collarbones where his knuckles rubbed against my bare flesh.

"Maybe later." My breathless whisper could be heard over my heartbeat.

His head nodded and he brushed his lips against mine. "The food smells amazing."

I cleared my throat and took a step back before sprinting back into the kitchen. Bubbles from the bottom of the heated pan broke through the surface of the risotto. I added more broth to the rice and cheese mixture.

"Are you ready to eat?"

"Of course."

A shiver shot through my spine as I envisioned things that had nothing to do with food.

I grabbed the shrimp and added them to the pan along with even more butter. "Great, it'll be ready in a couple minutes."

"Can I help?" He stood beside me with his sleeves rolled up, showing off his muscled and sinewy forearms.

"If you want to put this on those plates." I nodded to the two set beside the stove. "I'll finish these."

He nodded and plated the risotto.

Each shrimp only took a couple minutes to cook. Using my spatula, I scooped out the bulk of the shrimp and put them on his plate, giving myself another five and pouring the garlic butter over top of both the mounds of creamy rice.

He took each plate and set them beside each other on the table, standing behind his chair.

"Did you want water, soda or juice? We have Coke, Sprite, Cherry Coke, Cherry Coke with Lime, Vanilla Coke. We might have a slight Coke addiction in this house."

He laughed. "Water's fine."

"You sure?" I lifted an eyebrow and gently jiggled two cans in my hand, careful not to shake them. "The Cherry Coke is killer."

His lips twitched. "You've convinced me. Cherry Coke, it is."

I set them down on the table and Dare pulled out my chair and scooted it forward as I sat. "Thanks."

He sat beside me, his knee bumping against mine.

"Sorry we don't have beer or wine or anything. My mom's not much of a drinker."

"Don't worry about it. I don't need booze with every meal. I don't even drink half as much as most guys on the team."

"Really?" Skepticism oozed from the one word.

"Really. Do you think I'm a party guy getting drunk most weekends?"

I shot him a knowing look and his head dipped.

His mouth opened and closed. "Those were extenuating circumstances. I don't party like that. Football has been too important to me to screw it up over booze. I've managed to do that over more than enough other things." He picked up his fork and filled his mouth before I could ask another question.

"You made this?" The muffled words were hidden behind his hand.

"Yeah, I made it. Try not to sound so surprised."

"I'm shocked. What can't you do?"

"Cooking isn't *that* hard when you follow a recipe. And with my mom working so much, I wanted to do stuff around the house to help. Figuring it out took some trial and error, but it's not rocket science."

Watching him devour the food filled my chest with pride and happiness. I didn't think he let people do things for him often, and I was glad to be let in. Two refills of his plate and another soda, and dinner was done.

"Did you want to go home?" I took our plates and set them in the sink.

"Are you kicking me out?"

"No, I just didn't know if you had something else going on tonight." I took our glasses.

His hand wrapped around my wrist with his thumb brushing against the side of my arm. "There's nowhere else I'd rather be tonight."

A giddy, idiotic laugh shuddered in my chest, the kind of nervous laughter that couldn't be stopped no matter how hard you tried. "Do you want to watch a movie?"

He nodded, holding me in the tractor beam of his gaze with a smile that threatened to vaporize me where I stood.

Standing at the sink, I gave myself a silent pep-talk. *You've got this, Bay. We're just watching a movie. In my house. At night. All alone. No biggie.*

25

DARE

Her silent pep talk wasn't as silent as she thought.

I went out into the living room to give her some privacy. From the minute I left my house, a lightness had come over me, and the second I touched her, the rest of the world went up in flames, leaving only us in the haven of her house. The place felt more like home than my own house, and I'd only been inside a handful of times.

The car repair season was upon me, and I was close to having enough to take her someplace nice. I wanted to take her someplace she'd remember, that would make me uncomfortable as hell, and where they'd probably kick me out for setting my elbows on the table.

Anywhere with Bay felt like a place I always wanted to be.

I grabbed the remote off the arm of the couch and clicked on her account. With a quick glance over my shoulder, I went to her queue. Game shows, a few rom coms, binge-worthy TV series from ten years ago. Action flicks as well as comedies were selected through the next few months. I'd love to sit beside her and spend the time we had left on this couch marking it all off her list.

Now the same nervousness she was trying to talk herself out of crept up on me.

Falling asleep in my bed with her had been one of the best nights of my life—championship included. Waking up in the middle of the night, I'd stared at her, watching the relaxed way she breathed and burrowed deeper into my chest like only I provided the warmth she needed.

Instead of closing the window, I'd wrapped the blanket around us. Warm, bundled and safe—that's how it felt with her in my arms. A landscape swung to mind, one with a setting sun that settled in your chest with a glowing peace.

Lying beside her, fully clothed with our shoes still on felt way closer than I'd ever been with anyone else, but it had been an accident. We hadn't planned it. I hadn't planned it.

Tonight, a lot more build up meant a chance for nerves to creep in. On the field and before a game, I didn't have any problems getting out the energy buzzing through me. But I didn't think Bay would approve of me jogging in place, shoving on my helmet and banging my head into the wall a few times.

"Did you find something?" She popped up beside me.

I jerked, heart racing, nearly knocking the two glasses of coke and bowl of popcorn from her hands.

My body recovered quicker than my brain and I snatched the two glasses from her shaky hold, leaving her to save the popcorn.

She bent over with the bowl clutched to her chest and let out nervous laughter. "Did you think a serial killer had shown up or something?"

I slid the glasses on the coffee table and took the bowl from her. "Sorry, I didn't hear you come in."

"Obviously." She snorted and dug her fingers into the bowl of chocolates nestled in the center of the pile of popcorn. "Goobers, popcorn and cherry Coke. It's my nirvana. Did you find something for us to watch?"

I leaned back and rested my arm along the back of the couch. "Not yet. I didn't know what you felt like watching." The smell of the buttery popcorn had my stomach rumbling. I turned up the volume to cover it.

She shrugged and flopped down beside me, falling right into the nook of my arm. The raspberry smell of her shampoo filled my nose.

She reached over me, her chest brushing against mine, and grabbed the remote, wedging herself even closer.

Every sense was overwhelmed by her, and I wanted even more.

Flicking through the screens, she glanced up at me.

I ducked my head like I needed to get an inch closer to her to hear her, trying to cover up the fact that I'd been in la-la land daydreaming about her and hadn't heard a word she'd said.

"Sure, sounds good." I looked back to the screen and my smile widened.

"Welcome to the party, pal." She clicked play and set down the remote before grabbing the bowl and setting them on her lap.

I leaned forward and dragged the table closer to the couch, bringing the drinks within arm's reach.

The opening frame of Die Hard filled the screen. It wasn't until I noticed her mouthing the lines right along with me that I said them out loud. This began our quote battle, which devolved into laughter and even more touching. Not a single complaint from me.

Halfway through, we shifted, moving so one of my legs

was up on the couch and one on the floor with Bay settled between them.

Her back was no longer against my side, but fully flush against my chest, and her ass in that skirt that nearly touched her knees was nestled right against my denim-covered crotch. It was a testament to how good the movie was and how much I didn't want to break the easy comfort between us that I kept my erection under control. But I managed to keep the leash tight on my thoughts and my body—chokingly tight, to keep the easy air between us.

Her nervousness evaporated and comfort settled in by the time McClane made it to Nakatomi Plaza.

"This is my favorite part." She grabbed my face with one hand and held my chin in place like I wasn't already watching the movie right alongside her. Well, I'd also been watching her.

A hail of bullets hit the police car as the cop threw it in reverse before flying over the edge of the concrete basin, climbing out of the car with Twinkie wrappers flying everywhere.

She put on her best McClane voice, welcoming him to the party.

I laughed and grabbed another handful of popcorn.

Bay sighed and dropped her arm to my leg. I was her own personal recliner, and I wasn't complaining one bit.

Her intense need for me to watch certain scenes had me smiling so wide my cheeks ached.

She shot forward. "How did he know he wasn't Bill Clay? I've never understood this part. It doesn't make any sense. On the office directory, it said 'W.M. Clay'. How the hell did he figure it out?"

"He's just that good."

She grumbled more about it making no sense.

The waves of her hair tickled against my neck and chin. Her head fit perfectly in the hollow of my shoulder. Contentment like I'd never experienced flooded me. It was unexpected, like my head was being held under water, and I'd discovered that I had gills.

She finally wore me down enough to try her Goober-popcorn abomination. It wasn't half bad, but most of the goodness came from her fingers brushing against my lips as she fed me the salty-sweet combo.

My fingers itched to caress her. I wanted to touch her, taste her, sink between her legs and show her how I'd do anything to make her happy. I wished I'd grabbed my sketchbook on the way out to step outside myself to preserve tonight between those ratty covers.

The credits rolled and Bay didn't move from her spot against me. Her weight settled even firmer against me.

"That's a classic." My voice came out strained. I cleared my throat.

She laughed. "The first time I saw the not-for-TV version I was pretty shocked."

I wrapped my arms around her. "Or just pretty."

The corners of her mouth quirked up.

Taking that as all the invitation I needed, I turned her, our lips meeting like we'd both been playing it cool throughout the whole movie. Her hands were in my hair and mine were in hers.

She held onto me like she never wanted to let go.

Good, because I didn't want to either. I delved deeper into her mouth. Her lips were so soft, and they tasted like a home-cooked meal and a decadent dessert all in one. I wanted to relish each moan and gasp. The nibbles of her teeth on my lip sent maddening sparks of need rocketing through me.

It was too much.

She was too much.

I broke our kiss that might've been going on for five minutes or the last hour. Panting, I rested my forehead against hers before dropping kisses along her cheek and down to her neck, running my lips along her shoulder, tugging at the wide neck of her shirt to give me full access.

She shuddered in my lap and I smiled against her skin.

"I've been waiting to do that since I showed up."

"What took you so long?" Her voice was shaky and breathy, the kind I could imagine her using while laying against my chest with sex-messy hair, coated in sweat, as we both stared up at the ceiling, sex-satisfied. "Was that making out?"

I shook my head.

Her fingers tickled against my stomach, palms resting just under my ribs. Under my shirt. Against my skin. She looked at me expectantly. Her eyes hooded with desire.

I licked my lips. My dick was on board with the sex plan, but my head and heart threw on the brakes.

Whether or not it was her first time, I wanted our first time to be special. I wanted rose petals, good music, the perfect atmosphere to make it a night she'd never forget. Not quick and dirty on the couch with some guy from high school.

I took her hands from under my shirt and put them back on my chest.

Her head tilted to the side like a confused puppy. "But I thought...don't you..." She ducked her head.

"Of course I do, Bay. More than anything, I want to push you back on this couch, shove the skirt up over your ass, grab the condom out of my wallet and make you scream my name."

Her head popped up with eyes wide. A hint of fear flashed across her gaze.

And that's when I knew I had to do the hardest thing I'd ever done. I had to leave before I did something I'd want to beat the shit out of myself for even thinking.

With the backs of my fingers running along her jaw, I pulled her closer, kissing her again. My body hummed, so ready to unleash every bit of my skill on her. The ticking clock hanging over our heads competed with the desire to make this perfect. Channeling all the demands my body was making on me to lick my way up her body, I deepened the kiss, stealing away her breath.

Her hands clenched tight around the front of my shirt, driving the buttons deeper into my chest.

My hand cupped her ass. Her skirt had ridden up. The soft cotton of her underwear snapped me out of the mission powered by my body.

I stood. Bay partially came with me, nearly falling to the floor before I grabbed her. Hunched over, I helped her stand.

"I've got to go."

"Dare..."

"Everything's fine." Walking was nearly impossible. With my back to her, I adjusted my erection, cursing the denim and zipper torture tag team going on down below.

"Why do I feel like you're always running away from me?"

I straightened with my hand on the door knob. "Because the last thing I want to do is hurt you, Bay."

Her fingers brushed against my shoulders. "I'm not scared."

"You would be if I told you what was going through my head while you were on my lap."

"I'm braver than you think."

"I don't have any doubt." My Adam's apple rocked up and down. Releasing my grip on the doorknob, I turned to her.

"But if you knew how hard it was for me to keep myself from ripping off those panties, throwing you back against the couch and slamming my dick into you until you were clawing at my back and screaming at the top of your lungs, you'd probably think it was better that I leave. You're a virgin Bay."

Blood pounded in my veins like a stampede of a hundred horses. My engine was revving all for the dark-haired girl standing in front of me, looking like I'd scared the shit out of her.

She sucked in a sharp breath, her unblinking eyes locked onto mine.

"Yes, I remembered. It would be pretty hard to forget." I squeezed her in a tight hug and dropped a kiss on the side of her head. "I'll see you later."

Did I run like a scared asshole? Yes. This pattern seemed to happen more than I'd like with Bay.

Don't fuck this up.

Don't break something that can't be unbroken.

Don't make her regret the day she ever met me.

26

BAY

Dare's confession had me in a daze long after he'd left. I probably stood staring at the closed door for at least ten minutes.

He hadn't scared me with his confession—okay, maybe a little bit. But only because I didn't know what the hell I was doing. The flutter in my stomach had travelled lower with each kiss. The rough pads of his fingers against my skin had felt raspy and powerful.

He wasn't avoiding me, at least. My mom had four days off, which meant no more movie nights, but a flurry of texts had kept me up late into the night.

I was pushing hard on the flirtation buttons, and every time Dare tried to steer me back to more neutral territory, I course corrected or at least tried to. My seduction bag of tricks wasn't exactly overflowing.

He'd made the annoying new move of only showing up when my mom was home, so he knew I couldn't jump his bones.

Piper came over, giving me the distraction I needed.

"Why won't you come to prom?"

"So I can be a third wheel? No, thank you. Go with Jon. Have an awesome time. I'll be here polishing my spinster wheel all on my own." I let out a witchy cackle.

"Stop making me feel bad."

"It was a joke. I'll be fine. I don't even have a dress."

"You can borrow one of mine. Or we could go shopping for a new one." She bounced up and down.

"No, not happening. I'm not a prom girl."

"It's senior year." She moaned like I'd said I was turning down a kidney transplant.

"I'll get over it."

Her gaze narrowed. "You're stressing me out. I need snacks and soda to handle this."

"Be my guest." I waved her toward the kitchen.

She got up with a harrumph and stomped into the other room. You'd have thought I told her *she* couldn't go to prom, the way she was acting.

Cabinets and the fridge opened and closed before she came back out.

"These really are killer cookies. Maybe you can open a baking side hustle at UCLA. I can't believe we're going to be apart." She sat beside me on the couch with her legs tucked under her, flipping open her notebook.

"I can't believe we're still studying." I slipped a cookie off her plate.

"Those are mine." She clutched the plate against her chest.

"I made them."

"Which means you can make more. My mom's been on a health food kick since I was five. This is one of the only places I can get refined sugar." She gnawed at the cookies like a beaver, sending crumbs flying everywhere.

"You have a cinnamon roll and soda every day for lunch." I brushed the crumbs off the couch.

"But it's the weekend. I'm jonesing, Bay. Don't do this to me." I could barely hear her around the cookie crumble in her mouth.

"Fine, but stop getting crumbs everywhere." I brushed more crumbs off the couch and grabbed the broom. The picture of my dad hung on the wall beside the closet. I wished more than anything that I could have one more talk with him. I'd ask him what he thought I should do with my life, what I should do about music, and school, and everything else going on. Would he think I should give music a shot, even though it had never panned out for him? Were the nights in the studio and a steady paycheck enough for him?

I plopped the broom and dust pan beside Piper and glared at her, going back to my spot.

The door opened and she inhaled, choking on her pilfered bounty.

Dare walked in and closed the door behind him like he'd done it thousands of times. Maybe not thousands, but much more frequently over the past couple weeks. Deviant pain in the ass. He'd probably spotted Piper's car outside. Clever girl.

"I'm headed to practice and I wanted to see if you wanted to grab something to eat afterward."

Piper stared at him, slack-jawed, half the cookie falling from her mouth and plunking straight into her glass of milk. It splashed her, but she didn't move a muscle.

"Definitely. Sorry I can't come, but I promised Piper she could help me with my last exam."

The corners of his eyes crinkled and he smiled at her. "Good to see you, Piper."

She gasped, hand to chest and everything. Her name had crossed his lips.

He didn't give me a *see you later* from the door or a wave on his way out—nothing quite so non-committal. He stood in front of my spot on the couch, towering over me before dropping his hands to the back cushions and trapping me under him.

He gazed into my eyes with a smoldering half smile. His fingers ran across my chin and he dipped his head, capturing my lips. The sparks flared with the swipe of his tongue against mine and then his lips were gone.

My body reacted, tugging me forward like we were connected by an invisible string.

"I'll see you later, Bay."

The door closed behind him and I brushed my fingers against my lips.

Turning my head, I stared back at a slack-jawed, frozen, and bewildered Piper.

"Oh. My. Forking. God." She shoved her glasses up her nose with the back of her hand, repeating the mantra like it was the only thing keeping her from losing her mind. The cushions bounced as she shot up, pacing in front of me.

"Please don't tell anyone." I braced myself.

"Dare came in here and kissed you!" The decibel level was bound to have dogs running into traffic all over town. Dare probably heard it even if he'd made it to his car already. The grin he only seemed to wear for me on full display. That asshole. He knew my reservations about others finding out didn't extend to Piper. What a power move he'd made in our relationship tug-of-war.

I laughed. "I remember, but please just don't tell anyone."

Her jaw dropped and she sputtered. "But why? You're dating Dare?" She screeched, nearly deafening me.

My head whipped back and forth as she shook me, panting like she was on the verge of collapse. "Shhh!" I pressed my finger against my lips like someone might hear this, burst in, and commit me to a mental institution for even thinking those words.

"We're the only ones here. Oh my god." She raked her fingers through her hair. Her head snapped up. "You said you didn't have anyone to go to prom with." The accusation came out like I'd confessed to murder. "This is why you weren't interested in Jon." Like she'd finally pieced together some big mystery she'd been investigating for months.

"No, I wasn't ever interested in him."

"Why would you be when Dare is walking into your living room?" She hopped up and down, squealing. "I mean come on." She bit her knuckle and stared at the closed front door like she could still see him. "I'm perfectly happy with Jon and he's totally more my speed, but holy shit, Bay. People are going to freak."

"No one is going to freak." I dropped my pencil and slid the notebook off my cushion beside me. "No one is going to freak, because no one is going to know."

Her mouth fell open. "How can they not? He's never even seriously dated someone before. That's all people will be able to talk about."

"Yeah, Dare dating The New Girl. That's exactly what I don't want. I'm not going to be the girl dating Dare. I'd rather they remember me as those initials because at least that's about me, not him." My insecurities about being the girl on his arm nudged at the edges of my mind. There was also that. I'd made it through high school without a single mean girl moment. I didn't need the scrutiny and ire of half of the student body raining down on me with minutes to go before the curtain call of my senior year.

"But come on. I never have gossip. We never have gossip." She gestured between the two of us.

"So no one will ever know. Plus, we're graduating in a few weeks. What does it matter? I'm going to school in California."

"But it's Dare." She was whining with exasperation that I was depriving her of some juicy Greenwood gossip.

"If you say that one more time…"

"Sorry, let me pick my brain up off the floor first, and then we can get back to boring bio." She crouched down, picking up an imaginary brain, and picked off a few pieces of imaginary lint before dropping it back into her head and dusting off her hands. "There, all better now."

"You're crazy, just so you know."

"Oh I know."

I grabbed my notebook and pencil.

"At the end of this problem set, you're going to need to spill everything." She flopped down on the couch beside me and picked up the textbook.

"There's nothing to spill."

She leveled her gaze at me and moved so quickly, I didn't even see it coming. With lightning fast fingers, she pinched my side, giving it an extra twist.

"Ouch!"

"Everything. You've been holding out on me since that first day he was looking at you, haven't you?" She smacked my arm with her notebook. "I knew something was up and you played it off like it was nothing."

I blocked her swatting, laughing and trying to grab the notebook out of her hands. "It was nothing."

"Liar!" Had they heard that in Chicago? "You're such an asshole! Spill all the details before I rip your arm off!"

"If we finish all these, I'll tell you everything, okay? But there's not much to tell."

"I want every sordid detail. Every wink, every glance, every kiss, every trip to Bang Town." She clutched her hands against her chest, eyes fluttering and her mouth twisted in a T-bone-sized smile.

"Sorry to disappoint, but that's going to be a short list. There have been no detours into Bang Town, as you so nicely put it."

"He's a granite statue of sexual madness and you're not all over him?"

"We're taking things slow." I ducked my head and tried not to think of how I'd been kind of throwing myself at him and he'd always detoured into Cuddle Town. Not that I minded him being cute and gentle, but I wouldn't mind a pit stop to Bang Town before we got there.

Maybe after the Bedlam Bowl. The plan formed in my head. It wasn't perfect, but it was damn close. If it didn't kill me first.

27

DARE

"I bet you draw all the girls you bring up to your bedroom." She rested her head on her hand. The waves and curls of her hair framed her face and cascaded down her arm, spreading across the sheets.

She wasn't angry or snippy about it. Her assumption that I dragged out my sketch pad as some post-sex ritual wouldn't have been crazy, given the stories whirling around school about me—rumors that had never bothered me until now. I didn't want her to think I was a man-whore only looking to score.

Her black Rolling Stones t-shirt matched her black shorts, which, even at mid-thigh, had me tightening the reins on my libido as I traced every line and curve of her body, from her hip to her knee to her sock-covered toes.

We hadn't had sex yet. Sleeping beside her and not letting my hands wander, not giving her what she wanted, was one of the hardest things I'd done in my life.

Holding on tight to those reins, I'd done everything I could to go slow. Probably too slow. And it was killing me. But once I started, I wouldn't be able to stop. I knew deep down that it would be like throwing the brakes on a train plowing ahead at a hundred miles an hour, never sure I'd get a handle on it. And the risk—the fear—of hurting her with all the craziness brewing in my head was too much.

I'd wanted to be *that guy* for her. But I was still me, even when I shoved those urges and my need for her down deep. The hungry, bordering on feral, force of nature that wanted to be her first everything kept me holding on tight to the reins, tiptoeing across a frozen pond as it cracked and I fell into the water below.

And her heart. My heart. Watching her go to school while I wasted away in this shit town, or in some shit job, where she felt she had to come back to visit my loser ass after graduation. If I didn't break her heart by fucking this up—because of course I would —then she would break mine.

How could I keep her and let her go at the same time?

The clock was ticking down to so many things in my life. My Titan Combine numbers from last month and the Bedlam Bowl in a week were all I had. This was my last shot —at least my last shot at a future that didn't involve pumping gas.

There were only sixteen days left in the school year before everyone would scatter, some never to be heard from again. And these would be my last days with her. When she looked up at me with her big brown eyes and wisps of hair brushing against her forehead that she never got with the first swipe across her face, I could hardly stand it.

Bay was...she was Bay. Getting under my skin and filling my head with the beauty of the world with her looks and her songs. Part of me wanted it to be only for me, wanted the songs and the looks to be ones she only shared with me in the comfort of a bedroom we shared where I made her the happiest she'd ever been. Crazy dreams that were destined never to happen.

She smiled at me, her question still unanswered.

A huff of breath shot out my nose. "No." I brushed the eraser remnants from the page and smudged the shading around her face.

I didn't need to sketch any other girls. I didn't stay in their bedrooms overnight, holding them close, breathing them in, trying to untangle my unsettling infatuation. Even thinking that word felt like a betrayal. I wasn't intrigued. I wasn't infatuated. I was in love.

It was a scary feeling that crept up and pounced on me like a tackle after the ref's whistle.

My hand flew across the paper, trying to preserve this moment with lead as if it would be wiped from my memory or stolen from me. Every hour, which had once been ticking down to my freedom and my future, was now ticking down to a bleak time where Bay wouldn't be one rickety wooden fence away from me.

I'd taken her to Ruby's, but she didn't want to sit inside. She'd slouched down, nearly breaking my passenger seat trying not to be seen by anyone in our school who might be hanging out in the parking lot.

After a few handshakes and talking shit while our order was prepared, I headed back to the car, not certain she hadn't stashed herself in the trunk.

We'd come back to my place, since her mom wasn't working tonight.

"Your mom thinks you're with Piper, doesn't she?"

The tips of her ears turned red and she took a long pull from her vanilla milkshake. Her cheeks were sucked in like a fish attached to a vacuum cleaner. "Maybe."

"Would she disapprove?" Not that I blamed her.

"She'd worry. It's what parents do, right?"

I nodded. *Good parents.* That's what good parents did. Shitty ones did far worse. I gripped my pencil tighter, the wood creaking in my hold.

Refocusing on the paper, I took a deep breath and settled back into the scene, shading at the peaks and valleys of the fabric of her shirt around her shoulder.

"Can I see it yet?" She leaned forward, tipping back the edge with her finger.

I snatched the sketchpad back, holding it closer to my chest, turning my wrist at an odd angle to keep the lines where I wanted them. "It's not finished yet." Why had I taken this out? I'd never let anyone know I was drawing them before. It had always been through windows, from the driver's seat of my car, or somewhere no one knew me —sitting here in front of her, intimately tracing every inch of the body that I'd become so well-acquainted with was a new experience.

But I'd needed to capture the way she looked at me. I hadn't been able to keep my fingers still after we'd finished our food.

She scrunched her nose at me. The indents from the glasses she'd set on my desk still showed on either side of the bridge of her nose.

I leaned forward, nudging her back onto the bed. The belt of my jeans jangled and her gaze shot to my crotch. Why didn't she just strip off her top and straddle my lap?

I bit back a groan. She tempted me in ways that made me question what the hell I was doing. Why hadn't I made a move? Climbing through her window or through the back door, watching a movie, and falling asleep with a girl in my arms wasn't exactly what I was known for, but it felt right.

Her hints hadn't exactly been subtle, but it wasn't the first time I'd played the oblivious jock.

"Is it going to be me with a giant head on a skateboard holding a lollipop?" She settled back into position on my bed. This was the first time I'd ever shown someone one of my quick sketches, but for her, I'd do it. For her, I'd do anything.

Laughing, I looked down at the pencil lines and curves that couldn't capture a tenth of her beauty. This girl did something crazy to me. She made me think crazy things about what I truly wanted in life, who I wanted to be, and who I wanted to be with.

I wouldn't be doing anyone any favors, though, if I ended up as a gas station attendant and kept her from doing what she loved.

Coach hadn't said anything, and I'd never heard of anyone signing a commitment letter this late in their career.

Apparently the word was out about me, because the calls stopped even after a check-in with the coach about whether I'd been signed. The team still interested had to be desperate—well, so was I. But Bay helped take those jagged edges away.

Her voice was perfection. It pulled something out of you, something hidden so deep down it scared you. When she played for me, the feelings were so raw and pure that it was the razor's edge between pleasure and pain. As much as I wanted to keep that all for myself, other people needed to hear her words, if she'd only let them.

Turning her in my arms, I took a sip of her lips. Like every other time before, one taste wasn't enough. 'Hungry' was the only word that came to mind whenever our touches moved beyond brushes.

Her lips were sinfully delicious, just like the meal she'd

made me and the songs she sung me. Bay had ruined me for anyone who came after her, and I didn't want there to be anyone else. It was like she'd been sent as a gift to me after so many years in the dark. A light, glowing and warm to guide me out of the trenches of my life.

She straddled me, grinding her hips against me.

My dick was in overdrive, rebelling against the restricting confines of my jeans and failing miserably. The pleasurable ache spread from my crotch to the rest of my body. I bit back a groan.

"Are you nervous about your game?"

I gripped her waist, trying to hold her in place to clear the sex fog clouding my brain. My erection had a one-track mind, and it wasn't on football. I gritted my teeth and tore my gaze away from our fabric-covered collision and the throb of my dick. "All I need to do is what I always do."

"What's that?" She looped her arms around my neck and toyed with the hair at the nape of my neck.

A shudder shot down my spine. A creeping animal of bliss whispering in my ear that now was the time. Screw all my big plans, I should throw her down on the bed and show her how much she drove me crazy.

"Play like it's the last game I'll ever play."

Her fingers were driving me insane. So soft with a little tug every few strokes. "How much longer are you going to play the gentleman?"

I swallowed, choking on the air like my lungs had forgotten how to function.

"Let's play a little game." Her fingers unsnapped the button to my jeans.

I closed my hands over hers. "We—"

She pushed her finger against my lips. It tasted like the sour gummy worms she'd snacked on earlier. "The name of the game is Bay Gets to Do What She Wants." Her hand pushed inside my jeans over the waistband of my boxers.

Anticipation coiled in my chest like a snake waiting to strike.

Her hand wrapped around my shaft and it took everything in me not to buck her off.

Freeing my dick, she stroked it up and down with a look of wonder on her face. Her inexperience was front and center, which only made me want her more. I wanted to show her how good it could be, and not have someone else spoil all these firsts by rushing her or forcing her further than she was comfortable going.

One pump of her hand and I did nearly knock her off. Her grip was firm, but soft. I gritted my teeth so hard my jaw ached.

"Am I doing this right?" She looked up at me, her hand continuing to drive me crazy. The frenzy was building. "Can you show me how you like it?"

My chest squeezed tight like I'd caught an interception and ran it into the end zone. With a nod, I covered her hand with mine and pumped it up and down my shaft.

The look of determination on her face would've made me laugh, if I wasn't seconds from shooting off this chair.

All it took was a gentle swipe of her thumb over the head of my cock and I was done. The spasm overtook me like this was my first time. And it was—my first time with Bay.

She kept pumping me until I was oversensitive from her touch. Our hands were coated in the evidence of how good her touch made me feel. My head swam and a tingling warmth threatened to swallow me whole. But I wasn't going to end the game now.

Cleaning us up, I tried to keep my heart rate under control. "Now it's my turn to play the game."

She looked at me with a hum in her chest. "What do you mean?"

"Did you seriously think I was going to get my rocks off and leave you with nothing?"

"I didn't do it so you'd do anything to me. I just wanted to." The flush of her cheeks and way she ducked her head, showed me how right I'd been not to jump into bed with her. How I'd have probably scared the shit out of her and sent her running for the hills.

"Maybe, I just want to too." I tugged her forward by the waistband of her shorts.

She gasped, her lips parting.

My fingers moved to the buttons of her shorts. A shudder ran through her at the pop of the plastic against fabric.

I slid my hands around her, dipping under the waistband.

Her hands covered mine, holding them in place. "I—I don't think."

"Only as far as you want." I swapped to the bed from my chair.

Her eyebrows quirked.

Spinning her around, I sat her between my legs with her back pressed against my chest.

She glanced over my shoulder, the question still in her eyes.

I dropped a kiss onto her neck and ran one hand along her thigh, brushing against the bottom of the shorts.

My other hand slid over her stomach and dipped into the top of her unbuttoned shorts, past the waistband of her panties, and through her curls to the prize to make her feel every as good as I had.

Her back rested against mine. She sagged against me, as

I parted her lips and sank my fingers into her. First one then adding a second.

"Dare!" she yelped and squeezed her fingers into my thighs.

I only wished I could see her face. The profile view of her was beautiful. Her eyes closed, lips parted, small gasps and moans falling from her lips.

My dick sprung back to life, but I only had one focus.

Her fingers gripped me harder, and I used my fingers and thumb to keep the shivers and gasps growing. Her thighs clamped tight around my hand and I kept going, strumming her clit until her back arched and she shot forward.

I held onto her, holding her with an arm wrapped around her chest. Peppering her neck with kisses, I blinked back the tears welling in my eyes. She trusted me enough to put her pleasure in my hands. With every fiber in my being, I loved her.

And I'd never faced anything scarier than that in my life. She was my heart. Watching her leave would be like cutting it out and letting it out in the world walking around without me.

28

BAY

"The recording started ninety seconds ago." Freddy's voice crackled over the intercom into the studio. He didn't flick the light on, but I could feel his impatient gaze on me from the other side of the glass.

Had someone kicked on the heat in here? I tugged at my collar.

I stared down at the guitar, not wanting to look up at the window because then I'd see the reflection of myself and Freddy beyond. A shaky breath whistled through my trembling lips. I licked them, but my whole mouth was cotton-ball dry.

Why had I agreed to this? Freddy had all but locked me inside until I promised I'd give recording a single track a shot.

"What happened, kid? You've been playing in there for weeks with one of the biggest bands in the world and you didn't have stage fright. And you sang in front of them."

A flash of me on a stage nearly sent me flying off the stool and to the closest trashcan. "That wasn't my song I was playing. And what I did was barely singing."

He shook his head. "I'll take a break and give you some time to get yourself together. We only have an hour until the next guy arrives." Shoving himself back in his chair, he gave me a thumbs up before leaving the booth side.

I slammed my eyes shut and went back to the day on my back steps. I remembered the heat of Dare's gaze on me, even though I hadn't recognized it at the time. I was playing for him. Picturing him, I unclenched my fingers, and they settled into place on the guitar strings like they'd never left.

I'd chickened out over at his place. There wasn't a facepalm big enough for what I'd done. I'd been so gung ho about riding the Dare Express, and his attempt at oral reciprocation had nearly given me a heart attack. Not to say his fingers hadn't been magic. It was a compromise I'd take any day of the week.

The studio door opened again and Freddy walked back in. Light washed over Dare, sitting, waiting, watching.

Maybe I'd been a bit overzealous on the whole 'losing my virginity' thing, but he'd followed my lead and hadn't pushed me, even though I'd been the one pushing him. I dropped my head back and pictured the notes in my head.

The first one started as a hum in my chest before I opened my mouth and let out the lyrics I'd already committed to memory.

It was a song about the only person I'd been able to write anything about for the past couple months. The only lyrics that didn't feel silly and trite were the ones about him.

The vibrations from the strings hummed in my arms as I held on to the final note and opened my eyes.

The lights flicked on through the glass and I gasped.

Dare stood behind Freddy with his arms folded across his chest.

My heart pounded in overdrive. I licked my lips and took the guitar strap off my shoulder.

I pushed open the door to the studio, feeling like I was walking through sludge, or underwater with ten pound weights on my ankles. Making sure the guitar didn't knock on the door frame, I stepped out into the hallway.

He stood in the dim, silent corridor, the door to the sound booth closing silently behind him. He held my guitar case in his hand.

"How much of that did you hear?" My fingers flexed around the neck of the guitar. I held it between us like it could protect me from the embarrassment.

"Every note." He took the guitar from me and crouched down, placing it in the velvet-lined case reverently, like even a bump would be a disaster.

The latches clicked closed and he glanced back at me with a small, sad smile on his face. Standing, holding the case, he wrapped one arm around me, pressing his splayed palm against my back.

"You're going to blow them away someday."

He got a little blurry and I blinked back the sheen in my eyes, my nostrils flaring and a small sound escaped from my throat.

"I wish you could feel the way your songs make me feel. It's like you've cracked open my chest and you're holding my heart in your hands."

"That doesn't sound like a good thing."

"It's the craziest thing, and it makes me forget how to breathe when I'm listening to you. There's never been anyone like you before."

I scoffed. "There are plenty of other people out there like me, trying to make it big. And that's not my deal. I sing for who I want, about what I want."

"I'm on that list."

"It's pretty much an exclusive list of one."

His grin was blinding. Even in the dim hallway, it was movie-explosion loud, and the force of it slammed into my chest. Why was he the only one who made me feel this way?

Freddy popped out of the studio and handed me a CD of the session recording and said he'd clean up the audio files and send them to me digitally later.

"You did great, kid. Just say the word and I'll pull every string I have to make something happen for you."

I shook my head. "That world isn't for me. But maybe I'll do more studio work out in California."

He grumbled like he wasn't happy at all about it. "Have it your way, kid."

Dare and I walked out to his car with me tucked under his arm.

"Let's listen to it." He took the CD and tried to stick it in his stereo.

I snatched it back and stuck it on the dashboard. "No freaking way. I can barely listen to myself when I'm in there, I'm not listening to it through your sound system."

He laughed and threaded his fingers through mine for the rest of the drive back to my place.

"Fuck." Dare's head dropped and mine shot up.

A sinkhole opened up in my stomach, unexpected, unannounced, unfortunately at the absolute worst time.

Sitting in my driveway was my mom's hunter green sedan.

As if it weren't bad enough, the second we hit the bottom of the driveway, the front door opened. Still in her scrubs, my mom walked toward the car like each step might break the concrete walkway.

"Bay Eleanor Bishop, do you have any idea what time it is?"

Dare's headlights flooded over her glowering stance in the center of the windshield.

We exchanged glances and for a second I contemplated just telling him to gun it in reverse. I could sing on the street corner for cash.

He turned off the engine.

So much for a speedy escape.

She rounded the side of the car and yanked open the door. "Do you have any idea how worried I've been about you? I've been home for nearly two hours. How long have you been doing this?"

Her gaze drifted to the back seat of the car where Dare had gently propped up my guitar, complete with seat belt.

"You went to the studio?"

Before I could even think to refute it, the demo CD Freddy had given to me flopped onto my lap, like a gift to the parental punishment gods.

Her gaze darted between me, Dare, the guitar, and the disc glinting in the interior light of his car. "In the house right now." Each word was charged with the explosives of me never being able to leave the house again. She'd push the plunger on the detonator and I wouldn't be able to leave until my second semester of college.

"And Dare. I thought you were more responsible than this."

His hands gripped the steering wheel tighter. The muscles of his jaw pulsed and throbbed like he was a second from exploding, but he kept his gaze trained straight ahead.

I rushed to grab my guitar and end his audience to my embarrassment.

Walking in front of the car, following behind my mom, I

mouthed 'I'm sorry'. In the brightness of the lights, I couldn't see his face, but his engine turned over and revved before he threw it in reverse and shot out of the driveway as the front door closed behind me.

"I cannot believe you did that. How long has it been going on?" She stood with her arms crossed over her chest. "How long, Bay?"

"Since January."

"You've been doing this for five months?"

I ducked my head. "January of last year."

She gasped. "You've been lying to me for almost a year and a half. You've been going to the studio. I thought we had an understanding. I thought I could trust you."

"It's not like I'm out doing drugs or drinking. I'm working in the studio to make extra money and I'm—and I'm playing."

"And Dare?"

My shoulders dropped. "Sometimes he gives me a ride, so I'm not riding my bike so late at night."

"And that's all he's doing? Just giving you a ride?"

My head shot up. "Yes."

Her gaze narrowed. "I don't even know if I can trust you, Bay. Who knows what you've been up to for the past few months when I've trusted that you've been here safe at home?"

"There is no *safe at home*, Mom. There's no *safe* ever. I'll be gone in a few months and I could be doing the same exact thing. You'd have no idea. I was taking every precaution I could. But do you think there's anywhere any of us are safe?"

"I don't even want to think about when you're gone."

"It's coming, whether you want it to or not. Just like dad

being gone. You can work as much as you want, but that doesn't change a thing."

"Now you're giving me attitude because I'm working to put food on the table and a roof over our heads?"

"No, Mom, I'm not. But me playing music—you've never been able to stand it. It's my one connection to dad and you can't bear to hear it. Every time you've even seen the guitar, you look like you're reliving the day he died all over again. Of course I'm going to hide it from you. Of course I'm going to do it, because it's the only thing I have left of him, and sometimes my music is the only way I feel like I can breathe." I broke down, my tears choking me and my sobs pounding so hard in my head the ache felt like it would explode.

She wrapped her arms around me and pressed my head against her chest. "I was scared. I'm scared. So scared of losing you just like I lost him. How you feel about music? That's how I feel about you. You're what I have left of him and you're going to be gone."

I clung to her arm. "I miss him so much."

"Me too, honey." We sat in the middle of the living room floor in a heap until both of us had bloodshot eyes and my throat was raw.

She walked me upstairs with her arm wrapped around my waist. After changing into my pajamas, she sat on the edge of my bed and brushed my hair back from my face.

"We've both had an eventful evening. Get some rest."

"I'm grounded, aren't I?"

She smiled. "Oh yeah. Big time. The biggest time." Her laugh caught in her chest and she dropped a kiss on my forehead. "But we can talk about it in the morning."

At the door, she flicked off the light and closed it behind her.

As quietly as I could, I grabbed my phone from my bag.

A message from Dare flashed on the screen the second I hit the home button.

Dare: Are you okay?

Me: I'm fine. Grounded though.

Dare: For how long? We only have less than a month left of the school year.

Me: I'll find out from the warden tomorrow. I'm sorry my mom yelled at you.

Dare: That's nothing. I'm just glad you're okay.

Me: Tomorrow is a new day.

Dare: You left your CD in my car.

Me: It's probably better you keep it for now.

Dare: Goodnight, Bay

Me: Night, Dare.

I drifted into a headache-laced sleep where my nightmare unfolded in front of me. Standing center stage, I forgot the lyrics to the song I was supposed to sing. People were booing and throwing things at the stage until I spotted Dare in the center of the sea of people like there was a spotlight on him. With one look, the words sprang to mind. Not the ones I was supposed to sing, but totally new ones that quelled the writhing beast of the angry crowd until flowers fell at my feet. If only it were that easy. If only he'd always be my anchor in rough seas.

29

DARE

Not being able to see Bay was harder than anything else I'd ever done before. Her grounding lasted for as long as her mom wanted, and they're hadn't been any indication that it would end any time before Bay left.

Seeing her through my window, over the backyard fence, and texting had shaved the edge off my antsiness. In school, she wanted things to stay as they were. I hated not being able to hug her in the hallways or find a spot under the bleachers. I was left with hand brushes when we passed one another in the hallways or a long look in class and it wasn't enough.

I was focused so hard on Bay I hadn't noticed the street looked different. I opened the front door and the smell blindsided me.

My dad sat in his piece-of-shit recliner, already half a bottle deep. I'd have gone straight up to my room if the bright white of the paper in his hands hadn't contrasted with the darkness around him.

My body went rigid, like a brick wall laid in seconds. My stomach was a churning cauldron of ill will.

A slosh of alcohol dropped onto Bay's cheek, sliding off the edge of the paper and onto his shirt.

And just like that the brick wall was demolished.

"Get your fucking hands off that." I stormed across the room. Cursing myself for leaving the sketchpad out, I grabbed for the pad. These were my private thoughts. Private moments. Thinking of him seeing even a sliver of who I was sickened me.

"Look at you, doodling pictures of all the little chicks you're fucking. I'd have thought you'd go for prettier ones." He blocked my grab for the sketchpad, his grip tightening on my forearm.

I was getting sloppy. A wild grab for the book opened my whole flank.

"Fuck you, don't look at it. It's not yours."

Even now, after four solid years of lifting, he was taller than me. Or maybe I only felt like he was taller. I was suddenly an eleven-year-old kid when his whiskey breath hit my face, slowing me down, weakening me.

"Everything in this house is mine, boy." The punch was solid, fast, and precise. Like he'd been studying up on all the right places to hit someone when the fight might be even. The wind blew out of me like I'd been hit with a hurricane.

"Not that."

My fingers gripped the edge of the notebook and I jerked it out of his grasp, flinging it toward the stairs. My lungs burned, screaming for air that wouldn't come, like a vacuum switch had been flipped in the room and there was none left for me. A choking sound escaped my lips.

I staggered back, dots swimming in front of my eyes.

"You think because you're going away to college to play ball you're better than me?"

He shoved himself out of the chair, pulling himself to his full height. Still an inch taller than me. A cruel satisfied grin spread across his face like he'd been waiting to get me back after the last time we'd fought.

Joke was on him; I didn't even know if I was. My mind flashed to the game I was meant to play in less than twenty-four hours.

I wasn't running away. I wasn't going to let him take this chance from me again.

He came in fast and hard like he always did, but I was stronger and faster than him. Tight end training had taught me to take my explosive energy and channel it toward my opponent, but something cracked inside of me when my opponent was my own damn father.

In the middle of the room, I felt like the whole world was closing in on me as he bore down, charging for me again. I stood ready with my hands up, not willing to be caught off guard—again.

Tucking my arms in close to my sides, I took the brunt of the hit, my back slamming into the wall. The drywall gave way under our combined weights, cracking and buckling.

I shoved him back, blocking his swing.

Planting my feet, I panted. Blood dripped onto my upper lip from my nose.

"Looks like you finally learned to take a hit without all those pads."

My vision filled with red, a fiery burning that radiated from my side through my arm and to my fist as it connected with his sneering face.

His eyes widened a second before I connected, like he hadn't thought I'd recover so quickly.

The floor shook under my feet as his body hit the ripped and worn carpet.

Gasping and cradling my side, I scooped up the sketch pad and rushed up the stairs.

I'd gotten out of the habit of locking my door, always hopeful Bay would come in. I was out of practice. I wasn't a sentry to my own personal safety. He'd been through my room already, but the lock on the bottom drawer was intact. He'd spend too much time rummaging through my dresser to see past the clothes spilling out of the other drawers above it.

I unlocked it with sharp stabbing pain blazing across my body. Leaving was my only choice. I'd put this off as long as I could, but I wasn't coming back to another second of this.

Rushing around my room, I grabbed my bag, fire radiating through my side with each move, and filled it up with clothes. My sketch books went in next.

A groan and groggy sound came from downstairs.

I shoved my hand into my cash stash in the ceiling vent above my bed, biting out a curse at the long reach, which felt like someone had taken a fire poker to my side. The money, some paper, and some clothes were all I was taking with me. I gave a final glance around the room—the only thing I'd miss was the view.

My feet hit the stairs, sounding like a stampede of animals had broken free from the zoo, but it was only me. The spot on the floor where he'd been was empty. I tightened my hold on the bag. The only things that mattered to me were in there.

Bottles and glass clinked in the kitchen, but I didn't care. He could keep his ass in there, I was gone.

The slam of the door behind me felt like the slam of a vault, never to be opened again. Outside, I looked around, trying to orient myself. My car sat in the driveway. I shoved my hands into my pocket and pulled out the keys, throwing my stuff in and reversing out of the driveway, bottoming out at the end of the steep slope.

My back ached. My side screamed. And my head was fuzzy.

I needed Bay.

I needed to lay my head in her lap as she stroked my hair and kissed my lips, telling me it would be all better. If she said those words, I'd believe her. Glancing at myself in the rearview mirror, I saw my blood-stained teeth and a bloody nose. Droplets trailed down my shirt.

I wasn't going to bring this to her doorstep. I wasn't going to show up bruised and beaten.

There was only one other place I knew. I sent a message.

"Fuck, man. Please let me call someone." Knox rushed forward the second I got out of the car.

I shook my head. "It's done. I'm not going back. We graduate in two weeks. I'll sleep in my car if I need to."

"Don't be an idiot. Of course you can stay here. It's not like I haven't offered that before." He seethed. Knowing my friend was so pissed on my behalf helped a little. At least there were a few people out there who cared about me.

I took a step, hissing and clutching my side.

"Let's get you inside." Knox grabbed my bag and walked me around to the basement steps. "Do we need to go to the hospital?"

"No. I have to play at the Bedlam Bowl tomorrow."

"You can't play like this."

"I will. I'm not letting him take this away from me a second time." Each step was torture. I held onto my side.

"How are you going to play?"

"It'll be fine in the morning."

"You're shuffling. And hunched over."

I straightened up and bit back my hiss, clamping my lips shut. "I'll be fine." It came out like a wheeze.

"It's make or break, isn't it?"

My shuffled steps stopped. My head shot up and I met his gaze.

Knox shook his head with his arms crossed over his chest. "Let me go get you some ice." He jogged up the stairs and I sat on his couch, lowering myself down by bracing my hands on the arm and back of the seat.

He came back with some ice packs, towels, an athletic bandage, and a first aid kit. He cracked the ice packs in half and handed them over to me along with a towel.

"Why didn't you tell me?" He handed me the supplies and let me clean myself up.

"What was there to tell?"

"It was after you missed that game last season, wasn't it?"

A grim nod.

"Was this what happened?"

Another nod.

"Sonofa-fucking-bitch." He shot up from his seat. "Why didn't you tell anyone?"

"What would I have said?" I gritted my teeth and lifted my shirt.

He paced in front of me. "My dad's abusing me, can you help? What would that have done? I'm fine."

"Are you shitting me? This is not fucking fine." He gestured to the spreading bruise on my side.

I covered the area with the ice packs and used the ace bandage to strap them to me. "You could've stayed here. You know my parents like you more than me. Or stayed with any of the guys."

"I'm not a charity case."

"Fuck you. You're my friend and you know that's bullshit."

"It's done now. It's over. What's the point of talking about it now?" I needed to be at peak performance to prove to everyone I could be an asset to any team that would have me. Once again, my old man had found a way to fuck me over.

"How are you going to play tomorrow?"

"Pain is temporary. It'll be tender tomorrow, but for a couple hours, I can push through that." There was no other choice. I was out of options.

"You shouldn't have to. I can't believe you kept this from me." He slammed his hand against the side of his head. "I can't believe I didn't realize." The last part was more to himself than me.

"Me not saying anything doesn't make it your fault. It's not a big deal."

He stopped and sat in the chair across from me, scooting to the edge of his seat with his palms pressed together.

"The fact that you think that..." He shook his head, his lips in a harsh line. "What the hell is your problem?"

Anger bubbled up in me. "I told you it was nothing. Once I change, I'll get out of here." I reached for my bag, wincing.

Knox snatched it up from the table and dropped it beside him. "You're not going anywhere." He crossed his arms over his chest.

Footsteps padded down the stairs.

I dropped my shirt over the ice packs.

"Dare, I didn't hear you come in. I thought I heard voices. Are you boys hungry?"

"Mom, Dare needs a place to crash for a while." His jaw

clenched, working like he'd bitten off a piece of the world's driest jerky.

I'd never been one to beg for anything, but I pleaded then with my eyes.

Knox's gaze narrowed. "His place is being fumigated."

"Dare, we've always said you can stay as long as you need to. With your dad on the road all the time, and you all alone, we worry about you." The edges of her eyes crinkled with a kindness that made me long for a mom of my own. Was that what mine would've been like? Or would she have piled on with my dad? Or been another person I'd failed to protect right along with myself?

"I'm going to get another steak out of the freezer for dinner."

"Thanks, Mrs. Daniels." I called out past the lump in my throat.

"Take some of these. I'll get some more ice. Don't even think about going back to your house. I'll be right back." Knox disappeared back upstairs.

From the hushed tones and slightly raised voices, he was probably telling his parents everything. His mouth was a leaky sieve, but I was too tired to care.

I rested my head against the back of the sofa and closed my eyes.

A heavy hand on my shoulder jolted me awake. I cringed and held my side.

The smell of a perfectly seasoned and cooked steak wafted over from the plate on the table.

"You can take two of these after you eat. But heads up, if you have trouble breathing or anything else even feels off with you, we're taking you to the hospital."

I nodded.

We ate in the basement, Knox watching me for every

grimace or wince. Whatever he'd given me helped numb the pain, and the sofa bed called to me, ready to drag me down into the dark abyss of sleep.

"Do you have a CD player anywhere?"

Knox looked at me like I'd asked him for an 8-track or vinyl record player. "Maybe. Let me ask my parents."

He came back down with a Discman and some headphones.

"Thanks." I patted the black and silver player against my palm.

"All you ever had to do was ask, man. Of course I'd be there for you."

I nodded and lay down on the soft, comfortable mattress —the best one I'd ever laid on until Bay's. But that might have something to do with it being hers.

Rummaging through my bag, I spotted the clear jewel case. The streak of light from the top of the stairs reflected off the disc when I popped it out and slid it into the CD player.

Sliding the headphones on, I closed my eyes and pictured Bay's face. I pressed play, and my heart sped up, skipping a beat. Her voice washed over me, relaxing me and wiping away the last lingering flickers of pain. Sleep was a blissful oblivion where her song was only for me.

Tomorrow I'd deal with everything that came with it, but tonight, I'd have my peace with Bay in my head, even if she couldn't be in my arms.

30

DARE

Knox and I drove to the scrimmage together. He kept a watchful eye on me, like he expected me to pass out at any second. The pain relievers last night had made it so I could sleep.

My side was tender as hell, but I suited up, happy we were only playing touch since it was off season. It was a practice. I'd gone to practice bruised and bleeding before. It was just like any other time. Just practice. A glorified practice where my whole career hinged on the outcome.

The screen lit up on the phone sitting at the top of my duffel bag. Each message pinged onto the screen, rolling in one after another.

Bay: Break a leg out there.

Bay: Not actually. I've been around theater people way too much.

Bay: Kick some junior ass at the Bedlam Bowl. I'm working on securing my freedom. The warden hasn't said when it will be. I'm sure it will be just in time for everything in our senior year to be over.

Bay: Don't be nervous.

Bay: *I hope I didn't just put that in your head.*

Bay: *I'm going to stop now.*

Bay: *You've got this.*

I laughed, breaking some of the tension burning in my chest. Walking into the locker room, I responded to her text before setting down my bag.

Me: *I wish you were here too.*

Bennet pulled his shoulder pads over his head. "Someone's in a good mood."

I popped open my locker. "What's not to be in a good mood about?"

Knox shot me a look before dumping his stuff in his locker and grabbing his pads.

Bennet stretched his arm across his chest, pressing his shoulder against the wall. "I'm looking forward to a whole month of only needing to go to the weight room. It's going to kick my ass when I get to North Carolina, but it'll be worth it. Not like I'm going to be a starting QB in my freshman year anyway." He shrugged like it was no big deal, but at least he knew he had a spot on the team.

His head swung in my direction when he switched up the stretch. His grimaced. "Sorry, dude." He ducked his head and leaned in. "Listen, I know what went down last season and I know you're keeping it quiet. If someone doesn't pick you up after this, they're out of their fucking mind. We've got your back out there."

With a tight nod, I finished putting on the summer pads. Not nearly as bulky, they allowed for even more movement and less sweat-inducing weight.

The locker room felt empty with only seven guys in here. This could be my last time in this room. I looked around at the lion logo painted on the cinderblock wall. Voices and sounds echoed in the nearly-empty room.

Lockers rattled closed and guys tested out their mouth guards, even though there would be no contact.

Knox came out and slipped his pads over his shoulders.

Coach pushed the locker room door open. "Were you waiting for an invitation? The other team is already out there on the sidelines."

Bennet, Knox and I traded glances and fist bumps before following him out.

Stepping out into the field, the smells of sweat, freshly cut grass, and liniment muscle rub brought me back to the first time I'd played for Greenwood. The stands were full —not at capacity, but more than most people would expect for an almost friendly seven-on-seven game.

In the stands were fans with jerseys waving banners in the air. And there were cameras. A sea of guys in non-branded athletic wear used their phones, but there were also those set up on tripods to capture the whole field. After winning the state championship four years in a row, the number of cameras had grown.

The tapes coach sent out were reviewed, but everyone had their own special formula for making their final choices, including coming here in person or sending their own scouts.

Coach called us into the huddle. "We have a lot of people here today, but it doesn't mean a thing. Some of you have already signed your letters, but today we're all out here giving it everything we've got. We need everyone for both halves of this game. Explosive energy. Do your jobs and don't do anything stupid."

Knox leaned in and mumbled, "Hell of a pep talk."

"Try having him as your dad." Bennet shook his head and put on his helmet. "Can't say I won't mind having another coach next season." He tugged at the neck of his shoulder pads.

Knox walked beside me. "You ready for this?"

"I don't have a choice. It's now or never." I shoved my helmet over my head.

Coach pulled me aside and grabbed my face mask. "I want to see explosive energy out of you on that first step. You hit and take every pass out there. It's time to be a little bit selfish." He held my gaze, more intense than I'd ever seen him before.

I looked over my shoulder at the rest of my teammates.

He jerked on my collar, so I was facing them. "Everyone else out there has already signed their letters or has at least a year or two to lock one down. This is your last chance, Dare. I know you've been dealing with more than the other kids on this team."

I opened my mouth like I always did to deny, deny, deny.

He growled and shook his head. "This is your chance to get the payoff for all the hard work you've put in. Don't let this slip through your hands again. We don't always get second chances and now you've got yours. This is *your* life. Do you understand?"

He smacked the top of my helmet and dropped back to the line of coaches.

I jogged out to the rest of the guys in our pared-down line of scrimmage, getting head nods, and took my spot at the end.

My fingers sunk into the warm ground and I zeroed in on my only goal.

Adrenaline shot through my veins. These weren't my teammates. They were the obstacles to me making it out of this shit town and out of my shit life.

The heat beat down on the back of my neck, sweat beading.

The center called out the play and I punched through the non-existent defense as explosively as if I'd needed to take down a three-hundred-pound linebacker. My side screamed like I'd been punched all over again. I dug deep, my cleats gouging into the turf and took off, coming up not too far behind the wide receivers before turning back and looking for the pass.

Bennet let go of his throw and the ball ripped through the air like a bullet. With quick feet, I shook the defense and palmed the ball, before bringing it in tight to my chest and rushing for the end zone.

First play down and I could feel the attention riveted to me. I tossed the ball back to the ref and got back to my line. My field. Finally, my time.

I flung my door open and flinched, bending to get out of my car. The adrenaline from the game and last night had worn off, draining me, but seeing Bay through the kitchen window still made me smile. The rib wasn't broken, but this would fucking suck for the next couple weeks, especially after the scrimmage today.

Coach had brought me in after and said anyone would be a fool not to pick me up after what I did out there on the field. It made every gasping breath worth it. And now I got to see Bay, which made any day a thousand times better.

I grabbed the key from under the flower pot on the back step and let myself in. Gently closing the door behind me, I walked through the screened-in back porch and into the living room. "Bay?" I hadn't checked to see if her mom was home. I didn't want to wake Molly, if she was still asleep.

Inside, the stillness and peacefulness of the house calmed me. No one raged here. There weren't abandoned bottles of rum clattering against one another on the floor. Now more than ever, I could appreciate this place—because I no longer had a home.

Her voice drew me farther into the house.

The words were indistinct and lost over the distance of the walls between us. But the feelings were there like always. They warmed and soothed me like a balm rubbed on my heart.

I closed my eyes and gave myself over to the untroubled melody growing louder.

"Dare!" Bay shouted.

My eyes snapped open.

A spoon flew from her hand and I caught it in the air.

"Did you attack me with a spoon?" I waved it in front of her.

She grabbed for it, but I kept it out of reach running my finger through the peanut butter.

"'Attack' is a strong word. More like 'yelped and flailed, letting go of my spoon.'" Her lips fluttered with laughter she tried to hold back.

Her peanut butter and green apple snack was in her arms, along with her notebook.

"You've been writing." I nodded to the worn green cover.

"Some." She tugged the spoon out of my grip and spun, headed back to the kitchen. "Do you want some?"

"Of course I do." I watched her walk away, hating it even when it was only to the other room.

We sat beside each other with our backs against the wall, destroying the bowl of peanut butter and apple slices.

It made me feel like I was seven and hanging out in Knox's basement again.

"You've been here all this time and you haven't told me how the game went."

Plucking the last apple slice from the bowl, I shrugged. "It went okay."

"Okay? All you're giving me is okay?"

"You know. Run of the mill."

"Tell me." She dug her fingers into my side, pulling up my t-shirt.

I bolted from the bed, pain radiating through my stomach and chest. The hammering throb sent bile racing for my throat.

Collapsing into the chair by her desk, I shielded my side, biting the inside of my mouth until I tasted blood.

Fuck my old man, and fuck me for not being fast enough. He shouldn't have been able to get the drop on me like that.

Bay's gaze was trained on the ground. She swung her legs off the bed and braced her hands on the edge of the bed.

"Did you get that at the game?" She peered up at me in that way only she could, the way that made me feel like I was naked in front of her, all the bruises and scars laid bare.

"I'm going to go. You've got stuff to do." This was where I got up. This was where I got up and left this room, making damn sure she wasn't within touching distance until things weren't so raw.

"Don't do that. Don't just shut down and shut me out."

"I'm not even supposed to be here. Your mom will freak if she sees me here."

Her mouth opened and closed. "He hit you—hits you."

She dropped off the bed to her knees and skimmed her hand over my arm.

I hissed and jerked it away from her. "It doesn't matter. I'm out of here in a few weeks."

"It matters. Of course it matters, Dare." Her hand hovered over my leg before she dropped it back into her lap.

"What would happen? I'd get shipped off to a group home? He's gone most of the time anyway. Usually, I crash on someone's couch when he's back, and now that I'm older..." I clenched my fists against my thighs. "It's not like it was before." I looked away, staring at her brightly-painted walls with framed pictures of her and her parents. "It's not like when I was younger."

"And that makes it right?"

I shot up from her chair. Pain radiated from the spot on my left side like a glowing 'do not touch' button. The chair clattered against the desk, pitching and toppling over. "Why is everyone trying to make such a big deal about this? You don't think I know that? But it's over now. It's finished. There's no going back to fix anything, and college means I don't ever have to see him again. I'll go pro, and he can eat shit and die for all I care."

"Leaving doesn't mean all this goes away. Moving doesn't change the stuff going on in our heads."

"Moving out will for me. I don't have to see him. And if I do..." My hands clenched at my sides.

"Maybe you should talk to someone." She stood from the bed and crossed the room to me.

"And tell them what? Yeah, my dad used to beat the shit out of me, but I worked my ass off in the gym to get bigger, and now he only throws wrenches at my head from a safe distance because he knows I'd fuck his shit up if he got closer."

"Obviously not."

"Fine. That I only need to be on guard on days he comes home when I'm not expecting him. I'm not going back there while he's there, Bay. Don't worry. I'm leaving town as soon as I can." I'd sleep in my car on the side of the road if I needed to. A few more dented car doors and bumper repairs and I'd have enough to support myself for a couple months somewhere warm.

"You can't just close the book on this and shove it on a shelf somewhere. It's going to affect you."

"I didn't realize they offered a degree in psychology at Greenwood Senior High."

"I'm not..." She ran her fingers through her hair. "I'm not trying to push you."

"It's exactly what you're trying to do. I don't hit anyone unless it's on the field." The few knock-down fights I'd been in off the field had all been justified, not whaling on someone who couldn't fight back, but Bay didn't need to know my whole dirty, bruised, and bloody history.

She didn't need to know that more than half of my bruises had nothing to do with my games. Or how I'd been essentially living on my own since I was twelve. It had been a hell of a lot easier mowing lawns as a cute kid for extra cash back then.

Once I'd started high school, I'd had to make the hard choices between practice and making money for food, and there were many nights I went to bed hungry, bummed food off someone, or went to a party just to eat. I wasn't above letting a fan pay for my meal so I wouldn't have to chug water to get myself to finally fall asleep at night.

"I didn't say you would, but... you shouldn't feel like you have to hide this from me. Don't be ashamed."

"You want to see the dirty details."

"It's not like that!"

I jerked my shirt up, my head shooting back, and I ground my teeth together. "How about when he hit me so hard, I couldn't see out of my eye for a week when I asked him for money for a field trip? Or when he broke my arm when I was in the sixth grade? Or how about the time he broke one of my ribs in tenth grade?"

Her hands shot to her mouth, her eyes horror-movie wide.

The mottled bruise had spread. My side ached and throbbed. It was hot, and her gaze on it made it unbearable.

"Now you see it. Now you know. I can go for more if you like." My hands flexed at my sides and all I wanted to do was escape.

Tears glistened in her eyes.

They hurt. Her tears and her horror. It hurt knowing she'd always see this when she saw me. I dropped my shirt.

"Are you happy now?" The words were nail-gun sharp.

She shook her head fiercely. "No! Of course I'm not. I don't know how to make this better."

"You can't. I'll be fine in a few days. Maybe a week."

She lifted her trembling hand to my cheek, searching my face. "I don't mean the bruises." Her throat worked up and down. She ran her palm over my chest. "I mean what he's done to make you think this is something that goes away when the bruises fade."

My heart skipped into overdrive.

I backed away and dropped my gaze, keeping it trained on the floor. "How many times do I have to tell you I'm fine?"

"You can say it as many times as you want, but that doesn't make it true." There was a pleading tone in her voice that shook me deep down.

Letting my guard down was something I'd never been good at. Surrounded by football players, no one would ever even think to bring up shit like this. My armor was always up, except around her. I didn't have to pretend, but I also didn't have the luxury of living a life where my armor hadn't been forged in the fires of rage and blood. Dropping it around her had opened me up to this, a lance in my side just as I'd dropped the metal to the ground and opened my arms to her. I couldn't do this, not with her. I didn't want to do this. I didn't want to go to that dark place I'd never wanted to touch my time with her.

My back hit her dresser. "Stop pushing. Would you just stop?"

"Dare." She held her hand out in front of her. Tears swam in her eyes. Without warning she shot forward and wrapped her arms around me, careful of my side. Her arms surrounded me in a bear hug.

My arms were trapped at my sides. My nostrils flared and I shook, trying to hold myself together. I wanted to shove her away. I wanted to get back in my car and drive until I ran out of gas. A noise ripped from my throat, but she kept hanging on. Holding onto me and not letting me go.

I brought my arms up to her back, pulling, clawing at the back of her shirt and burying my face in the crook of her neck.

She pressed her weight into me, and suddenly I wasn't the one being held. I was holding her like I was afraid a breeze would blow her away.

I held on tight, tears running down my face and onto her skin like Gatorade poured overhead after a win.

Her soft, gentle voice pulled me from the tears and the pain, and I clung to it like a life rope. She ran her hands up and down my back and I squeezed her until my fingers ached.

She didn't say a word, just held me until tiredness swamped me.

"Bay." A quick knock at her door and her mom's voice sliced through the moment. "Dare?"

I jerked back, dropping my arms and turning my face away from both of them.

"I'll be right back." Bay rushed from the room, closing the door behind her.

I scrubbed my hands down my face. Complete fucking idiot. That's what I was. Keeping my gaze off her mirror—I didn't need to see what the hell I looked like right now—I sat on the edge of her bed. My gaze shot to the half-open window. I wanted to climb out of it so I didn't have to face anyone ever again.

The door opened and I looked up; my eyes felt like someone had scrubbed them with a brillo pad.

Bay came back and closed the door behind her. She had a washcloth in her hand, a towel and glass of water.

My vision throbbed in time to my pulse hammering inside my skull.

"I brought you some water."

I took it and gulped it down like I'd been out on the field for two weeks, not two hours.

"Lay down."

"Your mom—"

She set everything down on the desk beside her bed. "She's fine, and she said you can stay as long as you need to."

I opened my mouth.

The bed dipped where she sat beside me. "I didn't tell her anything. Only that you couldn't go home and needed to stay here for a while." She held out the washcloth. "That can be for as long as you need."

I dragged it over my face, letting the cool water wash over my skin. "I'm crashing with Knox. I don't have to stay here."

"Can you, though?" She took the damp cloth from my hands and rubbed the back of my hands. Her fingers smoothed over my tendons and sinew. "Lay down next to me."

My gaze darted to the door.

She wrapped her arms around me and pulled me down.

I held her close, breathing in her fresh scent mixed with paper and wood. Her guitar sat beside the bed. "Can you sing something for me?"

Her fingers skimmed along my forehead. "I can sing for as long as you'd like."

I fell asleep in her arms with the story of us humming in my ears. No matter what happened next, I couldn't let her go.

31

BAY

I'd stayed up the entire time Dare slept. My voice was rough and scratchy by the time I stopped singing.

He'd left before five, saying Knox's parents were cooking dinner for them. The way he'd clung to me had felt like someone was trying to rip my heart out.

So many things I'd thought about Dare were wrong, and I didn't know how to handle this new information. My brain was still on the fritz trying to reconcile what I'd seen when he lifted his shirt with the cocky guy who was a member of the ruling class at school.

Watching him pull away down the driveway, I'd wanted to run out and tell him to come back inside where he'd be safe.

But there were other people who cared about him. Maybe Knox could talk some sense into him.

I'd stood in the door long after his car was gone. Mom kept shooting me worried glances throughout dinner.

Her hand fell over top of mine. "Does he need help? Did he tell you what happened?"

My fork screeched across my plate. "I—I don't know. He didn't say." I wouldn't put her in a position of needing to do something if Dare didn't want anything done, so I kept my lips pressed tight. "It just seemed like he needed somewhere quiet to be for a while."

Her lips pinched and her gaze shot to the wall like she could use laser vision to see straight through to Dare's house.

We'd spent the rest of the night in silence, and I dragged myself to bed feeling like I'd run an impromptu marathon.

It had been three days since Dare showed up at my house and I learned the ugly secret he'd felt he had to keep from everyone. He hadn't been to school, and my texts asking where he was were met with cryptic answers.

I poured my worry into my notebook and kept myself from riding over to his house, only because the lights weren't on there—ever. They hadn't been on since the day of the Bedlam Bowl.

When my mom was out, I'd pick up the guitar and quietly go through the lyrics, scribbling down the music to go along with them. Staying away from him hadn't been easy, but I'd spent at least part of that in a cocoon, binging on cookies and ibuprofen, so it wasn't the absolute worst not to have to explain to him why I was wearing a hoodie and using a hot water bottle every minute I was home.

With him gone, even at school, I hadn't had a moment or two with him. No furtive glances and smiles in class or in the hallways to tide me over.

Those talent show flyers flapping in the hallway seemed

less like a taunt and more like an arrow pointing to how I could leave a lasting impression on this place. I could wipe TNG off the map.

Maybe sensing I needed to leave the house, my mom let me go over to Piper's on temporary release to help her get ready for the prom. I stepped out of the pictures with her and Jon until she insisted on one and asked if I wanted to be smuggled in under her dress. Considering it was a mermaid-style gown, that might have been a little tricky.

"Oh crap! My other dress. I have to return it tomorrow by ten am or they're only going to give me store credit. My mom's going to kill me. She told me to take it back weeks ago." She looked up the swooping staircase in her house.

"I can take it back. It'll give me a break from my prison sentence."

"You're the best." She hugged me and came down with the dress on a hanger with a plastic bag over it.

Their limo dropped me off at my house on the way to the all-night dance extravaganza.

Back at home, there was a twinge in my chest as I watched them drive off. I couldn't say I was sad to be missing an overpriced rite of passage that most people said was overrated to begin with, but a part of me wondered what it would have been like.

I went back inside and sent Dare a text.

He'd been quiet all day.

I'd thought I didn't have the words to talk him through any of what he was going through, but the words came to me right along with a melody. I rushed upstairs and finger-picked the strings, keeping them quiet, and scribbled down all the thoughts I wasn't brave enough to tell him.

My mom's footsteps came up the creaky steps. I slid the

guitar under my bed with the heel of my foot. She rapped on my bedroom door and pushed it all the way open.

"You're still technically grounded." Her arms were folded over her chest.

I looked back down at my notebook. A new song had been gnawing at my chest from the time my head hit the pillow beside Dare. "I know."

"But I do know how important these high school milestones are." She dropped her arms and held out one hand.

Out of the shadows, Dare stepped into the doorway of the room beside my mom—in a tux.

I shot up from my bed. "Dare! You're here. Where have you been? Why are you here?"

"I'll take these one at a time. I went on a last-minute college visit."

A college visit. I grinned stupid-wide at him, so excited his dreams might still come true. "You could've told me."

"I know, but I didn't want to jinx any of it. And for your last question...I came to take you to prom." He held out a corsage.

Mom clasped her hands to her chest, looking on the verge of tears.

Relief that something terrible hadn't happened to him, swamped my urge to shake him for dropping off the face of the Earth. I looked down at myself. "They're probably not going to let me in wearing this."

He looked to the hanger on my bedroom door.

My jaw fell open. "You planned this."

"Piper helped." He pulled the plastic off the dress and there was a note pinned to the hanger.

There were three words on the paper in her big, looping handwriting. *No excuses now!*

I'd been played.

"Let's get you ready." Mom pushed into the room with her full makeup box.

Without much notice, there wasn't much that could be done, but we made it work. Using her costume jewelry hair combs she did a half-up, half-down style and put on only a minimal amount of mascara and lipstick. I'd probably rub most of it off by the time we got to the country club where the prom was taking place.

"Perfect." She stepped back and brushed at the side of her eye. "You look gorgeous sweetheart." A quick hug was all we could muster or I had no doubt we'd both be in puddles.

A pair of borrowed heels completed the look.

"I'll be waiting at the bottom of the stairs with my camera ready."

I turned and looked at myself. The pale green dress had a V-neckline with flowers sprinkled down one of the flowing sleeves that ended at my elbows. The chiffon made me look a little like a fairy who had sprung from a forest meadow awaiting a prince. Only mine was downstairs.

The dress brushed against the floor as I made my way downstairs, careful not to trip.

Dare paced in front of the living room and my mom stood at the bottom of the stairs with her phone at the ready.

He stopped when I got to the second step from the top. He looked like he was seeing a whole new version of me. I was too—the one reflected in his eyes.

At the bottom of the steps, in the heels, I was almost eye-to-eye with him.

The plastic clamshell with the corsage popped open. He took it out and slid it onto my wrist.

My mom spent the next ten minutes capturing us from every angle like she was going to have to turn these photos over for a police investigation.

"I love you. Be safe." She turned and wagged her finger at Dare. "And have her back by midnight."

"Of course, Molly. She'll be safe with me."

My stomach flipped like it was diving off a ten-meter platform.

He closed the passenger side door and walked around the front of the car.

I waved to my mom out the window as she disappeared in the distance.

We drove out of our neighborhood toward the country club, but Dare took a turn, heading in the opposite direction.

I looked behind us. "Where are we going?"

He took his eyes off the road and grinned at me. "You'll see."

"So we're not going to the prom?"

"We are."

"You disappear for a week and then you show up and stage a mild kidnapping. What's going on?" My heart raced, fluttery feelings made me feel seconds from taking flight.

"There are these things called surprises. Sit back and enjoy the ride."

The car revved up a steep incline. The headlights washed over a dirt road with a rocky wall on my side keeping me from seeing anything. He flipped off the head-lights and pulled the car forward.

I braced my hands on the dashboard.

He put the car in park. "This is for you."

Warmth enveloped my hand as he lifted it to his mouth

and kissed the back of it. Setting it back down, he opened his door.

The metal-on-metal slam rocked the car and enveloped me in darkness. Then my door swung open and I yelped, clutching my hand to my chest.

He helped me out of the car and pecked me on the lips. "Stay right here." With a quick cup of my shoulders, he disappeared into the darkness and left me standing in the pitch black. In the distance, the lights from the city glowed like an alien space ship seconds from landing. Crickets chirped and my shoes shuffled in the dirt. Where the hell were we?

The butterflies in my stomach were getting antsy. I tugged on the elastic of the corsage around my wrist.

A rumble broke through the eerie silence and a metal *thunk* accompanied the spot I stood in being bathed in a warm, glittering light.

My hands shot up to my mouth.

Strings of white lights were strung up along the metal structure I couldn't make out. A curtain of them twinkled and winked in a slow rhythm, like stars had been brought down from the night sky to make this night even more special.

A table sat under a canopy of the string lights with a small bouquet in the center. There was a cozy corner made of blankets and pillows, and a white sheet hung up like a screen.

Dare walked the perimeter of the space, flicking on lanterns, before meeting me at the car.

"Surprise."

"You did all this." I stared at him, not believing he'd planned and coordinated all of it.

"I figured you deserved more than a regular prom. Plus, tickets were sold out, and I didn't know how you'd feel showing up on my arm." He clasped his hands behind his back.

My fear of what people would say had made him doubt how much I cared. "I'd have loved to be your date. But I won't say this isn't better. I can't believe you did this."

"May I escort you?" He held out one arm.

I looped mine through his and walked alongside him.

Pushing back the curtain of lights, he and I stepped into our own little world. It was like finding a magical wardrobe in the attic.

"How long did this take you?" The white, wooden folding chairs had floral garlands wrapped around the sides.

"Piper helped me out. Something about me needing to kidnap you for you to consider going to prom with me." He smiled with a hint of uncertainty.

My jaw hung open and I sputtered. "I—not you specifically, just the prom in general."

"I know I didn't throw you into the trunk of my car, but I hope this'll do." He looked up at the lights.

Ripping my gaze away from him, I took it all in. The perfect night. The perfect date. The perfect time. "It's beautiful."

"And Knox said to make sure he got credit for his help too. He wasn't going to do all this on his own without some details, so I told him it was for someone I really wanted to impress."

"Job done."

He tapped his phone screen and slid it back into his pocket.

Amos Lee's 'Arms of a Woman' began its gentle build with the slow guitar finger-strumming.

"May I have the first dance?" He gestured to the small dance floor made up of large carpet swathes overlaid to give us enough space.

"Would you look at that? My dance card has an opening." I took his hand and placed the other on his shoulder.

He settled his arm on my waist and led me around our makeshift dance floor.

Staring into his eyes, I couldn't hold back the feelings welling inside me. The love, something I'd been trying to deny for so long, but now I knew it was true. Not because he'd planned this amazing evening for me, but because he looked at me like no one else existed for him.

I'd been so ready to leave. My bags had practically been packed since the tenth grade, but here I was, less than a week from graduation, trying to figure out a way to slow down time. I wanted to make this last and never have to let go.

I'd have to, though, and so would he. But standing under the twinkling lights, listening to the gentle whine of the guitar, with his hand in mine, I knew we could make it deep down in my bones. Dare had become so intertwined with my soul that walking away would be like leaving a piece of myself behind. We might not be thirty yards from one another after graduation, but leaving him would be like chopping off a limb.

"What's got you making that face?" He smoothed a finger over my brow.

"Nothing important." My smile widened. "Does this exceptional date also come with a meal of some kind? Maybe some snacks?"

"What kind of date would it be without food?" The song ended and he kissed me before heading back to his car.

The latch of the trunk popped and slammed shut.

He walked out of the dark with a silver, insulated bag. Sliding out two containers, he waved me closer to the table.

"I thought you might like one of these."

The clear lid to one container had 'B.Well' written on it. The other said 'L.Thermidor'.

"You didn't. How'd you even think of these?"

"They stuck out in my mind when you invited me over for dinner. You said it wasn't like you were making Beef Wellington or Lobster Thermidor. I figured if you'd mentioned them, they were probably things you'd like. Or at least things you'd thought about."

He pulled out my chair and opened everything that had come with the meals.

"My dad and I would always watch cooking shows together. When he got home from work, we'd hang out on the couch while my mom read and watch chefs prepare amazing meals. And there was one where they made these two dishes. He said for my birthday we'd find a restaurant that served them and go all out."

I dropped my gaze to the linen napkin in my lap. I fiddled with the edges. "But then he died and we never got to go. I always swore I'd have them one day, when I had something big to celebrate."

Dare covered my hand with his. "I didn't know you were saving them to have for a special occasion." He looked down at the food like he wanted to chuck it all back in the bag and hide it away.

I turned my hand so our palms touched and threaded my fingers through his. "This is the most special occasion I can think of."

His neck reddened and he lifted his fork. "We should

probably dive into this. The lobster has been in my trunk for a bit. I don't want either of us being done in tonight from trunk lobster."

I laughed and grabbed my fork, taking the first bite. I closed my eyes and hummed as the creamy, buttery goodness coated my tongue. "This is the best thing I've ever had in my life."

He laughed and scooped half of the seafood dish onto my plate.

"Don't. You need to try it too." I tried to ward off his spoon.

"I did try it. It's great, but I much prefer watching you enjoy it. Plus, there's more than enough of the beef for me."

It was on the tip of my tongue to argue with him, but then I had another bite and my taste buds won the battle.

After we ate our food, accompanied by even more music and a death by chocolate cake, we made our way over to the cozy nook in front of the screen. Dare took off his jacket and wrapped it around my shoulders.

I sat between his legs, leaning back against his chest.

The small projector hummed to life and the screen filled with a blank blue rectangle.

"What's our movie for the evening?"

"Since you're a classic action movie fan, I figured we'd start with the best sequel of all time." He flipped over the DVD case and the half-cybernetic, half-human face looked back at me.

Doing my best Austrian accent, I punched the air. "Come with me, if you want to live."

He laughed and pressed the mini remote, bringing the screen to life.

When the bowl of popcorn and goobers came out along

with the cherry coke, I didn't think the night could get more perfect.

Under the sea of twinkling lights, as Arnold lowered himself into the vat of molten metal, I could have sworn Dare brushed a tear from his eye. I snuggled closer against him as the credits rolled.

"I could watch the movie on a loop."

"There are a lot of things I could watch until the day I die."

I smiled. "How do you always know the right thing to say?"

"You'd be the first person to accuse me of that."

"Maybe everyone else doesn't know you like I do." I wrapped my arms around his waist. The stone-cut muscle was barely softened by the smooth dress shirt.

"And they don't know you like I do." He twirled a lock of my hair around his finger. "There's a whole world of people out there who have no idea how amazing you are."

I stared into his eyes, still feeling like I'd wake up at any second and the past three months would all be a dream. "The most important people know."

He smiled the kind of smile that made me forget to breathe. The hint of dimples he'd deny until the day he died dented his cheeks and softened all those sharp, hard lines he wore most of the time.

Then his face turned serious. He stared into my eyes and licked his lips.

"I don't want you to say anything, okay?"

"Like, ever again?" I smiled, but he still wore the serious face that made my stomach leap into my throat.

His finger ran across my lips. "Smartass."

I nodded.

He let out a breath like he'd been holding onto that for a while. "I love you, Bay."

My startled gasp was muffled by a long deep kiss in our private prom at the overlook. The L word.

The words lodged in my throat. I'd already lost so much, and in two weeks we'd graduate and I'd lose even more. Leave it up to Dare to make me wish I had longer in Greenwood.

We danced again and every time I opened my mouth to say the words, he kissed me instead. It wasn't the worst way to shut me up. On the drive back to my house, we held hands like he never wanted to let me go.

I never wanted to be let go.

Stepping out of his car, I took his hand and he walked me to the front door.

Still wearing his coat, I rested my hands on either side of his neck, brushing my thumbs against his skin. His pulse jumped wildly under my touch.

Leaning in, I pressed my lips against his, delving deep into the full Dare tasting menu.

I infused that kiss with the three words I couldn't say —not yet.

His hands were on the sides of my face and his lips were hungry, seeking and deepening it until I was lightheaded, clinging to him to keep my feet under me.

Resting his forehead against mine, he gave me one more kiss as I stepped into my house and closed the door behind me.

The flash of his headlights ran across the front of house, and then he was gone. Walking up the steps to my bedroom, I couldn't help wondering if there hadn't been another first we'd somehow skipped over tonight. He'd been the perfect gentleman and I swore, if he penned a letter asking my mother if she could accompany us on our next promenade around the grounds of a manor neither of us owned, I'd lose my mind. All my best-laid plans to get laid hadn't worked, so it seemed I'd need to take a much more direct approach to keep my football player boyfriend from leaving town with the lingering question of who would be my first still hanging in the air.

32

BAY

"Dare, do you want to sleep with me?" I propped my head up on my arm. My bedroom had inched up at least a degree from every minute we were in here together.

The pencil dropped out of his hand, rolling across his notebook and onto the floor.

"Bay." There was a teasing warning to his voice.

"Dare." I mimicked his tone. "I'd expected us to do it at the prom."

"I didn't do that to sleep with you."

I crawled across my bed and onto his lap. "Then why did you do it? You know we have less than a week left of senior year."

Tugging his shirt up, my breath hitched. Since it seemed nothing was going to change his mind about slowing things down, I was going to have to go after it myself.

"Because you were too stubborn to let me take you to the actual prom."

He didn't fight me as my fingers skimmed his torso, dragging his shirt along with my creeping touch.

"It was too expensive." And there were too many eyes. On Dare's arm, everyone would know my name, but not on my terms.

He let me drag his shirt up and over his head.

I let it fall to the floor. My heart pounded in my throat, a drum beat in cadence with the throb between my legs. The ache kept growing with every second his hands weren't on me.

His head tilted to the side, observing my every move like a documentarian not wanting to interfere. Only I wanted him to interfere. I wanted him to do more than interfere. I wanted him.

Inching forward, I settled my hips right over his. The bulge in his jeans told me I was headed in the right direction. Maybe he only needed a little nudge.

I rested my elbows on his shoulders with my hands on the back of his head, raking my nails across his scalp.

His head dropped back and he groaned.

"You're making this hard as hell, Bay."

I swiveled my hips, drawing another groan from his lips. "That's sort of the point." Grinning, I kissed the bottom of his chin, peppering his jawline with kisses.

His arms wrapped around my back, squeezing me tight and hugging me close.

My mouth marauding continued, first to his ear, then down the side of his neck to the front of his chest. Each change in location drove his hands higher up my back. With a flick of his wrist, my bra was unsnapped.

I reached down between us to undo his jeans.

His fingers pressed hard against my spine, anchoring me in place.

Looking up, I stared into his eyes. They were a beautiful

chaos of conflicting emotions and a storm of desire brewing. Now I just needed to make it rain.

Taking matters into my own hands, I ripped my shirt off and dropped it to the floor beside his.

His nostrils flared and his gaze dropped to the swell of my breasts covered by the now-loosened bra. Tracing a meandering path up my back, he reached my shoulders and flicked down the straps.

I let my arms fall to my sides, taking the plain purple fabric with them.

He sucked in a sharp breath and brought his hands up. They shook before cupping my heated flesh.

We both let out a sound somewhere between satisfaction and torture. His callused fingers toyed with my nipples, rolling them, teasing them, pinching them.

I locked my arms around his neck, and his head dipped to take each one into his mouth. Rolling my hips, I brought a sliver of relief to the throbbing ache between my legs that would refuse to take anything less than the complete package—his complete package. Flickers of pleasure raced across my body.

My happy sigh was cut off when his hands shot to my waist.

One second I was on his lap, the next my ass was on the bed and I was staring at his back.

He stood, raking his hands through his hair.

The strained muscles of his bare back were facing me.

"Dare—"

"I wasn't doing any of this to sleep with you."

I got up onto my knees, moving to the edge of the bed. "I didn't think you were. The way I threw myself at you wasn't the first clue. But I'm probably not the first one to do that." Suddenly, all the insecurities and doubts came flooding in.

Was he only into the chase? The hormonal, irrational eigh-teen-year-old in me was coming out.

"Fucking this up for you..." His biceps flexed and he dropped his hands from his head.

"You're not going to fuck anything up."

He turned to me with hunger flaring in his gaze, along-side restraint I didn't have. His Adam's apple bobbed up and down.

"Are you sure, Bay?"

I pulled him closer by the buttons of his jeans.

His knees butted against the edge of the bed. With a gentle nudge to my shoulder, I lay down, my back against the cool blankets.

He crawled up my body, his bare chest broad and tanned above mine.

Catching my breath was nearly impossible. Would my tombstone read 'here lies Bay, dead from sexual anticipation'? I was on the road there, and every second the waves swelled higher.

The belt from his jeans jangled and skimmed across my bare stomach.

"Then we're doing things my way."

I reached up. My hands hesitantly cupping his cheek. "I want it to be you."

He shuddered under my touch and nuzzled my hand. And there was a cold vacuum left behind when he shifted his weight and left the bed.

Wasn't that what I was supposed to say?

He grabbed his wallet out of his back pocket and pulled out the reflective piece of foil.

My stomach was in chaos. My heart threatened to leap from my body, and my brain fixated on the devastating way he looked at me.

"First, I'll need to get you ready."

I tilted my head to the side, probably looking like a confused puppy. "What do you mean by—"

My answer came when he dropped to the ground at the foot of my bed and dragged me closer to him.

His fingers tugged at the edges of my underwear, dragging them down my legs, one excruciating inch at a time.

"You don't have to—" The words were lost in a gasp. His knuckles rubbed down the length of my thighs and over my calves.

"I want to, Bay. I need to." His fingers sunk into my thighs, pulling them apart. He was applying enough pressure to move them, but gently enough that I could stop him at any time. I didn't want him to stop. I wanted him to keep going.

He flung my legs over his shoulders, bringing his mouth inches away from the apex of my thighs. The pulsing throb of desire thundered in my veins, centered around the part of my anatomy he was about to become intimately introduced to.

"Are you sure?" His hands ran up and down the outsides of my thighs, both soothing and adding fuel to the insatiable fire building inside me.

"Yes."

He grinned. It was the lemonade grin, the one that threatened my ability to breathe. This time, though, these were lips I'd tasted. These were lips that were about to taste me. Taking his time, he parted my folds and lowered his head, keeping his eyes on me. Was he trying to keep me in a trance, or ensure I was one hundred percent on board with this? Either way, I needed him to stop the achy feeling shoving me toward the edge of the shoestring control I'd been able to maintain.

My fingers tightened around the comforter beneath me and I gasped.

He painted my pussy with his tongue. Rhythmic, perfectly-placed licks sent my back arching off the bed.

His lips wrapped around my clit and my hands shot to his hair. The sensations were overwhelming—too much, but not enough. My body was on fire—crazy, rushing-through-my-veins fire, all-consuming and unquenchable.

He hummed. The fucker hummed with my clit between his lips, sucking, and I shot up, screaming his name and feeling like I was seconds away from dying, the pleasure was so exquisite. Razor-sharp bliss. I couldn't stop shaking.

Collapsing onto the bed, I was deaf to everything, but I could feel each breath, each scrape of his body against mine, and my heart trying to escape my chest.

He ran his fingers along my hairline and stared in my fluttering eyes. "Are you okay?"

"Is that going to be the new question of the night?" I chuckled.

Concern creased his brow. "I don't want to do anything to hurt you, Bay."

His words sorbered me a little from my orgasmic high. "You're hurting me by not trusting me. I'm telling you, I'm good. I want this. I want you. I love you."

His hold on my cheeks tightened and his eyes glistened. "Sometimes I feel like no one would ever love me for who I really am."

"I see you, Dare. I love you and I want tonight is special just because you're here with me."

I reached down between us into his open jeans and wrapped my fingers around the appendage that told me every-thing I needed to know about how much he wanted me too.

He kissed my temple and slid off the bed again. This time to shuck his jeans. They fell to the floor and he stood at my feet in his muscled, ripped glory, so perfect and gorgeous it was hard to believe I was here.

Rolling the condom on, he held my gaze.

I opened my arms. "I need you, Dare."

That broke him from his holding pattern. He covered my body with his and settled his hips between my spread thighs. I hooked my feet around the backs of his, pinning him close.

"Tell me if—"

I quieted his concerns with a kiss. His tongue plundered my mouth and I urged him on, rocking my hips.

His cock slid against the seam of my pussy. The sound of my arousal didn't even embarrass me. All I wanted was for Dare to be my first.

He took a deep shuddering breath, keeping his lips on mine. A shift of his hips and the thick mushroom tip of his cock split me open.

I wrapped my arms around his back, breaking the kiss and crying out as he invaded me. A slicing pain radiated through me. I'd been unable to hold back the yelp despite how thoroughly he'd prepared me.

He froze. His advance stopped and he began to retreat.

My whimper turned into a moan. I tightened my hold on him. "Just wait." I clung to him with my arms and legs, waiting for the pain to subside.

His arms shook, braced on either side of my shoulders.

The initial shock had worn away and now the warm, glowy feeling was back. The same one I'd experienced with his tongue.

"You can move now."

"Bay." His voice was restraint laced with misery. "We shouldn't—"

Using my hands on the sides of his neck, I lifted his head to stare into his eyes. "I'm good. I need you to move." I shifted my hips and he sank back in.

We both moaned. My eyelids fluttered. I did it again and he hissed.

"Bay." The warning in his words sent a tickle of determination racing down my spine.

"Dare." I challenged right back. Shifting my hips, I did it again and again.

His hands shot down to my waist, trying to stop me, but not pulling out or running screaming from the room.

I hitched my feet around his waist and kneaded his ass with my heels.

His head snapped up and he stared at me with an intensity I couldn't even understand. He grabbed my hands from around his neck and pinned them above my head, thrusting my breasts higher, closer to his mouth.

"I was trying to go slow."

"We tried slow. Now I'm ready to try fast." My voice was needy, breathy, and demanding all at once.

His grip tightened around my wrists. He reared up and drove his cock into me. My pussy walls clamped around him, each thrust reverent and possessive. My moans became ragged gasps, clinging to the edges of my reality which melted away into a decadent and unstoppable crest.

My orgasm ripped through my body, turning me into a trembling, writhing cell, overloaded with every feeling Dare thrust into me.

He held me tight, wrapping his arms around my back and crushing me to his chest. His final, sloppy thrusts prolonged my orgasm and seared a bright white curtain in front of my eyes.

We collapsed into a tangle of arms and legs Sweaty, spent, and deliriously happy. I basked in the afterglow of what we'd just done.

"So that's what it feels like to have sex." I stared up at the ceiling, smiling at the giddy feeling broiling in my chest. If someone had told me two months ago this was where I'd be, I'd have taped their mouth shut with electrical tape, but here I was. Lying in bed beside Dare, I smelled him on my skin. The minty punch of a muscle heat rub, a hint of motor oil, and freshly cut grass.

Dare ran his finger down my arm. "No, Bay, that's what it feels like to make love."

He took my chin between his fingers and tilted my head, capturing my lips in his.

I wouldn't have changed a thing. Except for the part when Dare told me he needed to leave before my mom got home.

My heart would never be the same. A piece would always belong to him and I wasn't sure if I'd ever be able to let him go.

33

DARE

All my conviction couldn't stand up to a direct assault by Bay. All my plans to do things the right way evaporated once she put her hands on me. All my love for her was channeled into giving her every bit of me and making her first time something she'd never forget.

We had less than a week left. Part of my reason for dodging the sex questions had been because I knew once I'd had her, watching her leave would be even harder.

And she would be leaving me, leaving us behind, unless I packed up my car and parked it outside of her dorm in California.

Coach had been silent until last night. He'd called late to let me know there had been no news. Three other juniors and a sophomore had gotten letters after our game, but the mailbox remained empty for me.

I rolled over on the sofa bed, wincing when my sketchpad dug into my side.

Last night, after my final text to Bay, I'd gone out back into the woods surrounding Knox's house and let loose for a while. I didn't remember what exactly had happened, but my knuckles ached, my shoulders throbbed, and my head screamed.

I needed to see her sweet smile, to hear her laughter and feel her gentle touch. I needed Bay.

Me: I'll pick you up at 7.

Bay: It's okay. I'll meet you at school.

Me: Why don't you want to go with me?

Bay: Of course I do, but I need to go over something with Piper this morning, so I'll see you at school

That didn't sit right in my chest. It put me on edge. Her not wanting other people to know about us was something I'd dealt with, but right now I wanted to grab onto her and hold on tight.

My bruises were a mottled green-and-yellow mess now, still tender, but nothing I hadn't made it through before. I wouldn't go back for more. But my aches and pains now were my own doing. I poked at the cut in my lip. Whatever the hell I'd done last night, apparently the trees had hit back.

The pageantry and preening of the school parking lot had lost even more of its shine with the knowledge that, after the summer, if anyone here saw me around there would be whispers and rumors about me. The back of my neck heated and I clenched my fists at my side. I'd be another name on the long list of hometown heroes turned hometown losers.

I left, parking my car.

"At least we get to miss everything after third period." Knox called over the roof of his car.

"For what?" I yanked my backpack out of my passenger seat.

"Talent freak show is today. Remember last year where Bobby McMillan almost lit the entire stage on fire?"

My high school recall was never as sharp as Knox's. Maybe I could chalk that up to getting my bell rung way more times than he did as a receiver.

He stood beside me. "What the hell happened to your hand and your lip?"

I glanced down, flexing them. A drop of blood rolled down the back of my finger.

"It's nothing. I'll meet you inside."

I left before he could respond and I ignored people calling my name as I passed by with my hands shoved in my pockets. It felt like they were lined with razor blades.

Bay wasn't at her locker. Or first period. What the hell was going on? Things felt like they were spiraling, closing in on me and strangling the breath out of my lungs.

"Dare, you're bleeding," someone called out as I passed.

I stared down at my hand. Ducking into one of the bathrooms, I ran them under cold water and wrapped a paper towel around my fist.

The second period bell rang and I searched the hallways for Bay before heading to class.

Slipping my phone out under my desk, I sent her a message. No response.

"Dare." Coach stood in the doorway to my second period classroom and waved me forward.

I scooped my backpack up off the floor and rushed out of the room, but I stopped just outside the doorway at the grim, tight look on his face.

"Let's walk." He nodded in the direction of the gym. "We're down to the wire now and I didn't want to leave you hanging."

I licked my sandpaper-dry lips. "No word from any

schools." He'd have told me straight out if there were a chance.

He lifted his baseball hat and settled it back down like his head was overheating.

I knew the feeling.

"We've heard back from almost every school, and we don't always hear back from everyone who initially expresses interest. This late in the game there's not much more we can hope for. Walk-on spots are still a possibility for you."

"I didn't get into any schools."

His lips contorted with a grim shake of his head. "You can try again next year. Your tapes are still good and if you keep up your conditioning, you still have a shot. Retake the SATs. Redo your applications. The admissions committees might be more forgiving with the football coaches on your side. You've kept your nose clean these past two years. Keep doing that."

When I looked up, we were standing outside his office.

The bell to end second period blared.

"You can hang out in here if you'd like." He held his arm out toward his office.

I shook my head. I needed to find Bay. "No." I licked my lips feeling like all moisture had been drained from my body. Just like my hope. "I'll be okay." No, I wouldn't.

Walking back toward the classrooms, the tide of people was strong. Everyone flowed toward the auditorium, and I was a fish swimming upstream. Knox's head bobbed. He waved, signaling to the second set of doors. But it was the dark head of hair, wavy and shiny, disappearing into the side door of the auditorium stage that caught my eye.

"Bay."

She froze and looked over her shoulder at me before she was pushed inside by the other people behind her.

I charged forward, pushing through the stragglers, trying not to stiff arm anyone and send them careening to the floor.

Opening the door, I was met with the disapproving glare of Mrs. Tripp. "Dare, this is for stage crew and performers only."

"I just need to—"

"We're starting now. Anything you need to say can wait until after the performances." She closed the door in my face.

I pounded my fist against the wood and glanced around. Taking a deep breath, I teetered on the razor's edge of losing my shit. I should leave. Just get into my car and go for a drive until Bay got home, but I needed to see her now.

"Dare, we are still issuing detentions." Mr. Rourke tapped his detention slip pad against the palm of his hand. The last thing I needed was to ride out my last days of school sitting in a stuffy room watching the second hand tick by.

My jaw clenched and I flung open the door, stepping into the auditorium. The room buzzed with chatter and laughter. Everyone was happy for another reason to get out of class. But my muscles buzzed like I was being shocked. A tiny current, just enough to sting and keep me uncomfortable.

I should've camped out outside of Bay's second period class. I needed to see her, to focus on her face, to press my palms to her cheeks and kiss her. I needed to find the place where I knew everything would be okay with her touch.

Knox waved me over to the empty seat beside him a few seats into the row. Everyone stood, letting me pass. The too-small, hard wooden seats seemed designed for torture. I wedged myself into the seat, which groaned, just as unhappy about me sitting there as I was.

"Who's going to burn the place down this year?" Knox braced his heels against the back of the chair in front of him, rocking backward like he was trying to snap the seat back in half.

I searched the sound booth and the wings of the stage for Bay, but it was too dark to see anyone.

"Who are you looking for?" Knox drummed on his legs with two pencils.

"No one."

Mrs. Trip tapped the mic, shooting wild feedback through the room. If Bay had been handling it, that never would've happened. She introduced the first acts. Off-pitch singing, barely passable breakdancing. Someone attempted magic, which ended with a rabbit hopping across the stage.

Every time the screen of my phone dimmed, I tapped it to light it back up, waiting for Bay to check her phone and get back to me. My knee bounced up and down.

"And next, we have an original song performance by Bay Bishop."

My head jerked up. I barely kept myself from shooting out of my chair.

The stage remained empty. Maybe they'd gotten it wrong.

But then she came out with her head bowed, holding the guitar in one hand and the stool in the other. The guy I'd seen her with outside the auditorium ran beside her and hooked up the microphone. He squeezed her shoulder and whispered something to her.

My blood pressure spiked, and there was a roaring in my ear.

"This song is called 'Hurt' and it's written for someone very special to me." She cleared her throat and played a familiar melody, but the words were different. They weren't the ones she'd sung before.

When you look at me
I'm whole
You've given me my voice
The fire in your eyes
The fire in your soul
The bruises on your body
They were never in your control

"Oh shit."

The verses and chorus continued, but the sound wasn't reaching my ears.

Everything in me froze, like prey caught out in the wild.

A sea of people around me were being dragged into the depths of my own personal hell. A few heads turned in my direction. Whispers rippled through the crowd and I felt like all eyes were on me. Everyone was talking about it. After all these years, keeping it all wrapped up tight, never letting a word out, she was flaying me on stage, ripping out my soul for everyone's amusement.

I shoved out of my seat. The low-grade shock I'd been feeling had turned jumper-cable hot.

34

BAY

Puking wasn't an option. Not standing on the edge of the stage with my guitar in hand. But it certainly felt like a possibility. Bile raced up my throat.

My fear of chickening out had been the only reason I hadn't told Dare. He'd have tried to make me feel better about it, if I did end up slinking back to the choir room behind the stage to hide out instead of actually getting my ass out there.

"You'll do great, Bay." Jon stood beside me with the mic stand.

Setting up on stage, I tried not to look at anyone. I sat on the edge of my stool and closed my eyes, not pretending they weren't there, but pretending it was only him. No one knew who the song was about, but I wanted him to know.

After today, I wouldn't be The New Girl anymore. I'd be Bay.

The pads of my fingers ached from how many times I'd practiced this song over the past two days. Ever since the night everything changed, I'd needed to get this out and show him he was the one who'd given me the courage to get up here and do this.

The more I played, the less I felt like I was going to puke. The stronger each note got and the clearer the emotions poured from my voice. Every note wasn't perfect, but it was true. It was real and raw and contained every bit of feeling packaged into a three-minute song.

I sustained the last note and held onto the melody drawing it out past the end of the music. The auditorium was pin drop silent. Opening my eyes, I felt freer and bolder than I ever had.

"Thank you, Bay, for that wonderful original song." Mrs. Tripp got on the mic and clapped, but no one followed her lead.

Dare stood at the edge of the stage. Every eye was either on him or me.

Happiness burst from every pore. I'd done it. I'd sung in front of the whole school. And he saw it. I'd known he was there, that was why I'd been able to do it in the first place. I couldn't see him, but I'd known he was there.

Did he feel the electricity? Did he feel the magic in the room and the way I'd belted out the lyrics I'd written for him? No one else knew that, but I knew and he knew. A song to tell him how much I loved him and how strong he was after going through everything he'd been through.

Panting and coming down from my high of finally making it, I looked around the room.

Confusion raced through my head. Why was he standing there? Why was everyone so quiet?

"The New Girl's got the hots for Dare?"

Someone laughed.

"Is she obsessed with him or something?"

"Damn, he's got a stalker."

More voices joined in, increasing in volume, their laughter and stares burning straight through my chest.

He walked to the stairs at the side of the stage and crossed the front until he was in front of me.

He plucked the guitar from my hands and wrapped his other hand around my arm, walking me off stage.

The crowd noise kicked up the second we crossed into the wings. Everyone else waiting for their turn or who'd already performed parted like the Red Sea letting us pass. No one said a word, they just watched. Suddenly, I wished I could be invisible again.

"Dare, what the hell is going on?"

I jerked my arm from his grasp, but he held tight—not biting, but tight enough that I couldn't shake his grasp.

He walked through the door to the choir room and into the green room that usually buzzed with activity during shows. The few people in there took one look at us and rushed out, skirting past Dare's imposing figure.

"Close the door."

The guy in a Hamilton t-shirt yelped and slammed it closed behind him.

Dare released my arm.

I rubbed it and took a few steps away. "What the hell, Dare? Your lip is bleeding." I reached up to brush it with my thumb. Had he gone back home? Had his dad done this? Anger riled in my chest.

He stepped away from my touch and stood still, eyes boring into mine with his fingers wrapped around the neck of my dad's guitar.

"'What the hell, Dare?' That's all you have to say after what you did out there?"

Muffled music poured into the room. Someone else was performing after me.

"What I did? What the hell did I do?"

The door behind him opened. "Is everything okay in here?" Knox popped his head in. The drum solo from the stage clanged off the walls in the claustrophobic room.

"Out." Dare growled. "No one comes in here. Do you understand me?" His thunderous gaze snapped to mine. He hadn't even known who was at the door. It could have been a teacher—hell, the principal—and he'd have said the same thing.

Knox didn't say a word. The click of the door was the only sound other than the heaving breaths coming from Dare. He paced like a caged animal, still not looking away from me.

With my earlier confusion no longer clouding my gaze, I saw him. I saw the bruised knuckles holding my dad's guitar.

I swallowed, still trying to figure out how things had gone so terribly wrong so quickly. Stepping forward, I held out my hands in front of me.

"Dare—"

"No!"

I jumped, his shout scaring me in the quiet room.

"What gave you the right?" His jaw was tight. His entire body rigid like he'd been turned to stone.

The urge to flee was strong, almost undeniable, but the rawness of his voice zapped away some of the fear.

"You went out there and sang a song about me."

Bile rushed for my throat again. He was pissed that I'd sung a song about him? I'd sung tons of songs for him. He'd asked me to—why was he mad now? Most of my songs were about him.

"Why is that a problem?"

"You sang about me in front of everyone." He jutted my guitar out like it was an offensive rag.

"No one knows it's about you, although they might have an idea since you showed up at the edge of the stage like you did. No one knew we'd even spoken to each other until you did that."

"That's my life you're up there singing about. I didn't give you permission." He jabbed so hard at his chest, I winced.

"I've sung songs about you before."

"When we were alone," he roared, panting like he'd been out on the field all afternoon.

I swallowed again, my mouth feeling like a saliva factory.

"You're going to leave, and I'm going to be stuck here with everyone, and now they know the song." His body was racked with something between a shudder and a convulsion.

"Dare, please give me the guitar." I held out my hand trying to keep my voice from wavering, but I failed. It trembled like a leaf in a hurricane.

My father's guitar. He had it and he was raging. All the things I'd thought I'd known about him were a lie. If they weren't, I wouldn't be cornered in a room with a guy towering over me and screaming like I'd ripped out his heart. No, that was what he was doing to me.

"The guitar." He looked at it and his head jerked back like he'd only just realized he was still holding it. "This guitar is more important than our conversation? Than what you just did to me? Everyone out there is staring at me. Asking about my fucking lip and all you can talk about is this fucking guitar? The instrument of my torture?"

The air left my lungs. I felt the movement, the shift in

the room, before he did it. Like the silent before a shock-wave hit, and I covered my ears.

"Dare, no!" My scream was lost, drowned out by the splintering of wood against concrete. I couldn't breathe. Dots swam in front of my eyes. I braced my hands on the vanity next to me.

His head snapped in my direction like a predator finding another bit of prey. I was next. I dropped to the floor in the corner, hoping someone would find me, and that this wouldn't hurt nearly as much as what he'd done to my heart.

35

DARE

"Dare!" Her scream pierced the veil of rage that had been protecting me from the pain and rawness clawing at my chest.

Ripped from the hazy place where I couldn't see, hear, or feel anything, I snapped back to the small room behind the stage. My fingers were wrapped around the broken, hanging neck of the guitar.

Strings stuck out at all angles. The body of the instrument she'd sat on stage singing with lay demolished, pieces scattered in a circle in front of me.

Her hands were cupped over her mouth, trying and failing to hold back the sobs wracking her body. With wide eyes filled with fear, she curled up in a ball as far away from me as she could in the corner of the room.

That wasn't the place you wanted to be when someone came after you. I should know.

Loosening my grip, the splintered wood clattered to the floor.

She jumped at the sharp sound when only our breaths

broke through the gentle murmur coming from the auditorium.

"Bay." I stepped forward.

She flinched, covering her head and face with her hands. Protecting herself.

I'd done that. Nausea flooded through me, and it was hard to stand, let alone look at her. I turned, faced with myself in the reflection of the mirrors lining the row I'd backed her down.

I bolted from the room, bursting through the other set of doors that led to the hallway. The cool air did nothing to stop the churning in my gut and chest. It felt like an animal was trying to claw its way out of me, ripping me apart with each breath.

Sprinting to the end of the hallway, I braced my shaking hands on the sides of the trashcan and puked, retching so hard my eyes hurt. A throbbing, thundering wound opened bright and bloody, ripping through my stomach, streaking a jagged path across my heart.

Sneakers squeaked on the school floors. The sharp squeals sounded like when Knox and I were late for practice.

"There you are, son."

My blood turned to ice cubes in my veins, but it wasn't my father's voice.

Coach jogged toward me with sweat pouring down his face and a red flush in his cheeks. "You okay?"

I stood frozen, unable to even nod with puke dripping from my lips. I wiped my mouth with the back of my hand. The sour, pungent bile filling my nose.

"You don't look so well." Concern creased the coach's brow. He braced his hand on the wall like he'd run all the way over from his office. Had he?

Pulling a handkerchief from his inside jacket pocket, he handed it to me. "Listen, go home and get some rest." He squeezed my shoulder.

"The news is they're sending over the paperwork for you today." His smile widened. "I'll get it to you as soon as I have it. Sleep and get over whatever this is." He gestured to my slowly collapsing body.

"You're lucky the college is into forgiveness and second chances. This time tomorrow, you'll be the newest signed recruit to Notre Dame."

My dazed look must have been interpreted by him as shock. It was, but not because of the dream I'd been afraid to hang onto finally coming true. No, it was because the reality of who I was had finally shown itself.

Monster. Just like my father. Worse, because I don't think he'd ever even loved me. I was never more than a kid he'd been saddled with. But Bay. I loved her. Love her. And I'd destroyed the beauty she'd brought into the world.

"The offer deadline for the coaches was noon today and no one emailed. But then I realized I hadn't gotten any emails since yesterday. I turned everything off and back on, and there was an email at 11:59am. Sorry for the scare."

Her flinch and cowering replayed in my head on a loop. Those eyes that had stared up at me like I held the keys to the universe were clouded with fear and the need to escape.

I turned and walked away.

"Dare?"

I didn't look back. I raced out of the building and into my car. My tires squealed as I peeled out of the parking lot.

The way the guitar splintered in my hand. It all came flooding back to me as penance for my crimes. As punishment for what I'd done. I could see every excruciating second, and the look on her face.

I flung open the door to my car and puked up nothing but bile.

How could I fix this? Fix the unfixable?

36

BAY

He was a wild raging force of destruction and I'd been his target. He splintered the wood. My father's guitar lay in pieces after he stormed out of the room.

I'd clutched at my chest, the tears coming down so hard I couldn't catch my breath. If I'd passed out, I didn't remember, but I unfroze from my spot in the corner of the room and walked to the crime scene he'd left behind.

Crouching, I picked up the pieces with trembling fingers and cradled the remains like they were a dying creature. But it was already gone, and no CPR could bring it back. The neck and body were splintered, almost shattered. Slivers of wood stabbed at my palm. Tears flowed down my cheeks, soaking the broken guitar. The instrument of my destruction.

On the other side of the wall, the music died down and the muted laughter and applause ripped me from the haze of ruin.

Gathering up the pieces, I walked all the way home with them in my arms.

Numb and unable to process what happened, I needed my bed. I needed my house. I needed my mom. And my dad.

I broke down again. With each step, memories of Dare assailed me. I passed the place where I'd fallen off my bike and he'd held out his hand and given me a ride home. Where he'd helped my mom by pushing her car. Where I'd given him that glass of lemonade and he'd smiled, making my knees weak.

The wood bit into my palms. I shifted and a splinter slid into my skin. Wincing, I stared at the broken instrument. Almost none of it was recognizable. It was beyond repair. There wasn't a single intact piece to build from. He'd demolished it.

He'd demolished me. I'd been so worried about fixing him, but I should've been preparing to fix myself when he shattered me. Cruel. Violent. Vicious.

I feared my choking sobs would drown me. My fingers wouldn't unlock from the beaten corpse of the guitar. Staring at the shattered pieces made the tears come even harder. It had been his. The spots on the fret board where my dad's fingers had run across the metal with the inlaid mother of pearl had still been visible. But now it wasn't an instrument. Now it was another body I had to lay to rest. My fingers trembled as I put the remnants of the guitar into the trash.

My mom didn't need to see this. She didn't need to lose another piece of my dad. I'd take the case with me to college like nothing had happened and pretend someone stole it. Better for her to believe someone had taken it and it lived a new life with them than that it had been destroyed.

I slid the lid on and dragged the trash cans to the front of the house. The garbage truck would pick it up before she got home from work in the morning.

Slipping inside the house, I peeled off my clothes and stood in the shower. The running water and spray of steam were barely able to drown out the choking sobs erupting from my throat.

As I wrapped a towel around myself, the phone I didn't even remember bringing in with me skittered across the counter and fell into the sink. Messages from Piper and Knox blew up my screen, but none from Dare. He'd sent his best friend to try to do his dirty work.

I rushed back downstairs and grabbed the emergency key from under the flower pot before slamming the door, locking it and putting the chain on.

Dare-proofing the house used up the last of the reserves I had keeping me together.

In my room, I curled myself into a tight ball on my bed, clutching the pillow against my chest. I buried my face in it. A flood of musk, bar soap and the gentle hint of cologne flooded my nostrils. I jerked my head back. It smelled like him. Everything smelled like him. The pillows, the blankets, even my own clothes.

I ripped the sheets off the bed and shoved it all away. A pile of the offending fabric sat in the middle of my bedroom. Back on the bare mattress, still in my towel, I brought my knees up to my chin and wrapped my arms tight around them, rocking back and forth.

Dare wasn't there. I'd looked into his eyes and it wasn't my Dare. It wasn't the one who'd touched me like he was afraid I'd break or stared down at me before I closed my eyes at night, tucking a stray piece of hair behind my ear. That wasn't who I had been backstage with.

Or maybe I'd been lying to myself. Whoever he was, that

was something I couldn't repair. It would take all my strength to hold myself together, to make it through the next week of school and out the other side unscathed.

I prayed for numbness. I wished for someone, something to take this pain away and turn me into a zombie who could go through the motions of life without feeling like I was being sliced with each step. But I wasn't so lucky. I fell asleep feeling every crack, every splinter, every break.

I'd played with fire and been engulfed in flames—first of desire, but now of pain.

All the little signs along the way pieced together to form a map to where I was now.

I'd thought a stupid song could fix anything, that it could help heal a little of his wounds after what he'd gone through.

I was a stupid girl with an even stupider heart. And I'd paid the price.

37

BAY

The Friday after the talent show, I sat on the football field transformed into the setting for our rite of passage. Graduation day. The overcast day meant we weren't baking in the sun, but my plastic smile felt brittle and tight. I sat beside Piper, taking measured breaths through all the speeches. My mom sat in the bleachers in her sunglasses waving the pennant with my name on it, trying to get my attention in the sea of other parents doing the same thing.

I held it together—barely. The glass was still fragile and the glue hadn't dried. It might never dry. It was a rush job of piecing myself together just enough to look at from afar. Close up, a strong wind or the wrong word might topple me over.

My row stood and walked the path, filing up behind the last row, taking their seats as they left the stage.

A hand captured mine.

My heart thundered in my veins. The rough callous of his touch brushed against the inside of my wrist.

I tugged it free and kept walking, not letting myself

look at him. Dare was in the row in front of me. At the far end. Three seats later and he'd have been in my row, feet from me after the distance I'd put between us since that day.

At the top of the stairs to the stage, I brightened my smile for the pictures and shook hands, taking my fake diploma and waving to my mom in the bleachers. Jumping up and down, she brushed the tears from her cheeks. As much as I hadn't wanted to come today, she'd needed it. And maybe I did too. It was a little closure to the place where I'd always been TNG. Only now I'd be TGG—The Gone Girl.

Unable to help myself, I glanced at the seat three from the end of the row ahead of mine when I made it to the other end of the stage.

Dare stared right back like he'd been waiting for a gap in my defenses to plead his case with his eyes.

They weren't filled with rage like before. There was only a chest-aching sadness, his lips parted to say words I'd never hear over the crowd, mic feedback, and congratulations.

I didn't need to hear them.

This was the end of a chapter. An end to us.

I returned to my seat beside Piper, nostrils flaring and tamping down the urge to look his way.

All the reasons I'd come up with before were even more in my face now. I was leaving and so was he. What would trigger his next freak out? A missed call? A picture on social media? Another song I wrote?

Piper squeezed my hand. At the instruction of Michelle, our class valedictorian, we shifted our tassels from one side of our caps to the other.

A sea of mortarboards flew up around me, but I didn't —I couldn't celebrate this day. There was no happy ending here, only two broken people who'd managed to break one another even further.

His gaze was on me. Even through a sea of celebrating classmates, I could feel it searing my skin.

In the past week, my window and doors had remained locked. I'd gone to Piper's way more than I should've, and kept to long looping paths to class.

Today, there was nowhere for me to run.

"Bay..." His voice cracked, pain radiating from it.

It hit me in the chest like a blow. I braced my hands on the back of the plastic chair beside me, so I didn't sway on my feet.

My name was on his lips like it had been so many times, but now I'd seen the real Dare—the one people talked about on the field, the one who put another player in the hospital. The one who had murder in his eyes and didn't care who got in the way. The one who smashed up people's cars. The one who broke things people loved. I'd thought it had been lies, or people not understanding who he really was. I'd been wrong.

I turned and ducked through the high-fiving and hugging crowd to get to my mom. His presence only steps behind me, I darted down one of the now-empty rows.

People filled the other end, trying to make room in the aisles for photos.

My escape was blocked in every direction, and he stood at the end of the row. I was trapped, unless I hiked up my graduation gown and leapt over the folding chairs, probably breaking both my ankles in the process.

"Bay." He approached me with his hands out like I was a rabbit with my foot caught in a trap.

I held out my hand to ward him off, still not able to look him directly in the eye. "Don't, Dare. Leave it alone."

"I can't." The begging tone in his voice was the same one I'd heard on the voicemails and from the other side of my door and window.

"You can. I'm not giving you a choice."

"Let me explain." His eyes were red-ringed, wild, and miserable.

"There's nothing to explain. You picked up my dad's guitar" —my voice cracked—"After saying all those horrible things, and you shattered it." My hands flew to my ears like I could block out the words echoing in my brain. "You don't get to do what you did and pretend you're the hurt one." I bit back the fiery words. My palm itched to lash out and free myself from the open-air pen I was stuck in, facing off against the boy I thought I'd loved. The one I had to pretend I didn't still love.

The look on his face made it seem like I had, like I'd grabbed one of these chairs and cracked it over his head. "Your dad's." It came out like a pained whisper.

"I don't deserve your forgiveness." His voice broke. He took a step closer, standing less than a foot away.

I could smell him from there. That scent that used to comfort me was now choking me. My vision blurred as tears filled my eyes. My chest was on fire. "Get away." I pushed him back, trying to maintain some space between us.

His fingers wrapped around my wrists, his hands flattening against my fists as I clutched at his graduation gown. "I'm sorry, Bay." He traced his finger along the back of my balled-up hands, over my knuckles.

Letting out the breath I'd been holding, I shakily snatched my hands back, keeping my gaze trained on the center of his chest. I gritted my teeth and met his gaze. "I don't care. I'm not going to say it's okay or that I forgive you, because it's not, and I don't. You can choke on those words and what you did for the rest of your life. When I said you were wrong, I lied. No one could love you for who you truly are because you're an asshole who can't help but destroy the people around you."

"Bay!" My mom's voice broke through the throngs of people around us.

I knocked the chairs out of the way, rushing toward her, burying my face in her chest.

Her arms wrapped around me, squeezing me and rocking me. "Your dad would have been so proud of you, sweetheart. He's here with us."

That broke the last of the dam. I held on tight to her. This whole day I hadn't thought about my dad. What kind of shitty daughter did that make me? Instead, I'd been fixated on the boy who broke me. I peered over at the sea of people in navy and gold. There was one figure sitting in a chair with his head in his hands as people celebrated around him. I allowed myself one last look. It would be the last I'd ever give him.

38

BAY

Four Years Later

~

"**D**are." My lips were numb. My whole body was numb. He stood in front of me, as though saying his name had conjured him from my past, a memory brought to life and made manifest through sheer force of will. He wasn't a mirage or a dream, though. He was here.

As quickly as all those happy memories flooded in, right behind them was the pain and the heartache. The cracked-open chest with a gaping hole where my heart had once been, all because of him.

"Bay." He said it like a prayer.

A wet splatter ripped me back from drowning in the memory well.

"Oh, shit." Felicia clutched her stomach. Her legs and my floor were now drenched with water. No, not water, something much more terror-inducing. "That was my water."

"Oh, shit." A chorus of voices added to her own.

There was a flurry of activity. I shot off a message to her husband. He rushed over to the building, getting there just as the ambulance arrived to take her to the university hospital.

Her husband helped her into the back of the ambulance and she turned around, grimacing.

"Bay. Here are the keys." She slapped the Residence Director's keys into my hand.

"Don't worry. I'll handle everything. Don't worry."

She grimaced. Her husband yelped as she gripped his hand and froze just inside the ambulance. "Fuck, that hurt." She let out a deep breath. "Thanks, Bay, I guess you were right. Or you jinxed me." With a playful glare, she disappeared behind the closing doors.

I turned around, my heart finally dropping from my throat, and stood face-to-face with the man who had turned my life upside down.

He stood beside some of the team who'd arrived early, and the assistant coach, Hank. Our eyes locked. He'd be in my building for the next four weeks. The next four weeks in the building I now literally had the keys to.

I thought back to the last lines I'd written in the green notebook before I'd closed it for what I thought was forever.

Your love was gift wrapped in barbed wire, and I was stupid enough to believe I could open it without getting nicked. I don't know if the wounds will ever heal. You shredded me, Darren Keyton.

～

Bay and Dare's story continues in the second book in the Falling trilogy, The Sin of Kissing You!

You can pre-order your copy now!

EXCERPT FROM THE PERFECT FIRST

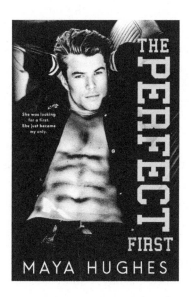

Seph - Project De-virginization

The jingle sounded again as the door to the coffee shop swung open. My head snapped up and my bouncing leg froze. The sun shone through the doorway and a figure stood there. He was tall, taller than anyone who'd come in before. His muscles were obvious even under his coat. He paused at the entrance, his head moving from side to side like he knew people would be looking back, like he was giving everyone a chance to soak in his presence. His jet black hair was tousled just right, like he'd been running his fingers through it on the walk over from wherever he'd come from. The jacket fit him perfectly, like it had been tailored just for his body.

I glanced around; I wasn't the only one who'd noticed him walk in. He seemed familiar, but I couldn't place him. He bent forward, and I thought he was going to tie his shoes, but instead he wiped a wet leaf off his pristine white sneaker. Heads turned as he crossed the floor toward me. Squeezing my fingers tighter around the notecards, I reminded myself to breathe.

He glanced around again and spotted me. The green in his eyes was clear even from across the coffee shop. Dark hair with eyes like that wasn't a usual combo. He froze and his lips squeezed together. With his hands shoved into his pockets, he stalked toward me with a *Let's get this over with* look. That didn't bode well. He stood beside the seat on the other side of the booth, staring at me expectantly.

My gaze ran over his face. Square jaw. Hint of stubble on his cheeks and chin. My skin flushed. He had beautiful lips. What would his feel like on my mouth? I ran my finger over my bottom lip. What would they feel like on other parts of me? My body responded and I thanked God I had on a bra, shirt, and blazer or I'd have been flashing him some serious high beams. This was a good sign.

He cleared his throat.

Jumping, I dropped my hand, and the heat in my cheeks turned into a flamethrower on my neck. "Sorry, have a seat." I half stood from my spot in the booth and extended my hand toward the other side across from me. The table dug into my thighs and I fell back into the soft seat.

Sliding in opposite me, he unzipped his coat and put his arm over the back of the shiny booth.

"Hi, very nice to meet you. I'm Seph." I shot my hand out across the table between us. The cuff of my blazer tightened as it rode up my arm.

His eyebrows scrunched together. "Seth?" He leaned in, his forearms resting on the edge of the table. He was nothing like the guys from the math department. They were quiet, sometimes obnoxious, and none of them made my stomach ricochet around inside me like it was trying to win a gold medal in gymnastics at the Olympics.

I tamped down a giggle. I did *not* giggle. The sound came out like a sharp snort, and I resisted the urge to slam my eyes shut and crawl under the table. *Be cool, Seph. Be cool.* "No—Seph. It's short for Persephone."

He lifted one eyebrow.

"Greek goddess of spring. Daughter of Demeter and Zeus. You know what, never mind. I'm glad you agreed to meet with me today."

"Not like I had much choice." He leaned back and ran his knuckles along the table top, rapping out a haphazard rhythm.

I licked my lips and parted them. Not like he had much choice? Had someone put him up to this? Had something in my post made him feel obligated to come? I hadn't been able to bring myself to go back and look at it after posting it.

Shaking my head, I stuck my hand out again. "Nice to meet you..."

He looked down at my hand and back up at me, letting out a bored breath. "Reece. Reece Michaels."

"Very nice to meet you, Reece. I'm Persephone Alexander. I have a few questions we can get started with, if you don't mind."

"The quicker we get started, the quicker we can finish." He looked around like he would have rather been anywhere but there.

Those giddy bubbles soured in my stomach. A server came by with the bottled waters I'd ordered. I arranged them in a neat pyramid at the end of the table.

"Would you like a water?" I held one out to him.

He eyed me like I was offering him an illicit substance, but then reached out. His fingers brushed against the backs of mine and shooting sparks of excitement rushed through me. Pulling the bottle out of my grasp, he cracked it open and took a gulp.

My cheeks heated and I glanced down at my cards, flipping the ones at the front to the back.

"I have a notecard with some information for you to fill out."

Sliding it across the table, I held out a pen for him. He took it from me, careful that our fingers didn't touch this time. I'd have been lying if I'd said I didn't want another touch, just to test whether or not that first one had been something more than static electricity. He filled out the biographical data on the card and handed it back to me.

I scanned it. He was twenty-one. Had a birthday coming up just after the New Year. Good height-to-weight ratio. Grabbing my pen, I scanned over the questions I'd prepared for my meetings.

"Let's get started." *Just rip the Band-Aid off.* Clearing my throat, I tapped the cards on the table. A few heads turned in our direction at the sharp, rapping sound. "When were you last tested for sexually transmitted diseases?"

Setting the bottle down on the table, he stared at me like I was an equation he was suddenly interested in figuring out. And then it was gone. "At the beginning of the season. Clean bill of health." He looked over his shoulder, the boredom back, leaking from every pore. *Wow.* I'd thought guys were all over this whole sex thing, but he looked like he was sitting in the waiting room of a dentist's office.

"When did you last have sexual intercourse?"

His head snapped back to me, eyes bugged out. "What?" I had his full attention now.

"Sex? When did you last have sex?" I tapped my pen against the notecard.

He sputtered and stared back at me. His eyes narrowed and he rested his elbows on the table.

I scooted my neatly lain out cards back toward me, away from him.

"No comment."

"Given the circumstances, it's an appropriate question."

The muscles in his neck tightened and his lips crumpled together. "Fine, at the beginning of the season."

"What season?" I looked up from my pen. That was an odd way to put it. "Like, the beginning of fall?"

"Like football season."

The pieces fit together—the body, the looks from other people around the coffee house. "You play football." That made sense, and he seemed like the perfect all-American person for the job.

"Yes, I play football."

"When did the season start?"

He shook his head like he was trying to clear away a fog and stared back at me like I'd started speaking a different language. "September."

"And..." I ran my hand along the back of my neck. "How long would you say it lasted?"

His eyebrows dipped. "It didn't last. It was a one-night thing. I don't do relationships."

Of course not. He was playing the field. Sowing his oats. Banging his way through as many co-eds as possible. Experienced. Excellent.

I cleared my throat. "No, I didn't mean how long did you date the woman. I meant, how long was the sex?"

The steady drumming on the table stopped. "Are you serious?"

I licked my Sahara-dry lips. "It's a reasonable question. How long did it last?"

"I didn't exactly set a timer, but let's just say we both got our reward."

"Interesting." I made another note on the card.

"These are the types of questions I'm going to be asked for the draft?" He took the lid off the bottled water.

The draft? Pushing ahead, I went to the next line one my card and cringed a bit. "Okay, this might seem a little invasive." I cleared my throat again. "But how big is your penis? Length is fine. I don't need to know the circumference, you know—the girth."

A fine spray of water from his mouth washed over me. "What the hell kind of question is that? I know you're trying to throw me off my game, but holy shit, lady."

∾

Persephone Alexander. Math genius. Lover of blazers. The only girl I know who can make Heidi braids look sexy as hell. And she's on a mission. Lose her virginity by the end of the semester.

I walked in on her interview session for potential candidates (who even does that?) and saw straight through her brave front. She's got a list of Firsts to accomplish like she's only got months to live. I've decided to be her guide for all her firsts except one. Someone's got to keep her out of trouble. I have one rule, no sex. We even shook on it.

I'll help her find the right guy for the job. Someone like her doesn't need someone like me and my massive...baggage for her first time.

Drinking at a bar. Check.

Partying all night. Double check.

Skinny dipping. Triple check.

She's unlike anyone I've ever met. The walls I'd put up around my heart are slowly crumbling with each touch that sets fire to my soul.

I'm the first to bend the rules. One electrifying kiss changes everything and suddenly I don't want to be her first, I want to be her only. But her plan was written before I came onto the scene and now I'm determined to get her to rewrite her future with me.

Grab your copy of The Perfect First or read it for FREE in Kindle Unlimited at https://amzn.to/2ZqEMzl

ALSO BY MAYA HUGHES

Fulton U

The Perfect First - First Time/Friends to Lovers Romance

The Second We Met - Enemies to Lovers Romance

The Third Best Thing - Secret Admirer Romance

Kings of Rittenhouse

Kings of Rittenhouse - FREE

Shameless King - Enemies to Lovers

Reckless King - Off Limits Lover

Ruthless King - Second Chance Romance

Fearless King - Brother's Best Friend Romance

Manhattan Misters

All His Secrets - Single Dad Romance

All His Lies - Secret Romance

All His Regrets - Second Chance Romance

CONNECT WITH MAYA

Sign up for my newsletter to get exclusive bonus content, ARC opportunities, sneak peeks, new release alerts and to find out just what I'm books are coming up next.

Join my reader group for teasers, giveaways and more!

Follow my Amazon author page for new release alerts!

Follow me on Instagram, where I try and fail to take pretty pictures!

Follow me on Twitter, just because :)

I'd love to hear from you! Drop me a line anytime :)
https://www.mayahughes.com/
maya@mayahughes.com

Made in the USA
Monee, IL
31 March 2023